BLOOD RED META

MICHAEL ARONOVITZ

GALLOWS WHISPER

ISBN: 978-1-937128-46-3

Text © 2025 by Michael Aronovitz
Cover © 2025 by Michael Squid

Design by César Puch
Edited by Curtis M. Lawson
Editor and Publisher, Joe Morey

Gallows Whisper
an imprint of Weird House Press
Central Point, OR 97502
www.weirdhousepress.com

I have committed bloody murder.

Many times.

It started when I retired from the People First Charter School in downtown Philadelphia, where I taught English to tenth graders and seniors for three decades. I was known as a good instructor, a pro, sharp with the product knowledge, quick with the comebacks. Rewarding? Damned straight. A rough ride at times? Absolutely. I had to write up all sorts of official discipline-slips throughout my tenure, the worst for a fight between twelve girls in the lunchroom that I was silly and idealistic enough to try and step between; I got socked in the jaw, gouged in the right ear, and scratched across the left cornea for my trouble. The second most serious was the student who hid an ounce of weed and a .32 Beretta Tomcat in the boy's bathroom up under the drop ceiling.

Since I have been "put out to pasture," you might have heard of me on the news, though local media outlets typically focus on local crime. Therefore, it is probable that you have only gotten a fraction of the story, as I am careful to choose impact locations in different cities to unveil my polished displays of beautiful slaughter. To be clear, however, I am no portrait painter, literally or metaphorically, and I never claimed to be a poet, yet common sense dictates that crafting a striking tableau of carnage must always involve an initial shock factor, aesthetic imagery, a dark riddle, and a pristine exit strategy.

I have killed six rapists, four abusive boyfriends, three wife-beaters, five racist teachers, and two smug C.E.O.s who did nothing to stop in-house bullying between lower employees. Of course, I know that these "businessmen" committed lesser crimes than the others, but they irritated me the most somehow. I shot both in the heart and took a pair of tin snips and a box cutter to carve out their eyes and replace them with their testicles sewn into the sockets. Both were dumped, or rather, placed in their given neighborhood zoo, in the monkey house, nailed to a tree, dangling, yet finally looking at things with a bigger set of balls, can I get an amen?

*Please consider my candidacy for **THE KILL OR BE KILLED PROJECT (PODCASTING FROM MURDERTOWN)**. Moreover, confirm that the grand prize for the last one standing is five million dollars and that the final roster of contestants will be capped at a nice and neat twelve.*

Respectfully,
The Red Headmaster

PART 1

Chapter 1

Cody Kennedy grinned.

"I like him," he said. "I dig his origin story, but don't you think 'The Red Headmaster' is a bit too—I don't know—over the top?"

The Professor put up his index finger.

"Hold on," he said. "Let me get out of the share. My desktop is slow, and your voice is delayed and machine-gunning." He clicked the keys, leaned back in his office chair, and waited until Cody's face again shared the full screen.

"The names have to be bombastic," the Professor continued, "like pro wrestling. That way viewers and listeners can go with it, sort of chuckling along and rooting for their favorites like superheroes."

Cody nodded. "Agreed. Realistic serial killers would disgust people."

"And bore them to tears," the Professor added. "Most of them in real life are tedious and dumb as a stump, like the Yorkshire Ripper, for example, real name Peter Sutcliffe, born 1946 and deceased in 2020. Sure, there was a lot of folklore at first, since he killed thirteen women, many of them hookers, as was the preference of his namesake, 'Jack,' but in the end, he was just a simple guy living in Heaton, Newcastle-upon-Tyne in Merry old England. He was a nobody, meandering between menial jobs like factory packaging lines and truck driving." The Professor adjusted his headphones. "It's sort of the reason," he said, "why the endings of mysteries always suck. The killer was—drumroll, please—Bob Finklestein! I mean, wow, nothing but a buzz-kill, right?"

Cody tucked his long hair behind one ear, then the other.

"Yeah," he said, "Boner-shrinker. Like you said, protagonists are supposed to be smart or at least clever."

The Professor smiled like a kid. "You sound like my college students."

Cody took a toke off his vape pipe. "You sound like my boss at the record store."

"I thought Spotify made you guys obsolete."

"Vintage vinyl is huge. Especially here in L.A."

"Well, here in the burbs of Philly, all they do is stream K-pop, country, hip-hop, and Taylor Swift."

"These are dark times."

"The worst."

"Metal is nothing but niche anymore."

"Yes indeedy. Just like the early to mid-1980s. People forget that the commercial norm back then was new wave—you know, skinny ties, shitty haircuts, and bad vocals on purpose. Glam metal and thrash were the underground, the underdogs, just like my band was."

"Who did you open for again?"

The Professor's eyes softened. Of course, Cody knew the answer to this one already, but he was kind enough to let things get sweet and wistful for the old fella for just a hot minute.

"We were the warm-up act for Metal Wolf at The Empire Rock Club," said the Professor. "They had an album out through a major label, and we were introduced by Lynn Kratz, a DJ at the biggest rock radio station at the time, WMMR."

"And you lit up the joint, didn't you?"

"Damn right we did. It was sold out, too, and the Empire was no joke. The next night, Cinderella played there. A week later, it was Skid Row, and a week after that, the one and only Bon Jovi."

"So close to the big time."

"So close."

Cody smiled sideways. "You know I wasn't alive yet in the '80s, right?"

The lines in the Professor's face flattened. "We're going to be a mighty strange pair of podcasters, aren't we?"

"Yes indeedy."

"I miss Ralph. And not just his vocals."

Cody paused and looked off to the right. "He would have wanted us to go on without him."

The Professor was temporarily wordless. Since 2009, besides teaching his college course load as an adjunct, he had been publishing horror books in the small market presses like Cemetery Dance and Hippocampus, and in 2015 he started writing rock reviews on current indie bands so he would have something to tweet about besides his buy-links. Ralph Romano's band Wolf Shadow was the subject of the Professor's first review, eventually leading to his freelancing the bios and press releases for the boutique label Eclipse Records. The Professor and Ralph became friends. It lasted years, and after the pandemic they did a number of podcasts and music reaction videos with Ralph's new guitar player, Cody Kennedy. Then Ralph died on January 1, 2023.

It was humbling and mind-numbing, and now it was mid-2024, and maybe this serial killer podcast idea was their chance to play phoenix-rising-up-from-the-ashes.

"So," Cody said, "who is the next psycho applicant going to be?"

The Professor had pen in hand, and he clicked it up by his ear.

"Someone who doesn't do factory packing lines or delivery trucks."

He went misty again, eyelids at half mast, and he started waving the pen in front of his face all slo-mo like a maestro.

"I'm thinking circus," he said. "I'm thinking clown."

Chapter 2

Cody signed off and took out the earpiece. Candi came in from behind him and put her hand on his shoulder.

"Dinner's on the stove in the skillet," she said. "I covered it with tin foil."

Cody's head drooped. "Sorry," he muttered. "Lost track of time."

She slid her palms down the front of his chest. She nuzzled him in the ear. She had a soft fragrance of lilacs about her that Cody adored even more than freshly mown hay or a grass ballfield with dew on it.

"The Professor always makes you lose track of time," she said. "It's his grand superpower." She straightened, and Cody put his hands over hers on his collarbone, talking to the wall.

"He's funny, both ironic and ha-ha," he said, "and he knows a lot about writing."

She gave the chair a slow push to revolve Cody around to face her.

"He also comes up with shit so gory and weird," she said, "that you're tempted to call the police. I know I am."

Cody smiled. The idea that this rebel of a girl would be tempted to call the police over mere stories and podcasts was hilarious. She was too smart in her own way, too willful and confident. She was long, toned, with straw-colored blond hair long enough to sit on. She had an hourglass waist and heart-shaped hips with that high flare just *made* for low-cut jeans, exposing the thong straps.

And her eyes. Talk about a beautiful rebel: her brows were sleek and slanted, and she had permanent cat's-eye makeup tattooed in dramatic, elongated lines and wingtips, forest emerald green eyeshadow, no blotches, no smears.

She sighed. "Did he talk about the good old days of the mid-'80s again, with the old rock and roll war stories?"

"Yes."

"Does he even know that you and Ralph rocked the Whiskey a Go-Go more than ten times, four as the headliner? That you played The Roxy and The Troubadour and that you slayed it at the Hollywood Bowl opening for Metallica?"

Her arms were folded, but her eyes were smiling.

"He never asked," Cody said.

"Does he know how much work you put into the music reaction videos you three used to do, like the set-up and the levels and the edits and the graphics?"

"No, not exactly."

She stepped in, sat on his lap, and he put his arms around her. She rested her chin on the top of his head for a second.

"So what's his harebrained scheme this time around?"

Cody kissed her shoulder, since it was the closest.

"A podcast called '**The Kill or Be Killed Project**,'" he said, "and the plot is that there are twelve homicidal maniacs locked down in a city block of abandoned tenements we're going to name 'Murdertown.' They go after each other like *The Hunger Games,* and the last one standing gets five million dollars."

She moved her bangs out of her eyes, pouting as if posing in front of a mirror.

"How would twelve serial killers stay trapped there?" she said. "What would stop them from bailing if things went sour?"

"An electric fence."

"And where are you going to get the five million dollars?"

"There is no five million," he said. "There are no tenements either. It's all a big hoax."

"Won't that piss off your audience?"

Cody nodded reflectively.

"I asked the Professor the same thing. He said we were going to pull an Orson Welles, you know, like *The War of the Worlds*, where you announce at the beginning that the whole thing is fiction, but after that you carry on like everything's real. Each week, we introduce a new killer that we've actually just made up out of thin air, and we read the miscreant's application response essay. We have the audience give feedback in the Comment section, and we vote contestants on and off once we have that initial twelve, dropping and adding."

"What happens then?"

Cody looked glum. "No idea."

She stood and glided over to the doorway. Halfway there, she turned back.

"So, what's your role in all this?"

He laughed. "You mean besides the set-up, the levels, the edits, and the graphics?"

"Yes, Captain Cryptic."

Cody pushed to his feet. "It's my job today," he said, "to create the next killer, who, of course, is a clown."

"Of course it is," she said, "because he's aware of your past."

"Yeah. Tell me, though, I forget, which music reaction were we doing when the subject came up?"

She looked at the ceiling, tapped her fingers against her chin, and then looked back at her husband.

"I think it was one of the ones you did on The Warning, 'Evolve Live' maybe, or it could have been 'Choke,' but I forget the context."

Cody shook his head as if clearing it.

"Well, regardless," he said, "he knows that my family was in the circus, and as a boy I was a real-life clown."

She smirked. "He uses everything, doesn't he? Resourceful! So it looks like we'd better start brainstorming."

He paused and gave a wink of a grin. "Basement?"

"Oh, yes."

"My jumpsuit clean?"

"Air-dried on the clothesline between the pipes the way you like it."

"My big ole parade shoes?"

"Under the stairs."

"The greasepaint?"

"On the workbench next to the hacksaw, the toolbox, and the WD-40."

"I love it when you talk dirty."

She put her hand on her hip, curled her lip.

"I'll get out my whips and the specialty knives and the war spikes and the throwing hatchets," she said. Cody pushed up from the chair and started creeping in close, giving her the one-eye. When they were nose to nose, his voice was an affectionate murmur. "Has the doggie woken up yet down there? Has he been barking in his crate?"

"Of course," she said. "He's an asshole Republican."

"All the better for the kill, my darling. And blood looks so gorgeous spattered on a clown suit. God, I love it when the stars align."

Candi pouted.

"What's the matter, babe?" Cody said.

"I don't know. Thinking on it, this seems such a waste to off him tonight, you know, since we've been starving and priming him, and he's still a few weeks too ripe for the gouging. I wanted it to be perfect. I got the titanium blade back from the sharpener for the bone saw, and I've been practicing on the cadavers at work. The human head is a canvas, and I can uncap the back of a skull like Rembrandt at this point. I can scoop out the waste like a pro and open a handhold in the back of his mouth so smooth it will feel like you are putting on a glove."

"I'm getting hard."

"Not kidding! It's a shame. In a week and a half even, his legs and arms would have been so spindly, he'd actually have looked like he was made of rickety Pinocchio-wood if you swung him around to your knee."

He touched her cheek. "There are plenty more Republicans, babe."

She shrugged. "I suppose, but I'm confused. What exactly are you going to tell the Professor? Don't you need a theme or some poetic sinister purpose?"

"Well, why not play it straight? Why not say that this is a clown, named 'Cody the Clown,' with a vision of having a humongous footlocker filled with lap-puppets made of real people? Eleven, to be exact?"

"Isn't that a little too close to the truth?"

"The best lies are chock-full of truths."

She considered with her lips puckered to the side like she just ate a lemon.

"Right," she said finally, "but our captures are boring now as they stand—you know, the ole isolate, distract, use a blackjack, then a needle, and the kill is just an insignificant knock on the back of the head. The point is to keep everything clean, no spatter, no mess. What I mean is that all our 'sinister poetry' happens in between, you know, when we're scratching at the sanity of the doggie in his crate with the circus motif, training him, thinning him. Of course, the human lap-puppet idea is a howl post-mortem, but wouldn't our clown have to have a more colorful kill-game?"

Cody ran his fingers straight back through his hair.

"Squirting flowers filled with muriatic acid?" he offered.

Candi giggled. "How about whoopee cushions that explode?"

"Chattering joke teeth that really bite," he said, laughing.

"A motorized toilet with a gun in the plunger."

"A clown car with a twin turbo V8 engine and poisoned spikes sticking out of the grille."

"Show off."

"You are."

They walked together out to the hall and went hand in hand down toward the basement.

Chapter 3

The Professor had just finished the best day of teaching this year, possibly the best of his career. The students at The University of Delaware were amazing, critically thinking, contributing, self-editing, and working magic in their free-writes within the guidelines he had given them to best frame their arguments. He had shown them two videos, the first Paul Gilbert recording his track on "Technical Difficulties," and then Zakk Wylde jamming to a recorded track on "Zakk Wylde Plays 'Low Rider' on EMGtv." They had to argue for one or the other for their first drafted paragraphs and then actually pick the other guy to sign to a record contract. That way, dismantling the opposition was easy, since the students already were the opposition, and they could take their three biggest points and find ways to deconstruct them.

Consequently, the Professor should have been on cloud nine, but he was brooding on the ride home. It was Cody and his clown bit. First off, he had portrayed himself as a character who discussed the show's internal workings, revealing the macrostructure's underbelly. Suddenly, it was a podcast about two guys planning a podcast, and, while interesting, it wasn't practical. Now they would have to cut most of the "giveaways" plus change the name of the character playing the clown, who was apparently notorious for imprisoning Republicans in basement doggie-crates.

Also, on more technical grounds, Cody had written this excerpt like a story or an actual fictive chapter with the multiple paragraphs used in the standard template for dialogue mechanics. It was supposed to be a summary, a formal letter with block paragraphing. How were they going to read this kind of excerpt on the podcast, even if rewritten without the meta stuff? Was the Professor supposed to take the role of the wife? Who read the narration in between? If one of them had to double-up, it took away the effect and made it too see-through, sort of like the initial problem of "showing their scaffolding" all over again.

Moreover, the clown character had admitted that his "kill-game" was ordinary. It was the doggie training and eventual lap-puppet thing that was of interest, and while it was colorful, it didn't necessarily make him a worthy foe locked down with eleven other assassins in Murdertown.

The Professor smiled at himself. His Red Headmaster didn't have a good kill-game either. The mysterious fella erected tableaux, and that was the point. This whole thing was supposed to be bombastic, over-the-top like Pro Wrestling, Monster Trucks, and the *Evil Dead* movies.

The Professor glanced at his gas gauge: quarter tank, good enough. He put on his turn signal and waited at the red light to make a right on 322. In all, the most important question was whether Cody would be miffed if the Professor suggested these rewrites in the first place. He hoped this wouldn't be the case. Their whole endeavor was based on the idea that the quality of the final product was more important than whose name deserved more airtime in the credits.

The Professor stuck his tongue in his cheek.

Maybe the deep-seated issue here was that Cody's chapter segment was pretty darned good, sort of making the Professor's Red Headmaster killer seem tepid. But wasn't that the point? If the characters were to compete, maybe it was fitting that their creators did the same. It would make the villains spicier and uptick the pressure to create the best product.

Still, all compliments aside for Cody's raw creativity, the Professor wanted badly to take a red pen to that chapter segment, or at least give him notes.

The name "Candi" was a bit much. There was supposed to be an age difference, and therefore wide cultural variances between Cody the twenty-something guitar player and himself, the aging professor playing the Professor, but the Cody character's wife didn't have to have a name like a stripper, for Christ's sake. Then there were her physical descriptions, the first paragraph fair to middling, sure, but the added paragraph about the tattooed-on cat's eyes didn't play for some reason, hard to "see," at least compared to the heart-shaped hips. Then, in the last part, Cody had his Cody character give Candi the one-eye just before going nose to nose, after which they proceeded to unload an entire conversation, their faces supposedly an inch apart from each other all the way through. But really? Uh … no, sir. You go up close like that, and there would be a soft kiss, a hug, a break, then some distance. Hey, logistics mattered.

The Professor turned left to go down West Chester Pike. He hit the gas and tapped on Sirius Radio, Hair Nation. A Dokken song came on, "It's Not Love," and the groove was just right.

Okay then.

He would give Cody notes, but only on the most egregious stuff. Cody was a big boy. And if he had comments to give the Professor on *his* characters, he was more than willing to listen, key word—listen. After all, he was the word man here, and Cody was sure to understand that.

Chapter 4

To be honest, Cody wasn't too crazy about the criticism. Like c'mon, *"Incorrect narrative structure instead of formal paragraphing … too much of it overwritten … other things underwritten … physical scenarios logistically improbable."* In other words, back to the drawing board, son.

It didn't make sense. Serial killers would not all be English majors who had had professional interviews requiring perfect three-paragraph cover letters. Cody had never needed one, so there, and therefore in turn, wouldn't it make sense for some of the "proposal letters" to be written like uneven, flawed stories suffering from a number of realistic mistakes like descriptive overload? Hell, these kinds of killers would be total narcissists, so therefore, overdoing things would be in their DNA. And if every application was a neat three-paragraph page, wouldn't the audience be bored shitless by the fourth or fifth candidate?

Cody pushed up and out of his mango-colored Mini Cooper with all the nicks and scrapes he had accumulated on the front and back bumpers trying to park and fit every which way but sideways downtown over the past year. A damned lemon, and worse, the Mini Cooper people were owned by BMW, so prices for parts and service were ridiculous. Last month, Cody had needed an engine gasket replaced, one little plastic O-ring, and it ran him five hundred. Fucking crooks.

He shut the door and made his way up the walk. They paid too much of a monthly for this place for it not to have a driveway, but he did like the personality. Sometimes he deeply missed his hometown of South Boston, yeah, wicked-pissah, he was a Southie, but he liked the idea that a lot of the houses in the L.A. area were low-profile Spanish bungalows with the terra cotta roofs made of rust-colored shingles shaped like half-moons. He liked the arched doorways and fancy-looking courtyards, even if this particular rental was altogether in need of a shitload of repairs. Their faucet dripped in the half-kitchen like the Chinese water torture. Same room, the long tubular overhead lights flickered for five minutes or so before coming on, and the bathroom ceiling had water damage in the far corner over the toilet.

But it felt like Cody was living in a Mediterranean fantasy land with the houses tucked in, beside and around each other like small villages with levels and gradations praising the landscape.

He reached into his shirt pocket for his Marlboros, then ambled left of the front door for the footpath he shared with his neighbor, the border-marker neither made claim to and therefore left abandoned to become overrun with chickweed and crabgrass sticking up between the old pavers.

He grinned sardonically. Though he wasn't lighting up in the house, Candi would know that he'd started smoking again; she'd smell it on his breath, on his clothes. But he was sure she wouldn't bark too loudly about it; she gave him his space, and he paused to light up, knowing the flame made the light flicker along the shadows of the early evening, so he looked like a dude in a movie. There was movement off to the left, and he peered through the baby palm trees and spiky yuccas up the short rise. It was Bill Robbins, his neighbor, out behind his house fucking with something he had in a tree on a low-hanging branch.

For a moment, Cody thought he must have been hallucinating. The sawed-off branch had an industrial black bag affixed to it, tied off on the upper side to a higher branch, and the thing sort of looked like a grass catcher you would put on a lawnmower, only more cylindrical. And spilling out of the wide mouth at the bottom was some kind of substance that bloated the width of its branch tenfold, all the way to the knot a foot down that elbowed back in toward the trunk. What the ... hey, man, the swelled excess seemed to be ... moving, dull-shimmering in idiot rhythms, in and out and around like a live thing with breathing skin.

Cody almost said, "Fuck!" out loud. It was bees. A swarm of bees, some that spilled out of the bag and had congregated on the branch beneath it.

Hoarding bees, huh?

Of course, like hey man, why not? Robbins was a quiet sort of oddball to begin with, the type that back in high school probably sat around on weekends all day in his beanbag chair in the basement playing the latest version of *Call of Duty* and taking a break once in a while, to feed dead mice to his pet snake named Medusa. He was a decade older than Cody, a musician as well, and he played the brand of guitar George Lynch had used in Dokken, the one with the skulls on it. Cody had jammed with him once. The guy knew a lot of '90s metal, note for note, bend for bend, but had no ability to improvise, making the session go stale in about twenty minutes. The dude had long-ass, bushy weeping willow hair he kept in a ponytail and a goatee that never quite grew in at the chin. He had a wandering eye, so you never knew if he was really looking at you. Candi called him "Captain Stink-Eye."

That said, he was a good neighbor, all things considered. He arranged his trash cans and recycling in a tidy row, never had his television volume loud enough to be a nuisance, and supposedly made good coin, working at the East Hollywood Dutch Brothers Landfill. He originally got the job because he was on the crew that built the flare methane tower, impressing the new yard ownership and becoming their new foreman, responsible for driving the skid steer loaders and operating the crane.

Robbins reached up to the bloated branch. It was dark enough to make his sleeve tattoo a wash of murky coloring, but Cody could have sworn some of the bees came off the branch to crawl over his fingers. Like pets.

Something in Cody's brain exploded. He snuffed out the cig. Dinner could wait. He had to type this into his laptop while it was fresh in his head.

The Beekeeper

Robbins, fondly known as "The One-Eyed Pirate," looked through the windshield at the entrance to the landfill. In the bald glare of the headlights, there were the swerves and divots that big vehicles with mammoth tires had cut into the dirt road leading up to a fence gate with a sign that said "Service Entrance." Robbins shut off the engine and got out to open the padlock. He would walk from here. Perfect testing ground.

To see if he really could talk to insects.

Before him was a rough lane cutting through gargantuan rises to each side: tires, twists of steel, brick piles, and what appeared to be a mountain of appliances cut to two sections: one with ovens and air conditioners, and the other old computers and television monitors.

From around the corner, as if on cue, two forms came skidding and redirecting, pawing the ground hard and galloping forward. It was Mr. Dutch's junkyard guard dogs, two hideous creatures Robbins despised right down through the soul. Every morning when he had to walk to the trailer to get the day's work order, these mongrels woke in their cages to the left of the front steps, barking, slobbering at the jowls, working up a lather. They were a pair of Rottweilers, one light brown with white spots on his chest and the other dirty gray with black tips on the ears. Both had steel-studded choke collars, and both knew only one set of objectives: Rip. Maul. Kill.

The dogs were about two hundred feet away and closing now, the brown one in the lead kicking up dirt, barking hoarsely. Robbins closed his eyes; he concentrated, and the weird visions came up in his mind, visions he was getting a lot of lately, visions he hoped he could trust.

In a pile of factory exhaust fans, there was a massive hive affixed to the inner right corner of an enormous industrial draft hood that came from the roof of a ball-bearing plant. Inside the paper-like labyrinth swarmed twenty-nine hundred and fifty-eight black-bellied hornets, two hundred and seventy subservient males surrounding their queen, and the rest a disciplined company of vicious asexual female mercenaries.

Robbins addressed the queen directly, and the hive around her buzzed. Recently, they had ravaged an eclipse of gypsy moths, and while it left some of them gorged, they accounted for such things by eating in shifts, and there were over twenty-two hundred soldiers still hungry, ready for war. The word went out quickly, scores of troops funneling through the honeycombs, secreting pheromones, and storming out of the entry hole, darting and weaving in a savage alarm dance.

Simultaneously, Robbins called out to the one thousand and nineteen German yellow jackets in the hive nestled in a crux at the bottom of a pile of splintered wooden utility poles and old railroad ties past the clumps of sheep sorrel by the cyclone fencing east of the service entrance. They exited, swelled, and shot down through the air.

The brown dog was hit so hard by the first wave that he was knocked sideways, rolling, howling, and the rest of the black-bellied hornets followed in an arrow formation that shot down and spread. For a moment, they took on his shape in the dirt, making it seem he had changed colors. He jumped up, pawing at the air and flailing, and the swarm rose and retargeted. Again, they stuck to him like a second skin, this time covering his eyes, and he fell to his side in jerks and spasms.

The gray Rottweiler had tumbled head over heels into a pile of rusted tin ductwork, and after the crash and shudder, he jumped from the wreckage, running in circles as if chasing his tail. The swarm of German yellow jackets mimicked his movements like a cape following a bull.

It was all over in a matter of seconds.

The brown one lay still twenty feet north at the edge of the lane on his flank, and the latter was ten feet closer on his back with his paws up. The insects were still busy, thrusting, working those abdomens like pump jacks, clockwork, machines.

Robbins was ready.

Ready for Murdertown.

Chapter 5

The Zoom was uncomfortable, to say the least.

"It doesn't sound like me," Cody said, "and we never agreed to write from the other guy's perspective."

"Still," said the Professor," with your 'Cody the Clown' in the bag, it was my turn. And to keep the thread going, it made sense to transition from the Cody character to the Beekeeper next door. It almost wrote itself."

"It's too detailed."

"And the clown's application isn't? Besides, like I told you before, you don't go dumbing down characters."

"Well, thank you, I guess."

"You're welcome, I'm sure."

"Yeah," said Cody, "but you wrote it in story-form, and you said the other day that it would be hard to use it on a podcast that way."

The Professor nodded. "True," he said, "but thinking about it, I changed my mind. Part of that comment was jealousy, I think, a rather distasteful surge of envy. I liked your mini-chap. I liked it a lot, still do, and I wanted to follow suit."

"But I agreed with you! Sorry, I'll turn down the volume. That was loud on my end."

"No apology necessary."

"Did I apologize? Sorry, didn't mean to. What I'm saying is … what do we do with this now? You don't have the 'multiple characters-needing-multiple-voice/actors' issue like my 'Cody the Clown,' but the reads are becoming too detailed, you were right about that. I agree that some people like it that way, but honestly? I have to admit that I can never listen to books on tape and shit. It either puts me to sleep or makes my mind wander."

The Professor leaned forward and folded his hands on the desk in front of his PC.

"Regardless of what I said before, I now suggest we don't stall the creative process because of formatting issues," he said. "We treat everything like a rough draft. Let's give this thing space to really fly and see where it takes us."

"You are an old rebel, aren't you?"

"Damn straight."

"You'll break all the rules even if you were the one to write them in the first place."

"Right on."

"But still, the new character has a supernatural power. Doesn't that change the basic setup too much? Wasn't the original deal that twelve real-life killers are going up against each other? Now the killer-bee guy can just lock himself in a room and off everybody."

The Professor smiled. "Not if we introduce an Exterminator."

"Okay, then what about the other ten? What's the Red Headmaster's supernatural gift?"

"No clue."

"And let's not fail to mention that you have Cody creating Cody the Clown, who then creates Robbins the Beekeeper. Does that even make sense? It's getting hard to keep track."

The Professor made a fist, eyes wide.

"Yes!" he said. "An echo, like a time ripple, like the movie *Inception*, going levels and levels deep. We could only hope to have such an appeal."

"Or such a big fat mess of confusion."

"Exactly. If we nose-dive, it will be in a blinding, earth-shattering, supersonic blaze of unadulterated glory! That alone might earn us some sponsorships."

"For the car accident."

"But how exciting the race!"

"A tsunami."

"Yet look at the grand spectacle of a ten-story wave."

They paused. Cody traced his index finger down one side of his moustache, then the other.

"Well," he said, "It's my turn then."

"What are you waiting for?"

"You asked for it."

"I did," said the Professor, but Cody had already exited the Zoom meeting.

Chapter 6

*Attention, creators of **THE KILL OR BE KILLED PROJECT** to take place as a podcast from MURDERTOWN. If you choose to read the cover letter enclosed, it will be at your own risk. If you reveal the name of the one described, the people associated, or the business he/she/they are involved with, you will be eliminated. We know where you both live. If participation in this contest is awarded as a result of this letter, you will refer to our candidate as "The Rock Reaper." You have been warned.*

Tito Quinones is the lead singer for the savage Latin metal band Saint Diablo, signed to Eclipse Records, and tonight he is going to brutally butcher another sexual predator. He will get away with it scot-free, and he will be wearing the blood of the victim in the great wide open, spattered on his face and up along his sleek bald eagle crown like war paint, his trademark stage gimmick. Since Saint Diablo are still considered "indie," they have no roadies, so after the set at the T.L.A. Theater on South Street, Philadelphia, he and the boys, wearing hoodies with the drawstrings pulled tight, hiding their faces, will clear all the gear and pack it into their two equipment vans. They will drive to Baltimore, check into a cheap roadside motel, and sleep off the night.

All except Tito.

He will shower, then open his laptop to call up the Baltimore State Police Website, tabbing to the list of convicted sex offenders, recently freed after serving their sentences.

Tomorrow he will go with the band to the Angels Rock Bar at 10 Market Place at 5:00 P.M. to store their equipment. He will then take his rental car and stake out the neighborhood, this time, of one Louis Tanner, an elementary school teacher jailed for sexually assaulting, on the same day at the same location, third-grader Bonnie McLaren and her grandmother, Elizabeth May, during a home tutoring visit. The bastard was released to a halfway house after two short years. Typical story.

The outdoors is painted with the gentle brush strokes of the early evening's dying summer sun, and Tito waits in his car across the street from Tanner's home residence, which is one in a row of yuppie apartments with fancy railings and flower boxes bursting with decorative foliage. Five doors down, there is an alley. A half hour before the warm-up act comes on to play their set at the Angels at 7 P.M. tonight, Tito will ring Louis Tanner's doorbell. He will say into the intercom it is a package needing a signature. When Tanner answers, Tito will keep the door open by planting his left elbow into it, take the pistol out of his pocket, flash the silver, and raise an eyebrow, like *You don't even want to think about running back into the house and having me chase you,* next jerking his head toward the street, convincing Tanner to come with him to the alley for fun time.

To make a skull-face.

He starts by taking Tanner's cheeks in his palms, the way your mother or auntie would do, but instead of saying in a boo-boo-voice, *"Ooo, you're so cute,"* he will dig in his thumbs behind the rapist's eyes, making them roll crazy like the googly-wiggle eyes on a teddy bear, and then he tears them out, slippery little bastards, both popping loose, no souvenir dice to take tonight. Hands drenched and hot, he grabs Tanner's shirt and trips the dude backward, dropping him to the cement. Though Tito is shredded with biceps like pythons and has a washboard for abs, he needs a better hold, better angle, better *traction,* so he gets out the slip-joint pliers from his back pocket, forces the mouth open, *Don't you even think of biting me, motherfucker,* and clamps the tool tight to the tongue. He puts the sole of his right sneaker flat to Tanner's forehead and gives a two-handed pull like starting a lawnmower.

There is a bright spray of glory like fireworks.

He drops the bloody appendage on the victim's chest. Most of these fuckers bleed out. If Tanner lives, the disfigurement will scare away the kiddies, so there will be no chance for grooming, hey, everyone prevails. Tito balances the scales.

He unties the black sweatshirt from his waist and slips it on, pulls up the hood, and walks out to the street. Across town at the Angels Rock Bar, the opener is two songs into their forty-five-minute set. In the tradition of Mushroomhead and Slipknot, the band called Jack the Zipper is rocking the joint, all of them wearing burlap scarecrow masks. The singer is supposedly Tito Quiniones himself, moonlighting as the lead singer of Jack the Zipper, where he has the opportunity to show off that old school feel with his brilliant tenor voice, unlike the vocal demands for Saint Diablo mostly based on the primeval growl.

Perfect alibi.

It is actually his cousin Nico, who could have been Tito's twin, same height and weight, and sporting that awesome tenor voice, smooth as honey.

If you choose Tito to represent in Murdertown, you may as well store the five mil in a locker with his name on it. You come after him, you better have a gun. You also best know that he's packing, and that he is a master marksman himself. So ...

Bring it on.

Bitches.

Chapter 7

The Professor was glad that his picture on Zoom was grainy and rather colorless. To begin with, he had rosacea, this sort of natural blush to his skin, and on top of that, he was embarrassed to give this critique for some reason.

"It's too much on the nose," he said finally.

"Say what?" Cody said.

"Sorry, movie-talk. I taught Introduction to Film at UDEL during the pandemic. It means that you are giving away too much in blatant exposition."

"Say what?"

"Really?"

"Not kidding," said Cody, lips thin. "Seems you're using words that will keep me outside the loop and stuck in the muck, always slowing it down, asking for an explanation."

The Professor put a loose fist to his lips and cleared his throat.

"Acknowledged," he said. "What I mean is, that when you name Tito and his label Eclipse Records, it offers the audience too much straight information. It plays like a cheap trick, a manipulation, as in a movie when the warden reads to the prisoner that prisoner's confidential file. Clearly, the prisoner already knows who he is, so reading the file aloud to him is quite obviously for the benefit of the audience. It happens all the time in movies, sort of what they do in *Rambo 2,* and at the beginning of *The Matrix.*"

Cody reached back to redo the knot on his ponytail.

"Well, I like both those films," he said crisply. "They were big hits, so

I don't see your point."

The Professor nodded patiently.

"Right," he said. "Okay, that aside, you can't give away an identity like Tito's, because realistically he would be arrested the moment we announce it." He fingered the bottom of his goatee, twisting it. "Or at least the audience would naturally assume he would be, so the character, within the world we have created, would never see the light of day in Murdertown. Additionally, it would wreck our credibility, as it would seem as though we are willing and eager to give away private information. Were this our M.O., no one would send us an application, and we wouldn't have a show anymore."

Cody nodded as if conceding a pawn that had been sacrificed.

"Fair enough," he said. "But why can't we read the same letter and use those cross-out marks everyone is so hyped about with national politics and investigations and shit. You know, those thick black lines blotting out the sentence beneath it."

"It's called a redaction."

"Right! We indicate that *we think* we know who it is for suspense, but the name and his record label have been redacted. It clears us for any aiding or abetting kind of a deal, and it gives a relevant flavor to it, adding to the mystery too."

The Professor leaned back in his chair.

"What about when the game supposedly goes live?" he said. "We are selling to the audience that we will have inserted cameras covering every angle of the city block of tenements. That is how we can narrate for everyone, battle after battle, that they can only hear and not see. The point is that *we* can see, and if we think we know who it is already, wouldn't it be confirmed to us when we recognized Tito? Then, according to the law, we would have to report him. If we didn't, we would open our liability in that plotline you just mentioned of aiding and abetting. And once that toothpaste is out of the tube, we would be obligated to follow it through to the end. Case in point, I don't think the two of us being arrested or getting one of our contestants arrested in make-believe land is the climax we were looking for."

"Well, who says we have to say that we recognize him at all? What if we eliminate that thread altogether? We don't know Tito, and he doesn't know us. He is a faceless indie metal-playing rock-god, period. And being that he is supposedly a public figure, to avoid being recognized by the Cody character and/or the Professor character and/or any of his fans, he could always wear a black hood, the bottom flaps sewn into the inside of his tee shirt at the collarbones."

Silence—a long one this time.

"You are forgetting," the Professor said, "the underlying issue that sort of dooms this 'character' by design from the get-go. Talk about shameless exposition … As you well know, the masked rock star-killer concept was Tito's idea to begin with, revealed to me during a Zoom we did when I wrote the bio and album hype for Eclipse to promote Saint Diablo's sophomore album, *Devil Horns and Halos,* in 2015. I think he would want some form of credit for coming up with the idea, and I feel guilty enough that I confided it to you in the first place."

"Didn't I do a good job with it?"

There was a pause just long enough to read as a pause.

"Yes," said the Professor. "Tito would be proud. Though—how do I say this?—I feel that this subject matter was … my turf. I feel I am the one who should have written this."

Cody deftly brushed aside the bangs off his forehead, left side, then right.

"I thought we were going to leave our egos at the door, man," he said. "Besides, you've had since 2015. How much longer was the world supposed to wait?"

The Professor smiled.

"Touché. Let me email Chris Poland and Tito to see if maybe they have an idea how to play this."

"Fair enough."

"Fair enough."

Cody's face brightened. "Hey, man," he said. "So now that we are all warm and fuzzy again, check this out and shower me with more envy." He reached down and brought into view a big violin with a guitar neck.

"What the fuck is that?" the Professor said.

Cody grinned like a child. "It's a 'guit-fiddle,'" he said. "See, we expanded the store from vintage vinyl to instrument sales, lessons, and the purchase and resale of antiques, and a few days ago a customer brought in this old violin hoping to preserve it. Man, it was shot, mostly the neck area, but during our inspection we saw that there was an inscription, or what violin makers call a 'label.' It said 'Antonius Stradivarius Cremonensis Faciebat Anno 1715.' In English, it meant that this instrument might be an actual Antonio Stradivarius, as in made by the one and only."

"And where did you see this label?"

"Inside one of the F-holes."

"My God, they call it that?"

Cody nodded, like *Okay, Okay ...*

"Yeah," he said. "Nerdy-dirty, I know. For your information, the F-holes are the two curvy, slim S-shapes on either side of the bridge."

"Yes, I figured. Is the inscription for real?"

"Nah, most probably a fake. We brought in an expert connected with Rare Violins of New York, and he insisted that the letter font was off. Couldn't specify how exactly, but we were all pretty sure at that point that it was just another violin."

"But it's fun to dream."

"So you're saying there's a chance ... "

The Professor adjusted his glasses. "Okay," he said, "so just in case the expert got it wrong, please tell me. What is so special about this violin maker?"

Cody beamed. "Antonio Stradivarius is known as the greatest violin maker of all time," he said. "That's why we called in the expert. If proven authentic, these instruments are worth a pretty penny, all kept like treasure under lock and key by different international councils for the arts, museums, ritzy schools like Juilliard, and a shitload of royal collections in a whole bunch of countries."

He angled the instrument for a moment, letting the light play off it, and then leaned down to the side to put it carefully, carefully back in what was most probably a guitar stand out of the camera shot. When he straightened, he had a look of mischief about him.

"If this was actually what the label says it is," he continued, "and if I am getting the timelines right, it was owned by the virtuoso Karol Jozef Lipinski. There is also an old urban legend that this particular instrument was cursed—you know, haunted. Still is, supposedly."

"How so?"

Cody put his hands to the side, palm-up, as if checking for rain.

"I don't know, man. I ain't no history major!"

The Professor was leaning forward, face filling the screen.

"And now," he said, "the instrument is yours."

"That's right. Once we bought it for a hundred bucks, I convinced everyone to let me adopt it, and I doctored on a neck from an old Fender Stratocaster, making this combo."

"And how does it play?"

"The sustain on it is absolutely sick. When you bend a note, you can hold on it forever, and when you grab your harmonic squeal, you can bounce it around the rafters like a majestic fucking clipper ship."

He bent to pick it up again and rested the butt on his knee, and for a weird moment he seemed to be this long-haired rebel musician from a fancy orchestra in another country in another century. Still, the Professor's attention and focus had already left the building.

"I'll see you," he said. "We'll make the Tito story work, no worries."

There was that awkward moment when the Professor hit the button to end the meeting, and Cody was in the middle of a sentence.

Didn't matter.

The Professor had a story to write about ancient curses and modern-day murderers, traditions, and folklore.

Chapter 8

Lucy Phirsgail played guitar, an Epiphone Prophecy Flying V, and her band had weekly gigs at QXT's on Mulberry Street, in the Crypt Rock Room, Newark, New Jersey. They were also booked twelve to fourteen times a year at the Red Lion in Manhattan, New York City, though the commute was a bitch, and they only made half the door. QXT's had good monitors, but you had to tip the house sound man a hundred bucks or he'd shut them off on you. As for the Red Lion, the stage was so small that Billy had to play as if his drumsticks were made of glass, and the opportunities for Lucy to get those big harmonic squeals were nil.

The band was called Lucifer's Gal, as they had fun with her name. She was pretty in a haunted kind of way, with dark eyes, dark roots, and winter-frost hair that she let hang in her face like Kurt Cobain when she played. She was lanky, no ass to speak of, but she looked good in a leather mini and knee-high black boots. They were a bar band that played arena rock, almost like a 1980s throwback, in a cross between Dogma, the sexy evil fetish nuns signed with MNRK Heavy, and ANA of Eclipse Records, one of the better female-fronted symphonic metal bands.

They had been seen by representatives from Warner, Nuclear Blast, Napalm Records, and Lava, but were told in each case that they "just didn't have it." Lucy practiced for three hours a night after managing the Greenblatt's Music Store on Union Street in Irvington, 8:00 A.M. to 7:00 P.M. As for her guitar playing, she was good but not great. She could never admit that out loud, but it was one of those truths in her head that she could never fully shake, like someone with OCD unable to stop thinking that they were blinking too much.

But, *God*, she wanted this so badly. She wanted the endorsement opportunities with E.S.P., Stratocaster, Ibanez, and Jackson, all the insider's experts advising her as to what effect boxes would give her which sounds, the bigger concert venues, the better lightshows, real roadies, the smoke machines, the roaring crowds, the green glow sticks and beachballs they chucked and bounced around, the weed and the free booze and the KFC or Bud Light sponsorship ads flashing on the concrete facing of the second deck in the break between the opener and Lucifer's Gal, the lot of them waiting at the bottom of the metal stairs leading to the stage with their landing points specified by X's of glow-in-the-dark Gorilla Tape, a safe distance away from the pyrotechnics ready to blow with the first power chord.

She had been at this for five and a half years now. She was almost thirty, and she was thinking of moving back home, thinking of going back to school, maybe following up on her bachelor's with a master's in music history. She could become a teacher, maybe an adjunct professor somewhere.

That Monday, she opened the store, which somehow always had the flat aroma of cobwebs and books, and she relocked the door to handle the preliminaries, flipped on the lights, and turned on the register. She made a note that she had to fill in two spots on the carousel with music books, both usually reserved for the drumming practice guides written by Carmine Appice, and on the pegboard adjacent to the display window they were short on EZ Play Pillow guitar strings and fifty-foot cords. She went to the back to turn on the central air, and on her way saw on the bench in the workshop, this busted old violin. Annoyed, she wondered when was the last time she told Denny Rawlings, her weekend assistant manager, not to take in used merchandise without calling her first.

She approached it with her head cocked to one side. The neck was broken off halfway down, making a splinter that could have easily been a weapon. Concurrently, there were no tuning pegs, no strings, yet the amber body looked to be sound. She came around to sit on the stool and picked up the wounded instrument.

The moment her fingers touched the wood, she felt something. It was a thrill that went straight to the spine, a rush under her jaw, behind her eyes. Suddenly she felt like an experienced craftsman from another time and earlier century, and she angled it up to move the shadows so she could look inside one of the F-holes.

Her breath quickened.

It said, *"Antonius Stradivarius Cremonensis Faciebat Anno 1715."* She gently rested it back down on the carpenter's bench. If this was legitimate, she had in her possession a product crafted by Antonio Stradivarius, considered the greatest violin maker, or "luthier," of all time.

The year 1715 was supposedly part of his Golden Era, and this broken instrument very well might have belonged once to virtuoso Karol Jozef Lipinski, he who got it from an elderly pupil of the late Giuseppe Tartini, a one - Dr. Mazzurana, who claimed that the violin gave him nightmares about teaching the devil to play but had increased his ability tenfold. Lipinski took it, welcomed it, and it supposedly darkened his life dramatically, as he performed for years as, ha-ha, second fiddle to Paganini, whose name most people would still recognize even today. In terms of story-cred, the affirmable history indicated that the two virtuosos did in fact know each other, that they respected each other and even played on the same stages together, but, because of the alleged Stradivarius curse, everyone always considered Lipinski to be the lesser of the two. Supposedly, it ate Lipinski alive inside, because he never touched the heart of the dream, but got so close he could feel the heat of it on his face, so to speak, forever possessed with this incredible talent and torturous, unquenchable desire to be number one.

"Well, I already have the desire," she thought. "Wouldn't mind a little taste of number one or two talent, thank you. I'd even be thrilled with top nine or ten, for fuck's sake."

On a whim, she looked back at the steel racking where they kept abandoned parts still intact. Next to the bell of a tuba and a snare drum with the head off was the guitar neck they had replaced on an Ibañez RG Prestige Super Wizard, for Greggie Hall, one of their regulars, a snotty thirteen-year-old who played chords and was doing a fair job with scales, slow but sure. He loved his birthday present, but he wanted gold frets they had to special-order. The Ibañez had the thinnest neck on the market, and Lucy walked over to give it a fresh look.

"One plus one spells fame," she murmured, absently padding back out front to open the door, let in Rick Dooley, and give him the register tab. Once back in the shop, she walked slowly to the rack as if in a daze, and she brought over the neck and set it on the bench. She went to the stackable red repair bins that held parts and accessories and chose number 666, yeah man—fucking A. She made her way to the other side of the room and started opening cabinets and drawers, started gathering, first a pair of small flat chisels, a level, a needle file, a handful of tiny set screws, and a fine-tooth razor saw. She walked over to the mini-fridge, which desperately needed to be cleaned out, and not with a rag … we're talking Brillo, and she got out her favorite cup, the New Jersey Devils one (double yuk-yuk) that had the two little demon horns on the leak-proof lid. She dumped out the week-old diet iced tea into the rinse basin, then filled it back up with water, drank it down, and wiped the cup out with a paper towel twice for good measure. Then she started to work.

She lost track of time.

Hair hanging in her face, she filed, sanded, scraped, and cut. At one point, she went and got a Wilkinson guitar bridge, a DiMarzio Humbucker pickup with a nickel cover and black insert, then two volume knobs, and sometime later she got a hold of the smallest drill bits they had plus the Milwaukee brand cordless drill. She made a brace with a contour guard to match the curve of the body, and since the tailpiece with the fine tuners did her no good, she removed it and drilled six holes right through the bottom to pull the ends of the strings through.

By 7:00 p.m., she had a "guit-fiddle." It was beautiful. She vaguely recalled throughout the day coming out from the shop to settle a dispute over a double charge for a bag of guitar picks and calling three vendors to get things shipped next day air. But Ricky, and after school hours, Hannah Richards, had handled everything else.

Lucy told Hannah to go on home, then locked up and dimmed the lights to "after-hours" mode.

She went back to the shop and took her new creation out into the showroom area. She got down a cord and a strap and plugged into a Marshall amplifier. The store was situated at the edge of the Route 59 Thruway, and to the right was the Ritter & Sons Quarry and Quarry Supply, a massive open pit mine a mile wide and a quarter mile deep in the lower levels, with its bulldozers and massive mounds of topsoil sand, river gravel, and filler dirt, all darkened by now for all but a few security lights looming above the office trailer compound, and on the other side of the music store there was the small portion of the strip mall they were rebuilding all day every week day until around 4 P.M. Consequently then, loud amplification in here would not be a factor, even if she made the windows shake. Time to play. This was going to be an all-nighter.

It frightened her at first, but there was a face in the window. She had the Marshall turned up to seven, so loud it buzzed the back of her teeth, but she had never played anything with this level of resonance and ethereal sustain, painting patterns in her mind of exotic scales, magnificent runs, and multi-note sweeps never attempted before with human hands, at least not by anyone she had seen live.

It was someone looking in through the display window to the right of the front door, pale and ghostly, gaunt and wide-eyed, with his hands curved on either side to cut glare. She turned the volume knob down to zero and approached.

"Let me in, would you, Ms. Phirsgail?" he said, faint and muted through the glass. Her ears were still ringing, and she shook her head. He took that as a no and said,

"Don't you remember me? Hank Frazier. Last week, I bought the neck strap for my daughter, who plays clarinet in the marching band. I also got a tube of cork grease, ligatures, and a spare mouthpiece."

She remembered; she opened the door, the little bell ringing like a nursery rhyme, and she did a free-fall into a dream state.

Everything came to her in flashes and figments all out of order, some in slow motion and others in those horror movie jump-cuts where the dark figure had frames eliminated, making him skip time and space across a room right into your face.

On the broad glass counter, there had been nine New Jersey Devils cups with the demon's horns on the leakproof lids, all arranged in a pair of circles, one inside the other. In front of each was a place card one might see at a bar mitzvah or wedding, all with different names written in fancy cursive. They were famous guitarists, the closest saying:

"Eddie Van Halen."

Lucy drank from that cup, chugged it down, and it was warm and electric, vaguely tasting of copper, and she turned up the volume knob and started executing Eddie's world-famous tapping technique that featured his signature two-handed independence, with double hammer-ons twice as fast as he'd ever managed, precise and delicate as the fluttering wings of a hummingbird. Hank Frazier stood watching, mouth slightly ajar.

Then came a dark vision of the deepest level of the neighboring quarry, the sound of her breath rasping in her chest, the heaviness of the body slung over her shoulder, his arms hanging down loosely and rhythmically bumping into the backs of her thighs.

There was the shop, and Frazier with his hands tied behind his back and his feet bound together with a twelve-gauge extension cord, and he was hung upside down like a bat on the heavy-duty hook by the rinse basin. He was pleading, frothing at the mouth, yammering on about what had just infected his mind, all about conflated texts, mixed legends, religious blasphemy, and things turned upside down as he was, inverted, his panic at the mouth flipped to the mad grin of a jester, and was it not ironic to the point of ridiculousness that it was not Lucy Phirsgail who was the bat, and that it was not Lucy floating outside the window asking permission to enter, and that Dante's nine concentric circles of hell were presented here in a convenient two just for show, featuring—you said it, sister—the top nine amazing guitarists …

Even mixed like a deck of cards, these scenarios almost made sense, sitting just out of reach, and she was studying the New Jersey Devils cup out of which she had taken that long, satisfying draught, the precious nectar so velvety, so warm and so rich, and another inversion, when you turned the cup upside down to drink, the leakproof lid wasn't imitation devil's horns but fangs, like the two she could feel in her mouth.

There was no moisture left in the cup either, not even a streak or a drop, because she hadn't used it since finishing the water in it this afternoon and wiping it out with a paper towel.

Then it all came back to her, the missing playing card, and she saw herself on all fours canine-style, just below the struggling Hank Frazier hanging upside down by the rinse basin, and she had pounced up and in, clamping her teeth to his throat in a crescendo of hot crimson that spattered her face, and then, eyes wide, she thrashed her head side to side like a rabid dog with a piece of raw meat. She had severed straight through the internal and external jugulars as well as the carotid artery, and he twisted and writhed, his breath a red mist, and he finally shuddered to his end like a train on wet, rusted rails. She kept up on her haunches, raised her palms to his cheeks as would a lover, and then buried her jaws into that gash, sucking hard with verve and with lust, and she drank that poor bastard dry.

Her mouth tasted sour at this point, her knees ached, and she was covered with the quarry filler dirt that she had pawed over the body of Hank Frazier, and she looked at her reflection in the window that was a listless, shadowed anti-reflection. She turned to the counter, and there were eight cups left: Yngwie Malmsteen, Al Di Meola, Stevie Ray Vaughan, Paul Gilbert, Randy Rhodes, Allen Collins, Tom Morello, and Slash.

And suddenly she knew the paradoxical tragedy of what had become her life story. She was destined to play the guitar better than anyone in the history of man, but always to an audience of one who would never live to document her achievement.

But was she only successful if acknowledged by others?

Hell, she was a rock musician playing bars, hoping for arenas. Public acknowledgment was the fucking Holy Grail. She looked at the drinking cups. There were nine again now, the one at the front with the fancy place card naming the Swedish shred wizard Yngwie Malmsteen, and replaced was the Eddie Van Halen place card at the implied back of the line, the farthest point away in the inner circle, now reading the next logical entry: *"Steve Stevens,"* Billy Idol's old ace who did that pick-me-up Spanish flamenco strumming.

Lucy turned the Marshall off "standby" and strapped on the guit-fiddle. She started this new jam session by playing the solo at the 4:58 mark of Malmsteen's *Seventh Sign*, note for note with even more body and feel, and abruptly she stopped.

There was someone looking in the window, hands cupped up at the eyes to cut off the glare.

"Please let me in," the woman said, muted through the glass.

Lucy walked to the door. It wasn't about fame. It wasn't about trophies and Facebook likes and thousands of YouTube subscribers. All that mattered now was the blood, and the way her throat ached to swallow it down.

> *Dear Sirs,*
> *I feel that I am more than qualified to be a contestant at Murdertown.*
> *P.S.—I can't wait to meet the others, for I want to play them a lullaby.*
>
> *Lucifer's Gal*

Chapter 9

Cody was flat-out pissed off, to tell the truth. He also had trouble identifying any one specific cause, since the issues were *"conflated,"* and there you go! He was compelled to use the Professor's word from the "Lucifer's Gal" snippet, even though it sounded uppity, conceited, and patronizing.

So what was the tally now? The roster was almost half filled with the Red Headmaster, Cody the Clown, the Beekeeper, the Rock Reaper, and Lucifer's Gal. It was Cody's turn, but why did it seem so uneven? He felt he was being bested somehow …

And, for Christ's sake, what was this podcast even about anymore? They had moved from serial killers to those with superpowers, as in *supernatural* superpowers, straight into the old school clichés, you know, *vampires.* What came next—mummies, witches, and zombies? Godzilla and King Kong? The Phantom of the Opera versus Frankenstein? Cody thought they had been creating something new here, something different, something, I don't know … scary, right?

The Professor was turning this into a cartoon because he was more interested in how it looked "in writing" than how it developed as a workable guide for a live podcast.

Cody closed his eyes. This was his fault, writing the "Cody the Clown" piece in what the Professor had called "narrative form," and clearly the "monster" Cody created wasn't a clown, but in more practical terms the wide-open door he'd left for the Professor to walk through, going straight to his go-to, the narrative structure he pretended to complain about.

Cody sighed. He knew he'd fucked up the metaphor.

The Professor was the monster, not the door he walked through. But wait: didn't you walk through a doorway and not a door? Cody looked at the ceiling and took a breath right up into the shoulders. Word riddles for the anal; the Professor's mindset in a nutshell, and again, Cody chided himself for taking on characteristics of the one he was questioning. I mean, talk about a loser strategy, right? Shit, man, Cody could practice word games all day, but he'd never catch up. And that was the overall point, wasn't it? It seemed the Professor was molding and shaping this to maneuver Cody into a corner so he would end up being nothing more than a shitty replica.

He turned his head to the side, closed his eyes.

What the fuck did they call that ... the poor replica, the shadow, the joke? He looked down at his laptop, his expression gone dark. He didn't need to go on Google for this one. He remembered from tenth-grade English that it was called a "foil."

He frowned like an angry kid.

As said, the Professor wasn't helping to craft a podcast. He was writing a book about two guys crafting a podcast, and he was using Cody as the stooge, the puppet who provided him material he could criticize as part of the plot.

Cody sucked in his breath, making a hissing sound.

Wait.

Puppet.

Lap-puppet. Basement. Doggie crate.

His face flowered petal by petal to a wide, angry grin.

You want to go classic? I can go classic.

He pushed up out of the chair, out to the hall, to the stairs. Yes, my good friend, my dude, my bro. Let's go down where it's cool, where it smells of damp cement, old canvas, and sediment. I want you to meet someone.

The most vicious bitch on the planet.

On the way to the den, which was, of course, on the way to the basement, Cody's resolve started to splinter like a few loose shingles

41

coming off in a hurricane. He had said himself in the earlier draft of Cody the Clown that the best lies, and therefore stories, were chock-full of truths. But this was the bald truth, the real secret exposed, nothing "borrowed" or "reconfigured" or "re-filtered." Still, the metaphorical roof in a storm only lost a few of those shingles, after all. By the time he gave a gentle knock on the door, he had re-fortified his decision, because the real truth in this case didn't sound like the truth. It sounded like a cliché horror thing, and "hiding in plain sight" would be outrageously easy, his ability to write it better than the other snippets a self-made bonus because he would simply describe what was really happening.

Plus, in defense of exploring the clichés in this part of the genre, it seemed a natural progression to feel personally responsible to point out where the clichés were dead wrong. Similar to vampire fiction, the idea that everyone you attacked became the walking undead, cursed with your curse so they could perpetuate the cycle, was as stupid as a village idiot on *Jeopardy.* Common sense: a vampire sucks out all your blood, you're dead. Period. If every victim became a vampire and all their victims became vampires and so on and so on, the world would soon be ninety-eight percent populated with vampires, and the two percent immune would be the new monsters.

And a stake through the heart? Please. More believable would be a removal of the head, and these common misconceptions applied to Cody's cliché as well. He knocked on the door.

"Come," said Candi.

He entered, and she was at the makeshift bar that was really an old bookshelf turned on its side. She was mixing drinks. She was training to become a bartender. She had on a sleeveless Avenged Sevenfold tee, and her hair was done up in a long Viking braid coming over the shoulder.

"Whatcha making?" Cody said.

She was in the middle of the pour.

"A Corpse Reviver," she said. "It is tart and zingy with a hint of licorice on the finish."

Cody smiled to himself. The coincidence was almost too good for fiction. Almost. She gave it the straw test and smiled. "Not bad," she said.

"You're an ace."

"You want a sip?"

"No."

"You don't know what you're missing."

"I want to go to the basement."

Her eyes flashed, and blush rose into her cheeks.

"Now, honey?"

"Yes."

She flipped the lock back over her shoulder and made to come out from behind the bar.

"All right," she said, "c'mon, then."

She brushed past, and for a second Cody watched her go. He loved watching women go so he could admire that caboose. Candi's caboose was primo even in loose jeans. He followed and slowed his pace as she accelerated down the stairs, because at the bottom leading into the first floor foyer she'd just left the Avenged Sevenfold T-shirt half inside-out on the floor, and in the archway to the half-kitchen was the rumple of her jeans, and hung off the nail with the oven mitts was her Wink Unlined Balconette bra, and on the knob of the basement door her black Micro-Thong.

Sex was always best in the basement.

And the consequences, the most deadly.

Cody started through the kitchen door by the pot rack down the stairs, wooden and rickety, the third and fifth creaking under his weight, and he paused halfway down. He closed his eyes and turned his head to the side as if to listen better, and yes, there was that weird dripping sound like what you'd hear in a cave, the source impossible to identify even by Fitzwater, the landlord's plumber, so the band had felt it convenient and safe to store their equipment down here after Ralph died.

Cody came off the bottom stair and was greeted by the band's gear spanning the front wall corner to corner, all covered in sheets like burial shrouds. Cody's equipment was positioned to the left, the blunt shape of his custom cabinet with four Celestion Vintage 30 speakers making a bookend opposite Mikey Riley's Peavy Headliner 410 bass cabinet to the far right. Between them was Ricky Dromio's Pearl Roadshow drum kit, all covered with dropcloths and sheets draped over the two outer crash cymbals like ghosts leaning in, whispering secrets to each other across the blunt form of the tom-toms.

None of this was relevant now.

Except that fucking bass drum.

Cody bent and rag-rolled up the old canvas blanket and draped it along the top of the shell. On the bass drum's front head was the Wolf Shadow logo. A week before Ralph died, they had paid for horror artist Lynne Hansen to design the silhouette of a wolf sitting and howling, the moon, of course, the background by default. What a fucking waste of money it had turned out to be musically.

Not such a waste in terms of black magic, however, and as soon as Cody had exposed the graphic just now, Candi made a low, teasing growl in the back of her throat. She was at the far end of the basement in the doggie crate, a wall-to-wall cell with the bars as thick as those you would find in a prison with stainless steel lock and mounting hardware. The space inside was loaded with cushions and pillows, silk linens, fur and satin, a king-size mattress, and carpeting on the floor with padding underneath five times thicker than what would be in most living-room spaces.

The love den.

Before all that, however (you dogs …), back to those silly clichés. They started with vampires and, for some God-awful reason, seemed to transfer over to the next most popular monster. As said, the first shared cliché was that a vampire made other vampires, and therefore a werewolf's attacks made other werewolves. Untrue. A werewolf made a bunch of very dead humans. The next cliché was that a vampire was susceptible to a wooden stake in the heart, just as a werewolf could be killed only with a silver bullet. Untrue. Silver bullets didn't work either. The third ridiculous cliché was that vampires were rendered defenseless in the daylight, just as a werewolf was dependent on the cycle of the moon. Again, grossly untrue. A werewolf's mate controlled the cycle by first unveiling the Wolf Shadow logo.

And secondly?

Cody walked heavily toward the crate. This was going to be quick and violent, and he was less frightened of being injured than he was disgusted with himself for always getting harder during the process, even after her first two orgasms. He also had a purpose this time, and he had never tried to give Candi a directive once she had fully transformed. He had always either locked her in the crate or he had let her out to satisfy her craving to find some creep and have a rip-fest.

She was on the mattress, down on her front forearms, her ass poked up so it was Valentine-shaped. Cody didn't recall shedding his clothes, yet he rarely did during one of these encounters, as he was under his own kind of spell as the instigator. She pounced up to meet him, both falling to their knees, hands pressed to each other's cheeks, kissing and tonguing with hunger. She pushed him back, threw a leg over, and mounted. It was not slow and building, but a hot present tense, up and down, slick friction, her small breasts bouncing in perky starts that harmonized with the hair sprouting around her wrists, under the ankles, and between every toe.

She pushed off, went to her back, and pulled Cody onto her, into her, and she cupped her hands around his buttocks so she could pull and pump him in and out in hard rhythm, escalating, peaking hard like a thunderhead, and her nails bristled and grew into claws, and they cut into his skin back there. He hardly noticed. Before him, her eyes changed, misty almond-shaped blue to slanted and harsh ruby red, her jaw elongating, her button nose darkening, spreading to join along the top of the mouth to make a blunt snout in a lengthening muzzle, lips curdling, growling, fangs bursting from inside the enamel and curving down like knives used by bush thieves and desert outlaws.

He turned her, got behind to finish the job, and it took but a moment for her third multiple, the blonde braid seeping in and dissolving like rich compost, giving way to the barbs pushing through and standing like oiled quills altogether shaped in what seemed a natural mohawk trailing all the way down her back, and her pointed ears sprouted, and her tail snaked behind her, and she pulled away on all fours.

In the back left corner of the crate, she took on the initial positioning, down on her forelegs; paws forward, her hindquarters raised, ears up, and a low growl simmering in her throat. She was showing her teeth, red eyes filled with cunning, and she waited.

Cody moved to the opposite side of the cage so he wouldn't block the door. He thought about the kind of subtle mental warfare that went on between friends, with creative business partners like the Professor, with his little soft sell trying to redefine little by little what equaled "equal." Right. Fuck him. Schoolteachers and music store managers aside, it was time to get real. Time to get bloody.

"Sex and drug trafficker," he said to his wife. "Bring me his lungs and his scalp."

Chapter 10

The Professor took his glasses off and leaned back in his office chair, pressing his thumb and index finger to the bridge of his nose with his eyes shut. Cody was not a bad writer, not at all, and he was getting better. The problem—minus all the smooth rationalizations—was that Cody's improvement was not what people paid the big money for. They wanted conflict and characters that were distinctive from one another, both the killers and the hosts. Hell, Cody wasn't even developing a distinctive voice. Instead, he was sounding more and more like the Professor.

He tilted back forward. Wait a hot minute. What if that was the big twist—that this whole thing was a fantasy inside one guy's head, "writing" both himself and "Cody Kennedy"?

Uh, no.

It was too easy, too middle school. Moreover, if the Professor was questioning it himself at this juncture, so would the readers, and tah-dah-poof, there goes the surprise. There had to be a major what-the-fuck moment late in the story arc, that was a staple of the Professor's work, and if there was one thing he fucking despised it was telegraphing that shit.

The doorbell rang.

The Professor jerked his head in the direction of the stairs in the hall and froze like a dog with its tail up. He was alone in the house; he was divorced, his son Max was a systems analyst in Tempe, Arizona, and Killian, his King Charles Cavalier, died of congestive heart failure last Christmas.

It was also 11:30 at night, and the way the Professor usually played it was … if you ring the bell this late, your house had better be on fire.

The doorbell pinged a second time. He got up, the chair creaked, of course it did, and he started down the stairs mechanically, as if watching himself go through the motions of going to open the door just shy of midnight, quite possibly to a stranger. He could have taken the old Pat Burrell signature baseball bat he kept in the office. He clumped down to the first-floor landing, and he could have grabbed the three-pronged fireplace poker to the left of the fake hearth, and as he crossed to the door, he saw himself not retreating to the kitchen to grab one of the butcher knives in the block on the counter.

What good would any of those "weapons" really be? If the caller was a thug with a mission, the Professor didn't honestly think he could assess this in half a second, then come to the conclusion in the latter half of that second that he was going to attempt to murder a stranger at his door with a bat, a poker, or a kitchen knife, because by then he would have already been attacked by the thug in the earlier part of the latter half of that very same second.

He flicked on the overhead porch light and opened the door. Cool evening breeze, cicadas in the trees, a moth fluttering an erratic diagonal up and across toward the light. There were long shadows made by the lawn chairs on the patio and the dull sheen of a spiderweb between the hedge and the handrail leading three steps down to the walkway.

There was no one out here on the stoop.

Knock-Knock-Zoom-Zoom? This late?

The Professor tried to think of the middle schoolers or teens in the neighborhood, but Corey and Will had grown up with Max, and Jenny Baker was a year behind them, all moving on during and after college. The block wasn't spilling over with kids at all; in fact, most of the homeowners were retired.

He closed the door.

He looked at the knob.

The bell rang again, seemed to be right in his ear, and he ripped open the door in a grandiose sweep.

Nothing.

Stillness. He stepped down to the patio and walked a few paces forward, half expecting the door to slam shut behind him. He instinctively looked back over his shoulder. The door was fine, but the mailbox fastened to the brick had the lid raised.

A business-sized envelope was sticking up, back side showing. The Professor reached up for it, took it out, and flipped it over.

No mailing address, no return address, no stamp, and the blank seemed to have the same effect on the Professor as the Michael Myers mask had on its initial audiences in 1978, supposedly bearing a resemblance to William Shatner, but only a faceless, formless … blank. There was to be no reasoning with this. Reason meant mutual bargaining for compromise, and in reference to Michael Meyers at least, there was only bloodlust, hunger, and purpose. Behind the faceless mask.

He opened the letter.

Greetings, Professor.

I am not fond of you, but you are the burden I have accepted openly for sixty-two years. No more. To the point, I am your "Mr. Hyde." In the original story by Robert Louis Stevenson, Mr. Hyde was Dr. Jekyll's evil side personified, a dwarf, since Stevenson was trying to illustrate the idea that our good outweighed and "outsized" our evil. Of course, this made the sappy, empathetic, wholesome part win out most times in the everlasting internal war between the two.

The problem is, Professor, that my patience with you has been exhausted. Concurrently, most of your fiction has been saved by me in the end anyway, because I so easily edited out the heaviest of the emotional baggage and offered conclusions that more honestly dealt with both the given protagonist and the antagonist. Still, neither of us has created anything one could call "pure," since my own climactic moments and choices are forever diluted by your needy, cloying sentimentalities, and it sickens me, frankly. I am real. You are more flowery than "Disney," and this tug of war must end.

I do not trust in your ability, let alone Cody Kennedy's, to craft an engaging and thought-provoking overall climax and resolution in Murdertown. Since you don't outline and you therefore "discovery-write," you have no idea what's coming until the moment you write it. Please hear me. For now, you may retain me inside as a shadow, for without at least that much, you wouldn't have the courage to go take a piss in the middle of the night, but as previously indicated, things are going to change.

To business then:

Demand: *Make me Contestant #7 in* **Kill or Be Killed,** *to take place in Murdertown.*

Admitted Weakness: *We are housed in a human being and are therefore easily killed or physically manhandled.*

Internal Plan: *You and I will switch roles, and when we do, I will control our physical form with you as my shadow and my hostage. Unfortunately, you see, there is a need for both of us in order to create prose. Therefore, when the game goes live, you will help me document the Murdertown experience the way I want it, no "art," no "inflection," just raw facts about death. Consequently, when the game is over, the reason to write will have expired. Joyously then, I will be able to unleash everything you have made me keep pent up for so long, and I might live, and I mean really live, for the sweet red taste of extraordinary violence with the whisper of stealth as my handmaiden. Note: I will keep you on as a prisoner for the fucking fun of it.*

Game Strategy: *I will booby-trap the block of abandoned tenements in phantom pathways that would lead to the most satisfying, and therefore, devastating conflicts between combatants, pitting their most colorful strengths and weaknesses against one another. Still, that is all part of a hoax within the hoax ... to lead our listeners into expectation, excitement, and predictions, even betting pools and straight gambling, as they evaluate these pairings like the old UFC with no rules, rounds, or weight classes. And all* *the while, it will turn out that our unsuspecting audience will have become hideously vulnerable to the surprise plot-thread that was right under their noses from the start, the one they can only blame themselves for missing, in that once I am disclosed as a contestant, the balance of our make-believe characters will deem it highly unfair, grouping together to rally as a whole against the rigged system, and I will spill cancer between them, acid, hot poison, betrayal and hate, cruelty and revenge, all causing those ugly surprise confrontations, unexpected and wicked, bloody and ironic, all in absolute organized chaos. What the listeners really want …*

*   **Consequence for Non-Compliance:** *Permanent severance of me from you, "Mr. Hallmark," and so, in other words, to hell with fun and games. You see, there is a significant difference between our relationship and the one presented in Richard Matheson's Star Trek episode* The Enemy Within, *1966. In that teledrama, the "evil" Captain Kirk could not survive without the "good" one. This does not apply here. You are the Professor's conscience. I am the Professor's consciousness, meaning that I inherit the mind if I make the split permanent. You, in fact, would be the one to soon perish, and I would still be free to live out our new legacy."*

Do we understand each other, Professor?

Yours Truly,
The Dark Doppelgänger

Chapter 11

Cody had his face in his hands, and when he surfaced, he rubbed his hands together palm to palm. Jesus! The Professor was a lunatic. He was also royally fucking over the "regular townfolk" with his internal wars and his history lessons. The violin shit was cool, I mean, it was music, and a metal audience was part of the plan, given that Cody was a metal musician. But Robert Louis Stevenson? Classic literature? 1800s? The philosophical hoop-di-doo was hard enough to understand, but multiple selves? Cody had read it three times and was still unsure of the "rules" for this guy, the dopple-whoever. Why hadn't this character taken over the Professor's body before? Was he a dwarf like Hyde, or was he equal sized? Why did he need the "good side" for writing? He was a showoff who loved literature, so why was he going to cut off the writing part of his life after Murdertown? Wouldn't he want to write best-seller after best-seller describing his addiction to "the sweet red taste of extraordinary violence"?

Right. The character was written poorly, yet in such a snobby "academic" voice with such colorful, million-dollar vocab, that few would bother arguing with him, even on the soft points, at least not the average Joes of the world. The Professor wasn't a good writer. He was an expert at putting lipstick on a pig.

The fucker.

Cody got up to turn the burner off and take the small saucepan from the stove to pour the warm milk into his favorite coffee mug, the one with the Wolf Shadow logo. He knew warm milk was not going to help him sleep. He also knew that he did this because he liked warm milk and liked to have something comforting when he couldn't sleep, stumbling through the wee hours of the morning like a zombie on the asphalt with the heat rising off it.

There was a noise downstairs, in the basement: a bottle being knocked over.

A beer bottle; that was Cody's first thought. A beer bottle Ralph knocked over down in the basement, Ralph, who was an unfortunate statistic in the fallout of one of the world's oldest afflictions: alcoholism. He died of cirrhosis of the liver, though most of the time those around him wouldn't even know he was under the influence. He never knocked shit over during a practice or a show, never ever, but that was the image that came to Cody nonetheless. Maybe Ralph was different in the afterlife, having the unfortunate flaws bleed into the magic like penance.

Magic.

Ralph had been a magical human being. He was charming, down to earth, and an automatic friend unless you went out of your way to *prove* him wrong. Frankly, he was beautiful. He looked like Jesus, but more muscular, with long straight black hair, trimmed beard and moustache, and honest eyes, though he did bring a sort of Italian, New York influence to the look: nose, mouth, expression, those same eyes penetrating, as he would stalk on stage right before they played live, pacing in a circle, eyeing the crowd whether an audience of twenty or twenty thousand, pointing, talking with individuals he picked out of the crowd, not "at them," but with them. He was focused. He was sharp. He was an event in himself with a riser stage center he liked to play off of, sometimes putting a foot up to the edge or standing on it like a preacher, a prophet, a god, and he didn't just get across, "I can see your house from here," but more, he showed everyone that they lived *in his heart* from here, this venue, this stage, this moment we would all storyboard together.

"Give us thirty minutes to show you the world through our eyes," he would say, as if he and the crowd were one being, one soul, one song, all of us together carving our signatures into the stone.

Then he would start performing.

What a voice. What a talent.

Cody pushed up from the table and numbly walked to the basement stairs. He started down, and before getting to the bottom, where the ceiling over the stairway ended, he saw that the sheets and blankets had been taken off the equipment.

He came off the last stair, and Ralph was sitting on a bass cabinet that was turned on its side. He was wearing his performance clothes: black leather vest with eyelets and string ties up the sides, wristbands with silver studs, loose black leather pants tucked into lace-up black motorcycle boots.

"Hey," Cody said, for lack of anything else that made sense. If he ever got famous, they could write on his Wikipedia entry that when coming face to face with a spirit of the night, Cody Kennedy was calm as a windless lake on a hot summer day. He still had the mug of warm milk in his hand. Ralph looked him over, eyes clear and sober.

"This is going to get away from you," he said.

"What?"

Ralph normally would have laughed, but this wasn't Ralph. At the same time, however, it *was* Ralph, the total man, more like "Pure Ralph," as odd as that distinction seemed. He had been leaning forward casually, his forearms on his knees, and he pushed slowly to sitting upright.

"You have started something that will have a finish you didn't expect," he said. "In fact, the mutation is already growing, the disease spreading."

"What do you mean mutation, disease?"

Ralph put his feet on the floor and moved off, starting to back away toward the other side of the basement. Then, as was *so Ralph!* he put out his hands to the sides, but unlike the old Ralph, he didn't raise his eyebrow like a wink and a "between us" kind of a smirk. He looked more like a religious figure about to make some sort of grand testament.

"Three things," he said, pausing at the other end of the basement. "First, check your email. Second, try to remember that all of it … all of this … all of everything … has always been about love."

"And what's the third thing?" Cody said.

Ralph was almost washed black in the shadows.

"The third thing," he said, "is that I am contestant number eight, and you can mark me down plain and simple as *Ghost*."

Chapter 12

Cody emailed the Professor immediately.

The Professor saw the yellow prompt giving him the choice of ignoring Cody's current message or tapping in, but he was already into the first sentence of the email he had received himself, a few seconds earlier.

Attention Podcasters,

I am an expert in urban, jungle, and desert warfare. My specific skills first include an expertise in handling a wide range of explosives, and I additionally possess intimate knowledge of operations with Daisy Cutters, Smart Glide Storm Breakers, Incendiary Napalm, Cluster with Skeets, and Hypersonic Cruise Missiles. For short-distance targets, I get the most bang for my buck from the Mk 21 Hand Grenade.

In reference to guns, my preferences are: the Browning M250 Tripod-mounted machine gun, the Heckler & Koch HK 416 M4 Carbine semi-automatic, and the .300 Winchester Magnum sniper rifle. For closer range, my go-to is the Sig Sauer M17 Service Pistol.

In hand-to-hand combat, I am a specialist with maces, war clubs, battle axes, Viking hammers, broadswords, rapiers, sabers, and bayonets, as well as smaller blade-to-blade scenarios when I employ the Ka-Bar USMC Fighting/Utility knife, visible, and the Benchmade Mini Adamas Axis knife hidden, ankle sheaf or waistband.

In weaponless situations, I have mastered Combat Sambo, Defendu, KPAP, and Ninjutsu. I can drive dump trucks, bulldozers, skid steer loaders, and various current models of tanks, rigid hull inflatable military boats, and small jets.

I have eliminated one hundred and fifty-seven men, seventy-nine women, twenty-three teenagers armed with guns or explosives, and eleven babies held at the chest by said women using them as human shields and hiding firearms in the swaddling clothes. To be clear, none of these are examples of murder, but instead, positive and well-calculated risk management carried out in the interest of retaining a free and powerful America. Your game contestants are mostly criminals, no matter how romanticized might be their plea for the justice of vigilantism against other criminals. I will purge you of these offenders efficiently, effectively, and completely in the name of patriotism. This is about duty, honor, and country.

Please indicate the manner by which you will start this competition. Are we all to be first in the same open space, or are we given the advantage of entering Murdertown separately and digging in so we can establish perimeters?

Respectfully,
The Soldier

The return email address was gobble-di-gook: 6$@30n6u#5%@gmail.com, and the Professor tried sending an email there, immediately getting the flag:

Error
The address "mailto:6$@30n6u#5%@gmail.com" in the "To" field was not recognized. Please make sure that all addresses are properly formed.

He tapped into Cody's message and saw that it was a forwarded copy of the same message from the same "Soldier." Cody's note atop was:

"Prof, man, did you write this?"

The Professor wrote back:

"No, Cody. Are you claiming you didn't?"

Radio silence. Finally, it flashed 1 in the Inbox, and it said:

"Not my style, Prof. I am also struggling just to keep up, so if you think I'm playing games, you're reading me wrong."

The Professor mulled that one over for a moment or two. To stall, he said:

"By the way, Cody, the 'Ghost' character as Ralph is the best of your work so far. Gave me chills actually."

"Thank you."

The Professor wished he could continue this more carefully, but blunt was better, he supposed.

"Cody," he typed. "Not to mention what you already know, but you created the character who told you to look at your email."

"I know."

"So you are implying that someone or something has hacked us, and instead of going for bank accounts or Social Security numbers, he, she, or they made up a cover letter to be in our fictitious contest as a combatant up against fictitious characters in order to make America great again by cleaning our 'swamp' of miscreants and felons to win five million dollars that we don't have."

"Exactly."

"Wait a minute," the Professor typed. He had something … something odd, something familiar yet in an odd framework or context.

First, this "Soldier's" letter looked like a bunch of lists made off Wikipedia pages, and aside from that, the guy's voice was familiar … oddly similar to a character in the Professor's last collection titled *Just Disappear,* put out by Hippocampus Press. More specifically, the similarities could be attributed to the Professor's short story "The Application," about an assassin named John McMenomay fighting his way out of an AI attack of bots and computer-generated illusions. This "Soldier" character was McMenomay's twin, at least semantically and syntactically, so the entire email was made by AI, most likely ChatGPT, using a combination of online factual data and the Professor's published fiction. The question was, who was hitting the buttons prompting this thing …

Something moved on the computer screen, yet at first the Professor didn't see it clearly, a corner-of-the-eye kind of thing. It took an extra second or two, but he nailed it soon enough, the tabs, up top. A second one was there, though the Professor had only opened the one for his email.

The second tab said:

"Contestant Number Ten"

The Soldier had been number nine. Hell, Cody could always send emails from weird places, but he didn't control the Professor's browsing. On a hunch that felt like turning over a rock with ground beetles and safari ants swarming underneath it, he typed a reply email to Cody in their running chain.

"Look up in your tabs, Cody."

"Just saw it. Was about to tap in."

"What does yours say?"

"Contestant Number Ten."

"Talk to you on the other side."

He gave the tab a click.

Chapter 13

The Legend of Savage Alice

One thing was for sure: Alice Gates was no brainiac. When she was little, they held her back a year in first grade, another for third, and by the time she reached fourth, they had modified her IEP seven times. She was a skinny wisp of a girl, always looking a bit forlorn in her baggy shirt and loose dungaree overalls, with that plain dusty brown ponytail and old, worn Cornhuskers ball cap. In fifth grade, she got teased a lot because everyone was realizing that the differences between boys and girls were far more interesting than the books about nutrition and goal-setting they had to read in health class. Suddenly, any boy with a high voice got teased. A boy who couldn't throw hard got teased. Short boys were razzed constantly, and boys were tormented for days if they backed out of a fight on the playground. And hey, trust me, the girls didn't get away scot-free either. Any female with close-set eyes was targeted along with those with armpit stains, zits, glasses, duck-feet or bad breath, and above all, anyone claiming gayness or "trans" got destroyed, especially in a small town like Cripple Creek, Nebraska, where they had a convenience store, a public-school complex K–12, a church, a bar, and a stoplight.

Alice Gates had a "horse face," pretty bad too, but the shit she took for it stopped the first day of middle school. First of all, she was fourteen, and after a summer growth spurt on top of that, she towered over everyone in her new sixth-grade classroom. The teacher, Mrs. Keystone, put them in reading groups. Alice's was the slowest, of course, and later, when they did math drills, there was a strange moment when Alice handed in her worksheet way early.

First off, Mrs. Keystone had not planned on having to look at anything from the kids this period at all, because she was hungover from the robust wine-tasting the girls had set up after scrapbooking club last night. The "math worksheet" was her emergency lesson packet with a hundred and thirty-five problems, requiring students to show their work, thank you very much, enough to keep them busy all period. She had planned on sitting at her desk, closing her eyes a bit, and delicately massaging her temples.

She looked at Alice's worksheet. She shook her head, got out the answer key from her desk, slipped on her reading glasses, and put her elbows on either side of the pages in front of her. She started massaging those temples.

Every answer was correct, but that wasn't even the point. It was the work. It looked like the ravings of some crazy person who'd been hit over the head with a pipe wrench, with things like, "Five aggies cannot split two half-harvest moons, not under the diamond-tipped drill bits smiling in the roof of your wood shed," and "Torque and RPMs never squeal with knuckle-knuckle gears when they have an air pocket and piston-striker design that equals five orbits times three turns of a woodscrew," and "PSI sparks in the face of soft bonds cutting hard stone castles and hard bonds swimming happily in puddles of abrasive brick mortar."

"Ma'am?" said Alice.

Mrs. Keystone looked up sharply, startled. "Yes?"

Alice went pigeon-toed, looked at her feet.

"I ain't asking no favors, but I happen to know Jimmy Rutherford called out today."

"And how do we know this?"

She shrugged. "He works for my dad sometimes, when he ain't doing the maintenance here at the school."

Mrs. Keystone pursed her lips. "You're saying that Mr. Rutherford helps with the horses?"

Alice put her hands behind her back and swayed a bit. "No, ma'am. My poppa runs the horse farm. Mr. Rutherford works in the equipment barn. I help him sometimes. Fixing stuff."

"And what has that to do with today?"

"Well," Alice said, "I finished my math problems, and I don't like clapping erasers or dumping trash. If you let me into the school's maintenance shop, I can fix the stuff on the bench and on the shelves, the midsized tools on the floor in the holding area, and even the bigger machines out in the gravel yard."

Mrs. Keystone took off her glasses and quaintly put them in her purse.

"How do you know which machines need fixing?"

"He told me," said Alice. "We always talk repairs. Jimmy says to me that I listen to the mechanical stuff everyone else is bored with. He likes it that I don't roll my eyes when he talks about changing brushes and installing trigger-switches and such."

As if challenged in some kind of contest, Mrs. Keystone got out her phone to type in some quick information. Her smile was too bright and sunny.

"Now then," she said, "what are the smaller tools on the bench and on the shelves, please?"

Alice looked up at the ceiling for a moment, her mouth open a bit, her jaw long.

"Okee-dokey," she said. "There's a Makita grinder with a burning smell, a Dewalt cordless drill that won't hold a charge, a two-speed Porta-Band that has the blade slipping off, and a Milwaukee screw gun filled with drywall dust making it sputter. The midsized tools waiting on the shop floor are the Hitachi miter saw with a worn arbor making the blades wobble, a Partner cutoff saw that needs new belts, and a wood framing gun that has nails sticking in the magazine."

"And out in the yard?" Mrs. Keystone said.

Alice counted each on her fingers for no real reason.

"The Craftsman Ride Mower's gears are screaming, the Ditch Witch needs oil, the Bobcat shudders when it lifts up its bucket, and the John Deere tractor needs a tune-up."

Mrs. Keystone stopped typing and looked at Alice closely, lips thin. She leaned forward and lowered her voice:

"Alice Gates … the worksheet … how did you do it? Your— your IEP says—"

"IEP's wrong," said Alice. "No need to whisper in each other's ears, Mrs. Keystone. Everyone has an IEP nowadays, and mine just ain't kept right. I still have trouble reading unless it's a parts breakdown or there are schematic pictures next to the paragraphs, but I always been good at math."

"But your scores—"

"I have test-taking anxiety, ma'am, and they changed my special ed. person five times since first grade, all of 'em always saying the same thing, just to give me more time. But time got nothing to do with it. No matter how long you keep me at a desk in the corner, or how sweet and maple syrup teachers make the titles like 'PRACTICE,' or 'STUDY GUIDE,' or whatnot, they all still look like tests to me that I'll never be able to start, let alone finish."

Mrs. Keystone sat back as if she won something.

"Then how did you do today's math so quickly?"

"It was a worksheet."

"And how did *that* not look like a test to you?"

Alice smiled, but only barely, and she looked again at the floor.

"'Cause, Mrs. Keystone, it's obvious that worksheet's a time waster. The problems are meant to be a boatload of busywork, and you handed it out so you could rest—you know, take a break, 'cause you seem half-sick like my Uncle Remmy the next morning after he drinks Jack Daniel's with my poppa when they sell a Dutch Draft horse or a Shire." She put her hands into her pockets and muttered almost inaudibly, "There weren't no pressure on *me,* that's for sure."

Alice got sent to the office for that one. The principal was nice. His name was Mr. Davids. He had a big, round face with big, square glasses, and he kept clearing his throat as if it were sandpaper. Alice had explained the situation and waited for instructions that were interrupted by phone calls and Mr. Davids "handling stuff" and "putting out fires," and when the smoke cleared, he didn't seem to know what to say, so Alice asked if she could play Candy Crush on her phone. The clock was the type you could hear ticking, old school with a big red second hand, and Alice was winning, winning, and winning her game, knees up with her heels on the chair, and when the period ended, Mrs. Keystone burst into the office as if she had a score to settle.

When she got it out of Principal Davids that there had been no real punishment, she showed him the tool list she had copied into her phone.

He read it all once, then scrolled back to read it more carefully. "Let's take a walk," he said.

He opened up the maintenance shop and told Alice to do her thing. It smelled faintly of oil, burnt wires, and machine cleaner, and she seemed right at home. She also seemed to know where things were, but not as if told casually by Jimmy Rutherford back on the horse farm. By instinct, she knew where the best shop tools were and the other places their accessories were stowed, the bit cabinets, the sprays and the screws and washers, and wingnuts and bit tips and all the parts broken into various sections against the far wall. She was methodical and quick, and Principal Davids let her keep working long after lunch, after Mrs. Keystone had left in a huff.

It wasn't just that the girl had a magic feel, sort of running her fingers over the machinery as if they knew their way blind, but she almost appeared to make the tools behave like pet cats or dogs. The first was the ride mower that she leaned into and across like an old friend. Next, she cleaned up the Milwaukee screw gun using the compressed air duster, she fixed the miter saw, and she got that shuddering bucket going up and down smooth as silk on the Bobcat mini-dozer.

By the time she had gotten to the John Deere, Principal Davis had his blazer off, hung on a hook by the carbide blade pegboard, and he was playing assistant, at first grabbing Alice a wheel wrench, then a hose cutter, vice grips, wire snips, and the oil gun. The tractor's hood-release was gummed up and frozen, and Davids had his fingers under while Alice did the detail work under there, armed only with a flathead screwdriver and a utility knife, and when they got that sucker open, they cheered and slapped each other five. Davids had sweat beaded on the back of his neck and furrowed in a long stripe down the back of his white dress shirt. He wiped his brow with the back of his forearm. His hands were grimy, black machine grease even under the nails, and he hadn't been this happy since his own dad taught him how to change the oil in their pickup truck back when he was nine.

The last bell rang, and he walked Alice back. There were no buses needed as everyone lived so close, and Alice waved and walked home. Davids oversaw the adjustments in her IEP and always treated her with grave and sober respect.

That didn't mean that Alice didn't cause her share of trouble in high school. She was a kid, after all, in a small town, where people sometimes did things just to kick up some dust.

Plain and simple, Alice was a pyro. She loved fire, the flames, the way they wavered and played the shadows off people's faces, giving them first comic, then tragic expressions. She liked the color, more like pure gold than a man's wedding ring, or a sunset, or any kind of flower or shrub, and she had a special affection for the blue part, that fierce, yet somehow dreamy, flickering spirit that did its dance down by the wick, where no one seemed to pay it any mind, sort of like her.

When she was in tenth grade, she took a gas can down into the woodsy part of Crum Creek and tried to see if she could make the flames flicker on the water, if only for a second. She didn't get her wish, but she did manage to ignite the low branches of some overhanging trees. There was no forest fire, no need place a call five counties south to Liberty City to see if they could get a flyover (which would have been delayed for hours anyway), but the fire department had to use a drone, and Alice had to listen to lectures from Poppa, the chief of police, and a fire department lieutenant that it could have been a disaster if the drone had failed, since it was highly unlikely that they could have gotten their hoses all the way down there in the gully.

In her freaky phase in eleventh grade, she fell in love with heavy metal music, especially guitar-extraordinaire Sophie Lloyd, because she was a girl, and she was tall, and in her hit video "Do or Die" she spliced in a fire dancer named "Lula," who was even more pretty and breathed fire out of her mouth. At the same time, in school, the English teacher, Mr. Knowles, was reading aloud *Macbeth* and explaining every line while most of the kids had their heads down. Alice loved it. She loved the witches and the idea of spells and incantations and boiling kettles on top of robust campfires, and she missed her mom, so she went to the Saint Peter's Cemetery at midnight and brought along a shitload of Zippo lighter fluid canisters in her backpack in order to set the gravestone afire and raise her mother's spirit.

It didn't get her an audience with Amy Lynn Gates, but it did char the grass black in the entire back part of the "Rosewood" section, burning up all the keepsakes too: the dead flowers, wreaths, baskets, and grave blankets. Poppa promised Sargent

McMillan that he would discipline her, but when she told her side of the story there at the kitchen table, he took it more that she had had to grow up without a mother, without another woman in her life to show her the ropes on all the lady-things, and he let it go and left the room, walking slowly, rubbing the small of his back, more tired than angry, like usual.

Late in her senior year, it got ugly, bringing us to the story before the real story that made Alice Gates a legend far beyond the borders of Cripple Creek, Nebraska. There was a new boy named Gus Graham in her home economics class, and he was trying to regress her right back to fifth grade. For no reason whatsoever, he started passing by behind her and whispering things during workshop times when the teacher wasn't really teaching and everyone was making their own quiet conversations.

"Horse face" was the first one. It literally made her mind freeze like a math test. She didn't have a comeback, and even if she did, it would look as if she was the one who started it, because she'd have to call it across the room at this point.

"Hillbilly-No-Tits" was his second whispering stab. To that one she pulled up with indignation, twisted around, and gave him "the stare," but he went over to his new friends Johnny Burns and Cliff Gaines, the three of them now with their elbows up on the lab table, leaning in like a little sewing circle as Bobby whispered a joke, probably about her, and they all snickered together.

That Friday it was "Cunt-Licker," and the way Alice saw it, this was a "three strikes and you're out" kind of scenario. After school, she ran all the way home, stalked into the maintenance barn, and started gathering the serious stuff, the torque wrenches, an extra-large pair of blacksmith's tongs, long- and short-handled sledges, and the welding equipment. She used the key to get into the shed with the gas-powered specialty stuff, and she went into the parade stable, where they kept decorations and accessories used for horse shows.

Halfway through the process, she almost lost her nerve. To do this right, she had to trash one of the motorcycles and the afore-mentioned gas tool. As for the latter, she knew Poppa wouldn't care so much about it, since they didn't have a need to fell trees anymore after they sold the rights to the orchard back to the bank three years ago. A motorcycle, however, was one of those untouchables. They had five of them: all vintage. They were Poppa's pride and joy, and when he wasn't riding them around the property slow like a general in a jeep overlooking the ranks or around town proud as a peacock, he would go out to the garage with a few clean rags, a tube of oil, and a spray bottle of cleaning solvent, all just to worship his precious machines.

Since Alice was more a shop girl than a showoff and therefore more interested in fixing and aligning than revving and riding, it wasn't often that she drove these hogs. That said, she learned on the Suzuki and got to the point with the Monster that she could get it up to sixty and pretty much hold speed even on the twisting curves of the dirt roads behind the farm all the way to the water tower. She could tear donuts and pop wheelies with the best of them, though she knew she should always clean the cycles up good before putting them back in the garage where Poppa was bound to inspect them.

She had an idea.

There was the fat-tire electric trike they jerry-rigged to be a tow cart when Poppa was considering turning the secondary stable into a small warehousing unit. It could go up to twenty miles an hour, and in neutral it would roll down a hill like a runaway train. She smiled quietly. This was going to be fucking awesome. She just needed the right kind of circumstance.

Of course, that circumstance never came about. First off, she needed Gus Graham to be confined, and second, to be stuck and stranded at the bottom of some kind of incline. The best shot she had was across Route 33 and a half mile into the sleepy town of Ridgeway, off Main and down Union Avenue South, where there was an abandoned plot that used to be the Blue Castle Drive-In. Though the ticket shack, the two snack stands, and all the speaker poles had been removed years ago, the concrete parking area had never been subject to demolition on account of ownership and zoning issues still tied up in the courts. The wide bosom of the theater was therefore a forlorn spread of cracked cement overrun with crabgrass and bindweed sprouting up through the fissures. The gargantuan wooden viewing-screen framework was still there, but the screen itself, made of plywood sheets originally painted flat white, was missing the top left and bottom right-center, like the smile of a loser in a bare-knuckle brawl.

Behind the screen, there were two empty maintenance sheds fifteen feet apart. A lot of guys had gotten laid back there through the years, a bunch their first time, so a common phrase at Cripple Creek High was to "get her between the sheds."

The whole theater area was surrounded by woods, and coming in through the back wasn't too difficult, as there was a dirt road back there and a trail about twenty feet wide worn into the grass, coming out of the woods and down the short hill leading right to the maintenance sheds. If she could just catch him parking there, she could cut loose on him the contraption she had manufactured: a fat-tire trike driven by what looked like a scarecrow holding a chainsaw straight up in the air like a battle flag. The foggy plan was to douse the whole thing with kerosene or gas, start up the chainsaw, light the whole kit and kaboodle on fire, and release the emergency brake: let it roll at him right into his fucking back bumper.

Oh, she could just *see* in her mind so vividly what he would see in his rearview, *feeling* in her bones that chainsaw's inhuman whine piercing the night like a siren, the flames bursting apart the darkness at the top of the drop like Leatherface himself come straight from hell, burning, scorching, and tossing shadows everywhere like dark phantoms.

Gus Graham would piss his pants, cry for his momma, scramble out of the car like a little girly, and she would get it all on her cell phone from her position lying tummy-down on top of the shed with the cedar shingles, putting it on social media for the world to see. Then they'd all really know who the cunt-licker was, now wouldn't they?

But, of course, the "plan" was too flawed to execute properly. Even if she did know Gus Graham's schedule and he just so happened to try to get lucky between the sheds, Alice couldn't be two places at once, starting up the chainsaw, tying off the trigger, and lighting the contraption at the top of the hill and filming from the point of impending impact at the bottom. And what about the poor girl in the car? What of the potential damage to the vehicle? What about the police report? How about the fact that the scarecrow wouldn't hold its shape more than a pair of seconds, and most of all, what if the chainsaw exploded?

Alice looked at her toy wistfully before taking it apart and returning the Stihl TS 350 chainsaw to the place for the gas tools and the trike to the building where they kept unused machinery for the purpose of cannibalizing them for parts and accessories.

As for Gus Graham, he had seemed to move on from his snide remarks behind her back, graduating to giving her ugly looks now and then, especially when spring hit, and she started wearing her short jean skirt, or her pleated mini, or her faded dungaree cutoffs with the white frays and the pockets showing.

A lot of people said she should have seen it coming.

And there were multiple versions of what really happened.

It was a warm night on the last day of May 2024, when the Cripple Creek High baseball team played for the district championship at home against Sun Valley. Alice was a week away from graduation, and she had already landed a partial scholarship at the University of Nebraska-Lincoln for mechanical engineering. She had only lately begun experimenting with cosmetics, and tonight her eyes were absolute fire, with hot pink shadowing, heavy smoky liner with wing tips, and thick sooty lashes, and she'd gotten her hair done in flirty waves framing her face, and she was wearing a ribbed crop tank top, a white tennis skirt, and gladiator sandals.

She was drinking like most everyone else in town that day at the Red Eye Saloon, only she wasn't banking on the fact that the team's big victory would make the bartender turn a blind eye to all the underage high schoolers in here tonight. It was a plain old Diet Coke she had up on the bar next to her small black purse with the long skinny shoulder strap. The music was hollow but pounding, a Jellyroll song, and the dance floor behind her was packed with folks standing in pockets and talking and laughing, some swaying to the beat, singing along and clapping their hands overhead, the girls all looking oh, so damned pretty, and the boys with their collared golf shirts and designer tees and straight leg jeans, dress khaki shorts, and skateboard loose denims, and while many of the older folk occupied all the tables over in the restaurant and family area in the back and outside under the awning, the room with the pool table and the connected bathrooms was crammed with the baseball team and their posse of populars and jocks all enjoying burgers, dogs, and pitchers of lemonade, all on the house, all you could eat.

Two people pushed up to the bar on either side of her, and the one to the right tapped her on the shoulder. She turned, it was Gus Graham, clean-shaven, eyes a bit bloodshot, big cowboy chin.

"Hi," he said.

"Hi," she returned, looking sharply across the other side of her where Cliff Gaines had his elbows up on the bar; he was smiling, he made his eyebrows go up and down. She reached forward, grabbed her soda, and took a few deep swallows. Nervous! If she had only noticed the small spill of powder on the bar, some soaking and dissolving in the condensation left by her glass. If only she had turned a bare second earlier to catch the Gaines boy spiking her soda with the stuff in a small glass phial that he'd bought from a friend whose brother went to the Nebraska Methodist College of Nursing … But he had anticipated her turning a second earlier than she chose to do so, and he had managed to get about half of it into her drink. The old geezer on the far side of him ordered a perfect VO Manhattan straight up with a twist, and the bartender, making a snide joke about fancy-pants liquor, wiped down the whole bar five feet both directions, acting prissy like a British butler to everyone's overall merriment. She turned back to Gus and sipped through the skinny red straw.

"You're mean," she said. "Mean to me, and you are a total dick."

"Guilty," he said. "I'm sure sorry about that." He looked down at the bar in front of him and shook his head. "Never figured out how to make friends in the sandbox is all." He put out his hand. "Gus Graham," he said, "originally from Old Mechanicsville and replanted here in Cripple Creek."

She shook it firmly and looked him dead in the eye as her poppa taught her to do.

They started talking, Cliff Gaines included, and they laughed and rambled, and she didn't notice that both of them weren't only smiling, but smiling crookedly and laughing with red eyes that patronized and were not laughing with her, but rather, straight at her, and some short time later she could be heard bragging in a rather slushy sort of a voice that she could fix any machine on God's green earth, and Cliff suggesting something about the barn on the property next door, and she returned that comment with her own, chin up and defiant, and the three of them left together, out to the parking lot, where two witnesses, both farm hands with foreign accents, claimed that the kids were all arm in arm, with Alice in between, legs sagging then steadying as they helped her along.

A third witness, an elderly man in a gray suit with a straw hat and a Tiger's Eye walking stick, claimed to have seen the three walking across the meadow toward the huge red machinery barn owned by Rutledge Industrial, which was verified by the police report to have contained all sorts of heavy-duty commercial farming and foresting equipment as well as three hundred propane tanks for their exchange-stalls at the BP in Glendale, the Sunoco on Washington Street, and the True Value over in Ridgeway.

No one saw how they got into the barn, but in what police estimate was about twenty minutes later, there was a girl's scream from inside the structure, heard in the parking lot of the Red Eye by a young couple, both still in their work clothes, the female wearing a white uniform and a steamtable server's cap and the male in a garage mechanic's blue monkey suit. They were having a spat about dinner plans, paychecks, and overtime, and then came the above-mentioned scream. According to the couple, the sound of it was desperate and forlorn and at the same time enraged. Next was the sound of an engine, high-end, sounding like something with a rope-pull.

Then they claimed that in the blink of an eye, the barn was on fire, you could smell it all the way over here, coming from the inlets and roof vents, and there was the tinkle of breaking glass, and you could see the flames start licking out of the loft windows. Then the whole structure exploded, mostly upward, a ball of yellow with a thick black furling underbelly, loud as fuck, sending shrapnel whizzing over their heads and all around them, hitting some cars, busting some windshields, and punching holes and divots into the broad side of the Red Eye.

Still, there was another eyewitness, a young lawyer from Uniontown taking his early evening bike ride on his ten-speed around five hundred yards north and approaching, and he swore up and down that while yes, there was a woman's scream, the revving of a small engine, tinkling glass, and fire licking out of the windows at first, the major explosion didn't come until after the front barn doors burst apart in a shower of splinters, and through the smoking orifice came a girl on a motorcycle, covered in a blaze of fire head to toe and holding a live flaming chainsaw overhead like a war flag.

She tore down the entryway, kicking up dirt and sod behind in a plume, and she screamed across the road into the field of dead cornstalks, kicking up a wheelie, chainsaw held high and her hair sparking and her skin swimming like liquid steel in a forge, her eyes blackened runners of molten tar, and then the barn exploded in a whoosh and a deafening "BOOM" that shook the ground and made the biker recoil, cover up, and scream through his teeth. Hesitantly, then, he looked up to see what was left of the barn, a junkyard of trashed machinery, rubble, and debris scattered across a blackened foundation, with scraps of paper, twisted steel, and hunks of wood raining down from the sky as if in slow motion. He put his hand to his brow in a salute to look back at the cornfield, which was leveled now to a speckling of fires shimmering like reflections on the water, and the motorcycle and chainsaw were gone like a dream, leaving the girl's corpse in the middle of the dead stalks, most burned to stubs, and she was a rumple of scorched bone, flames licking at the remains, her blackened skull grinning and smoking.

Then her remains seemed to deteriorate, black dust seeping down deep to the soil of the corn.

A similar story was told to the police later that night by a woman coming forward with the claim that while driving home from work down Route 40 North, she had already passed by when the barn exploded, but before that, she'd seen the flaming girl with the flaming chainsaw burst out through the barn doors like a firecracker in a paper lampshade. Thing is, the witness claimed the girl wasn't astride any motorcycle. It was a majestic Andalusian war horse with flames shooting behind it like great golden wings. When they crossed into the cornfield, the girl pulled on the reins, standing that beautiful beast tall on its hind legs, and as the girl's face was sliding into itself like fluid steel in a die, she opened her mouth to a long black oval and raised that chainsaw up like a field general.

Over the next week, there were five more that came forward with eyewitness accounts, all similar to the former, though they were split—three motorcycles to two horses. As for Gus Graham and Clifford Gaines, their body parts were scattered all across the blast radius, and the medical examiner could only tell the police two things he was relatively sure of. First, some of the boys' extremities were not separated from the given whole because of the explosion, but rather, something pre-detonation that made straight, perfect cuts, amputations. Second, the shins and feet of both sustained the least damage, at least in terms of relative connectivity, because at the time of the blast, both boys had their pants down to their ankles.

Traces of Alice Gates were never officially found.

The Professor was zoned, enthralled, and he almost jumped out of his seat, when again something moved at the top of the screen. It was the first tab that just changed from "Inbox" to "Inbox (1)." He slid the mouse and could just *hear* the movie soundtrack with either the foreboding cellos or their evil stepsisters, the high piano keys, going, *blink-blink … plink-plonk …*

He hit the tab and clicked on the email that said "Not Good Enough" in the Subject line.

Blood Red Meta

Professor,

The killers in your stable are flawed. While I am not thrilled with your representations of men in general, you have gone out of your way here to show that the women need immortality in order to compete. That is nothing but a patronizing insult, and on top of that, you have created a bogus equation, giving the vampire and werewolf gifts that are too equal for either to be able to claim victory over the other. And I am not even including in this evaluation the biggest question mark of them all: Savage Alice.

First things first, though: Please tell me what happens, Professor, when Lucifer's Gal tries to suck the blood out of the neck of Wolf Shadow, who in turn tears out her lungs and rips off her scalp? What then? Does the imperishable, bloodied vampire duck to the exposed underbelly of the werewolf to sink in her fangs a second time in order to suck that wolf-bitch bone dry? How much back and forth do you think we can stand? How do you make this anything but slapstick comedy?

Okay. Let's first say, just for argument's sake, that since Lucifer's Gal is primarily human, she loses battle number one and is utterly consumed, bones included, by the physically stronger predator. Does the vampire resurrect herself out of a pile of dung? What if it goes the other way? What if Lucifer's Gal puts the wolf in a trance, then hangs her upside down on a hook next to the splash basin and in a frenzy manages to suck out all of her blood, toss her carcass up on the shop table, cut her and gut her, and next stuff the steaming innards, bone matter, organs, and bloody pelt into a sack to take down into the quarry where there is a shop for fixing the mining equipment, a mechanic's shop with better cutting tools than she has in the music store? Now she can hack that beast into hundreds of small pieces, not to bury, too easy to have unearthed by a pit-mine worker, but better, to either be flushed bit by bit down a few different toilets or shoved down a couple of storm drains. Does the wolf somehow resurface as a pack of wolf-rats then, swarming out of the sewers? I mean, no matter what, Professor, it seems we are dealing with shit, shit, and more shit, and while it might get a laugh, I don't see it earning you many subscribers.

Now let's talk about Savage Alice. I assure you that she is not excited about killing anyone other than rapists, but I feel I have an obligation to show you the math. Think about it. Aside from Wolf Shadow and Lucifer's Gal, who do you have in the lineup that could possibly stand up to the Great Mistress of Fire? Did you ever play Rock-Paper-Scissors, Professor?

Well.

What are the chances that Savage Alice would be even mildly challenged by the Red Headmaster, Cody the Clown, the Beekeeper, the Rock Reaper, the Dark Doppelgänger, or the Soldier, unless they could somehow make themselves nonflammable, which they can't effectively or permanently? But wait! Maybe they could drop her in the ocean! But oh, sorry, the contestants will all be restricted to a city block of tenements and businesses, locked in by an electric fence, no doubt, right, I forgot. Locked in with a fire-queen whose heart burns like the core of the sun.

So, besides what I mentioned already about Wolf Shadow and Lucifer's Gal, my only other question in reference to Savage Alice concerns Ghost, and not only because it is difficult to rank spirits with such different characteristics, relative powers, and internal motivations: angel of fiery vengeance versus a sentimental apparition that tells riddles. Speaking of which, I ask you … how could Ralph claim everything to be about "love" in a world where children with special needs are misdiagnosed so easily and abused so readily … where gay and trans kids get emotionally and sometimes physically tortured or killed ... where aggressive boys are rewarded and assertive girls vilified ... where intelligence is measured by chalking up wins as opposed to nurturing the souls of the kind, the generous, the timid, the depressed, the downtrodden, and the oppressed?

Frankly, your loser podcast in the making disgusts me. As I said, you only allot power to women in terms of "the fantastic," and portray their human sides as seemingly helpless, objectified clichés. Lucifer's Gal is not a good guitar player. She is mediocre. She doesn't kill worthy foes but clueless victims, and in her brief description, we are told she looks good in a leather mini and high black boots. And how about your partner in crime and his "Candi," our stripper-like, willowy sex-toy who turns wolfen only when her master, a man, seduces her with that logo on the bass drum similar to the way Cliff Gaines spiked the soda Alice Gates brought to her lips? And I feel I must mention the way this "Candi" was initially introduced to us as well. I mean, heart-shaped hips? Thong straps? Eyes tattooed on so she will look good for Cody in the morning when she rolls out of bed?

You bastards.

As writers, you both have a moral and professional obligation to portray women as strong and diverse, not needy and brimming over with sappy coquettishness. For God's sake, Cody has her pouting as if in front of a mirror! What kind of example is that for the teenaged girls who happen to tune in to your broadcasts? To be attractive, you have to have pouty lips and heart-shaped hips?

You are being warned. Abandon this sadistic, misogynistic enterprise right now, or I will send down Savage Alice as my personal assassin. Not as a character in your uneven and grotesque hoax of a competition, but as a glorious angel of death coming straight to your houses.

Please take this seriously. I am giving you twenty-four hours to abort. If this demand is not met, you will be drawn out of your respective homes and into the dark, and you will be suddenly lost, the terrain different, the air sharper, the woods thick and dark. You will be pursued, and you will crash through the brush, pawing away the low-hanging branches, scratching through the rough until you emerge from the trees and lose your footing, head over heels rolling down a short hill. There is dirt in your mouth, in your hair, down the back of your pants, and you are breathless, and when you open your eyes you will be looking back up the short incline, quickly realizing that you have shackles around both wrists and ankles, legs spreadeagled and arms crucified out to the sides, and you are suspended between the two maintenance sheds. Behind you, however, there is no drive-in movie screen, no shield, and five hundred cars in the abandoned parking area will turn on their brights, making everything stark and sharp in relief, tossing your shadow back up the hill.

Behind you there is the roar of hundreds of female voices, primed for the kill, heckling and taunting, and someone hits her horn long and loud, and it is joined by another in harsh unison, a trio, then a quartet, and soon the whole clearing is shrieking at you.

A sound cuts through it all, piercing, a chainsaw, and before you at the top of the hill is Savage Alice on her motorcycle, popping a wheelie and holding it there like a general on a war horse, the whole affair burning, roiling, sparking, and her black eyes are runners of tar, her mouth a dark oval liquified and dropping like the character in Munch's scream painting, and she's screaming and the chainsaw is revving, and she bursts down the hill to give you what's yours.

She will cut off each limb at its base, first the right arm and the left leg, so you remain suspended between the two sheds on a diagonal. Next will be the right leg, making you swing over and bang against the opposite wall, hanging there by your last aching limb. She will dismount and come in close for the last amputation, and when she cuts all the way through, burrowing into the steel, the saw will whine high, smoking and shuddering.

You fall to the dirt, a torso and a head, and you will not bleed out, because the heat of the blazing implement cauterized the wounds. You are awake for the finale, beginning with Savage Alice driving a heavy-duty sharking hook straight up in through your balls and out through your gut, and she chains you to the back of her motorcycle, to drag you full speed back up the hill, through the woods and straight down to hell, bumping you along behind her like tin can on a rope.

Goodbye, Professor. Abandon ship. I'm not kidding.

Yours Truly,
The Mod Goddess

The Professor was filled with such unexpected resentment that he was actually stupefied. It was the content more than anything, and he was less concerned with the "how" than the "who" or the "why." So who wrote all this? The Soldier character, as said, was something made with ChatGPT; the Professor would recognize that flowery garbage anywhere, anytime. But Savage Alice? What the fuck? Obviously, this was Cody's work, had to be, but taking into consideration everything the Professor knew about him, it was doubtful he could have possibly authored this. He just didn't have the experience, and one could tell from his earlier character writing that there was simply no way he could have jumped ten levels this quickly.

The Savage Alice story was good. Maybe not as good as Stephen King or Ramsey Campbell, but it was a hell of a lot better than the Professor's work. Jealous? You betcha. Stunned? Oh, yeah. And where on earth was their podcast supposed to go from here? Of course, the Professor knew damned well that he had been the one to suggest they just "create, no holds barred," but number one, Cody was starting to play head games, pretending he had nothing to do with the creation of characters that only *he* could have possibly invented, and number two, fuck it, Cody was the one who started it with his standard dialogue mechanics in the "Cody the Clown" bit! How in a million years would they bottle and sell this, except if they wrote a book about making a podcast, failing at it, and then criticizing each other? Hell, not only was it confusing, but it was weak at its base. Why would each podcaster listen to the advice of the other, a fellow failure, and concurrently, why would an audience promised blood and thrills settle for these weird Russian nesting dolls that were more and more outlandish with every reveal?

More vexing for the Professor, however, was the Mod Goddess. Again, this was certainly Cody's writing, as it had his "poker tell," with the use of the words "I mean" to link ideas. I mean (ha-ha), who else *could* have written it, unless this all was, after all, a bunch of experiences in the Professor's head and he *really was* in some asylum, in a room with padded walls with the doctors watching him through the two-way mirror glass, saying, "Oh, look! He's doing the Professor playing the Murdertown game again!"

Uh, no. Similar to rejecting this general idea earlier in terms of "story," telegraphing, and being predictable, he knew in the real here and now he wasn't insane. And fuck it, no, he would never stoop so low as to ever, ever write "It was all just a dream." The real was the real, a copout was a copout, and there were good and valid reasons for things in life and in fiction, always. That's what made the unexplained such damned fun.

Still, all that said, besides the "tell," the Mod Goddess just didn't *sound* like Cody. The syntax was wrong, the semantics whacked out, the feel oxymoronic, and the venom … too venomous! This writing came from an angry, dissatisfied, disillusioned shrew, not a guy who gushed, talking about cool effect peddles and his "guit-fiddle." It was also a rather strange idea for him to trash the "Candi" character that he himself had created. He had seemed so proud of it, even going back for seconds with only minor variations when he created Wolf Shadow.

And at the heart of this, Cody was just not the type to follow trends in gender culture wars. He had been in a heavy metal band, for Christ's sake, promoting horror themes and window dressing that was all goth, all sex and darkness, all day and night. Concurrently, during the music reaction videos the three of them had done together, Cody had never mentioned any sort of feminist perspective, and from his commentary on art, music, metal, and mayhem, it was clear that he would never adjust his art to pander to someone else's social or political sensibilities. Neither would Ralph, and neither would the Professor. He wrote horror, and his main objective was threefold: first, to be true to the story, second, to sell books, and third, to have a blast doing it. There wasn't much money in small press publishing, so if he was going to spend a year writing a book about witches, girl-zombies, or deadly ghost-hookers playing dice on the moon, the last thing he needed to be worried about was whether or not he was providing good feministic models for the positive psychological development of teenage girls. Especially not in a mock podcast about a contest featuring serial killers working their splatter-games … and on top of that, the Professor was a feminist!

Hence his stupefying resentment.

Fuck it, he was about to shut down for the night, go get a beer, try to relax, and zone out on the back half of the Phils game, when he stopped halfway out of his chair, sort of suspended there. Slowly, he sat back down. Who else realistically would have access to the information that had been exchanged between himself and Cody Kennedy? How about Cody's wife, a woman the Professor had never met, never seen on a Zoom. Of course, it was possible that Cody was never married in the first place, and the fact that the Professor was fairly sure at some point Cody had mentioned his wife offhandedly, now it was not all that clear.

How much did the Professor really know about Cody Kennedy?

Not much, actually. In 2015, the Professor had written the article on

Wolf Shadow, and at that time the guitarist was a different guy named Brett Rocket. The ongoing relationship with Ralph over the phone was something the Professor treasured, and in 2020, when the band got signed by Pavement Music (Puddle of Mudd, Ted Nugent, Candlebox), the Professor was one of the first people Ralph contacted. The Professor wrote a mammoth five-thousand-word feature article for *Metalheads Forever* magazine, and it looked as if Wolf Shadow was on the brink of "making it big." Later, the Professor would find out that Cody had been managing the band at that time, sort of moving in and out of the circle with different roles, and then the pandemic hit. The band splintered, soon to reform with Cody on guitar, and while being locked indoors like the rest of the world, Ralph and Cody filled the time writing new music and making podcasts about music and life. In October of 2021, the Professor put out through Cemetery Dance Publications what would be his biggest seller, titled *Dancing with Tombstones,* and Ralph and Cody invited him on their podcast to talk about the book. He and Cody hit it off, and the Professor became a semi-regular on their program.

Of course, presently, one might think two guys planning a new podcast like **Kill or Be Killed** *Live from Murdertown* would have been familiar with all the background family stuff, but in this case, the Professor had never asked nor been told any of those particulars. And, yes, thinking about it, he had certainly noticed the jab at him in the "Cody the Clown" chapter, when the wife character mentioned that the Professor didn't know that Cody had played the Whiskey, the Troubadour, and the Hollywood Bowl, for fuck's sake.

The Professor pushed back in his chair, working the swivel lock that allowed him to lie back almost horizontally. He webbed his hands behind his head and looked up at the ceiling.

Welly, welly, welly, as Alex had said in *A Clockwork Orange.* Would it be at all feasible, then, that Cody's real wife had been watching all this, maybe guiding him at times, pissed at him in other instances, kind of chirping over his shoulder and then finally stepping in boldly to take the metaphorical pen for herself?

Blood Red Meta

Welly, welly, welly. There was one contestant's slot left to fill for the podcast, and the Professor was savoring this like a true victory before he even started writing it.

Oh, I'll have something for you, poor little Alice.

And something special for the Mod Goddess, too.

Chapter 14

Cody read the Savage Alice chapter-portion with a bit of jealousy and a shitload of awe. He got through the Mod Goddess part and wanted to put his fist through the wall. He hated gender politics. He loved women in general, almost unconditionally, and that's why it stung so bad to be lumped in with the users, abusers, and rotten rat-bastids.

He took a tight drag off his ebony vape pipe. The thing that he felt most defensive about was his "Candi" character. She was a sweetheart, supportive, independent, and sexy, and he felt that in terms of describing her sexuality, the Mod Goddess accused him of coming off like a perv watching porno on his phone at a PTA meeting. What was her problem, anyway? I mean, how about *Fifty Shades of Grey,* and *Gerald's Game,* and *Basic Instinct, Duck Butter, 365 Days,* and *Lust Stories?* Was he supposed to ignore the general presence of feminine beauty in the world? Cody was a sucker for a pretty girl; he just was, it was instinctive and baked in, and so a lovely woman wearing a short summer dress in the produce aisle at the grocery store made him glad to be alive. And this is what made him a selfish, insensitive prick?

Well, fucking kill me now, he liked women who pouted checking out their lipstick in the mirror, primping their hair, and deciding to go bold with the liner and lashes, and women who were athletic and looked totally boss with their ponytail coming out through the back of a baseball cap, or the business women in black skirts and fluffy white blouses, and he loved women who loved to smile and laugh and talk about any number of things. He liked it just as much when women were coy and seductive as he craved a good conversation with a bird over a beer, or going bowling with a babe and laughing and eating stale pretzels, or dancing with a doll till last call at a rock club, or just making small talk at the bus stop with a total stranger after working her shift at the pizza place, the hospital, the law office, or the boutique.

Cody had never seen nor met a woman who wasn't beautiful to him, at least at first, until she proved him wrong with cruelty or something. He recalled working at Continental Rental one summer loading trucks out of a warehouse, and the receptionist in the office, while looking at a *Sports Illustrated* swimsuit issue, remarked out loud while he was punching the time clock that anyone as fat and homely as Cody Kennedy was incapable of recognizing beauty in the first place. No, Cody had not muttered a comeback. No, he hadn't sent her a nasty email or called his local congressman, because better than dwelling on stuff like that was celebrating the fact that he celebrated the female majority. Every woman was a storybook, a portrait, a gem, or at least a good rock song, fucking right, fucking A, and so thanks for making me feel like shit, Professor, thanks a whole heck of a lot.

Suddenly, he stopped playing the pentatonic scale he was riffing on. He was still in his chair by the computer with the awful Mod Goddess story glaring at him like some old nun who caught him with his hands in his pants and a nudie pic of Margo Robbie in his desk.

So wait a minute here … new thought, new angle.

Exactly how many characters had the Professor just rattled off in one master stroke, anyway? In his mind, Cody pictured the list, stopping with Ghost at number eight. At that point, they had been even with four apiece. Now the Professor had added the Soldier, Savage Alice, and the Mod Goddess, so the count was going to be Cody with five and the Professor with seven, and *that* was only possible if the Professor conceded that it was finally Cody's turn at this point. If not … if the Professor was going to insist that he didn't invent the last three characters at all and claimed the next one for his own …

Cody smiled and nodded bitterly. Of course. The old crum-bum was going to make it so the ratio stood at: Cody with four, the Professor with eight. Cody leaned over to put the guitar down, straightened back up, and dug in his heels in baby steps to pull the chair closer to the PC. Enough. He reached and started hitting the keys, backing out of the Mod Goddess email and tabbing in to write a new message to his podcaster partner who was about to become a lonely man with a failed idea on an island where he had no one to blame but himself.

Cody paused, however. He was doing that a lot lately. It made a beat in his head … run … stop … jump … pause, and he forced himself not to zone out into a songwriting universe, because unlike a head space in which he thought about things and simultaneously practiced scales, a song-crafting galaxy often held him in the stars all damned night.

Slow the roll and wait just a second …

He thought about the line of reasoning that he had immediately rejected forty minutes ago, that the Professor wasn't lying, and some supernatural force had hacked their conversations on email and was fucking with them.

And no, of course that wasn't it, couldn't be. Cody didn't believe in that shit, not really, though he had once dated a self-proclaimed witch. The reason the idea had popped into his head again, all ghost stories aside, was that maybe the point here was that someone else wrote these stories … not a spirit, not some evil phantom, but someone tangible, someone … real.

Cody rested his elbows on the desk, chin in his palms. Right, made sense. The Savage Alice story was too good for the Professor, at least considering the tales he'd put in so far. Cody was no literary genius, but the Professor's characters were all either vaguely unlikable or sort of neutral, as if you didn't feel one way or the other. Savage Alice was a character you rooted for from the get-go. Also, the planting of the abandoned drive-in and the pyro stuff all coming together at the end like a coordinated fireworks display, nah. The Professor didn't do those acrobatics, didn't have the chops, wasn't capable.

Cody closed his eyes and nodded to himself.

Of course. Hadn't the Professor mentioned that he had an ex?

Cody forfeited a short, hollow laugh, like, *You almost put it past me …*

Right. The good old Prof was a figure in academia, and so his ex-wife was probably some snobby intellectual, a poet with a Ph.D., or the chair of a bunch of snooty committees, altogether a book-nerd and ice-queen. *Hence, our evil authoress,* Cody thought, sort of proud of his ability to be "Shakespearean." Maybe she had a screw loose. Maybe she was just bitter. Maybe she was punishing Cody because he was guilty by association, and once she spread her poison, it was every man for himself.

Cody refused to believe that maybe, at least to a degree, she might have had a point.

He was too busy creating in his mind the character that would stand up to the creator of the Mod Goddess.

Chapter 15

The Professor had a problem from the start, and he was finding it harder and harder to work this through to any sort of completion. Plainly, in a mock contest where violence was everybody's middle name, it was difficult to create some sort of character that would harm the Mod Goddess. It was the Professor's nature to protect women. He taught college freshmen, and though he did not consider the female students his "daughters," there was certainly a paternal factor to his livelihood. And let's be honest. This wasn't even about harming the Mod Goddess. It was about harming her creator by giving back a sharp stab of the same sort she had clearly enjoyed giving him.

He initially thought it would be easy to plan this, like those Pokémon games he so enjoyed back in the early 2000s when Max was a preschooler—you know, water beats fire, fire beats grass, grass beats rock, etc. Yet no matter how he drew it up, it always came back to inflicting pain on a woman, so, no way, ain't no-how ... this kind of shit was never acceptable in any context.

Also, Cody was his friend, and did the Professor really want to go sticking it to the guy's bride?

No.

But she had sure stuck it to them, hadn't she?

He slept poorly that night. He was a nighttime worrier to begin with, often lying awake, overheated under the sheets even with the air conditioner blasting, his mind an animal predator sniffing out, digging up, and re-exposing everything he hadn't gotten done that week at Immaculata ... that tutor at Delaware County Community College he was having a gripe with … what he was going to say tomorrow in lecture at the University of Delaware, Main Campus-Newark that he had divebombed with the day before in his Wilmington AAP class … a student he needed to confront for plagiarizing an analysis of "A Good Man Is Hard to Find," a Kohls charge he had to let go unpaid until next month, and on top of all that was his next-door neighbor who was mad at him for trying to get ahead of things by emptying his glass recycling in the back garden alley at 5 in the morning before rushing off to teach.

Tonight, he was waking up every hour or so, forehead glistening with sweat and stomach in knots, because he hadn't solved the current writing riddle. As unimportant as it sounded, the fiction writing was of weighty importance to the Professor's overall psyche, in that he used story creation as a strange sort of self-therapy. When he was onto a good idea and in the middle of writing, say, a chapter over a one-week period, all the worry got magically transformed and filtered into creative bursts and volcanic eruptions that were absolutely delicious. When he woke up in the night, there was no anxiety, no guilt, no toxic bullshit, because like a gambler having a lucky night at the casino, he was *at the table.* He was *in the game,* a player, a winner, and he most assuredly *did not* stress about office disagreements, students plagiarizing, or his fucking recycling. Instead, he was blessed with the ability to automatically reroute and remind himself that he was sitting at that *brilliant, dazzling, elegant table,* a player free to work out the next paragraph or line of dialogue, or nifty, poetic story-idea.

The (often) long pauses between projects, however, were torture, and once he had begun one, the Professor tried his best never to stop a writing session at the end of a chapter! If he wasn't sure what was supposed to come next, it was an absolute misery for him, all the real-life issues *plus* the writing block coming together to form a massive black mountain sitting on his chest, making him tense and nervous almost to the point of panic.

He sat straight up in bed in the darkness, and it was dark as a tomb, the way that he preferred it, the only things visible: the red numbers on his digital clock on the nightstand and the tiny red charge light on the mobile phone for his landline. The air conditioner had stopped. By accident, he must have set the mode dial on "Econ" instead of "Cool," and it was the sudden lack of sound that was tense and foreboding. It had invaded his dream—that he was at a crowded keg party at some dude's house when he was seventeen, a friend of a friend, parents out of town, and the Professor's young self had ventured inside to take a piss, and when he returned to the back deck, it was deserted, deadly quiet, red plastic beer cups all around like ritual candles on the deck railing, the pair of card tables, the top of the grill and next to the lawn chairs, and there were two big rustic wooden snack bowls, one half full of chips on the white wicker patio bench and the other almost spent of Doritos on the cushion of the hanging egg lounge chair, and the keg was almost emptied, leaning hard right in the sawed-off barrel it was sitting in, and the floor of the deck was littered with cigarette butts, candy wrappers, and dead leaves.

It was startling, the way the dream had allowed the silence of the air conditioner to manipulate it, making the Professor jerk awake, feeling hopeless, frightened, abandoned, and lost.

Slowly, his breathing calmed and his heartbeat slowed back to normal, and more than the fear was the lingering feeling of desertion, isolation, and loneliness, damn it, an incredible empty-canyon, desert-wasteland vertigo in the black hole type of loneliness.

Wait …

No …

But …

His expression slowly changed into the apple-slice grin usually reserved for some melodramatic villain in a top hat and coattails, stalking women in the fog or tying them to the train tracks.

He had it now, the basis for contestant number twelve in a game that had become oddly personal. It wasn't about hurting Cody's wife in any physical way whatsoever.

It was about neglect and betrayal.

It was about making her jealous.

Chapter 16

Of course, Cody had more than quickly realized that fictively harming the Mod Goddess in any physical way only made her digs at him more true and more real, and it was while he was eating breakfast that he thought of the best way to screw over the Professor's ex-bride. He was gorging himself on Captain Crunch, refilling the bowl and repouring the whole milk until he would finish half the box, then take it with him and gnaw on it dry all morning, his once-a-week gluttony cheat. This awesome, disgusting, orgasmic, cheap-shit sugary chem-filled cereal, of course, always made little cuts in the roof of his mouth that made lunch and dinner annoying sweet pains in the ass and it was so boss because it reminded him of childhood, at least the good parts when he was playing in the South Boston Little League as a ten-year-old on the Carpenter's Local 327 Padres, or when at age eleven he won the championship as starting catcher and cleanup hitter for the Metro Energy Athletics.

God, he missed it, even nowadays, the way baseball had been a haven where he didn't get teased for his weight as he did in school, or on church group picnics, or free swim at the Y. He was respected, especially by his fellow fifth-grade champion Athletics, because he could block the plate better than anyone in the league, and nothing got past him, even Adam Wasserman's wild pitches when he was just on the brink of developing a curveball. Cody batted .765 that year with twenty-six home runs, one that bounced off the roof of the snack shack fifty feet north of left field and another one clearing the scoreboard in center. He could remember it as if it was yesterday, the buttery smoke of the barbecue they had burning at the edge of the parking area in these fifty-gallon drums turned on their sides cut in half, and the kids riding their bikes, ringing the handlebar bells and making that flicking noise with baseball cards in the spokes, and the loud and hollow-sounding cheapo speakers on top of the equipment shed playing current country hits and classic rock, and the dugouts smelling like sweet damp cellar dirt and old leather, the shouting, the cheering, the sweat and the thrill of the kill when Cody Kennedy bashed one over the fence and came in to stomp on home plate, his team all around him, jumping up and down as if he was a rock star or some kind of gladiator.

His mother had been obsessed with health food, you know, god-awful plant stuff made for rabbits and lab rats, so Cody was extra psyched when as a reward for a dinger Pop always managed to convince her to let him pick his favorite cold cereal and splurge, half in the kitchen, half up in his room where he could eat, read comic books, fuck DC, it was Marvel all the way, and he would listen to rock records that made him feel grown, like System of a Down, Tool, and Velvet Revolver.

Music eventually became Cody's passion, and though he played Little League and on through Babe Ruth and a year of all-star travel at age fourteen, it was all but over when he bought his first guitar. Music became his new cathedral, his sanctuary. As for baseball at that point, to be fair, the game was already passing him by, and he didn't even try out for high school JV.

But Little League would always be special to Cody, as he thought of it as the central symbol of his boyhood when he was the king of the diamond, and to this day he was an avid Red Sox fan and a staunch hater of the local posers, the Los Angeles Dodgers, the Anaheim Angels, and all the California teams actually. And since he couldn't afford the kind of television that might bring him games from the boys in Beantown, his one guilty pleasure besides stuffing himself once in a while with Captain Crunch was women's college softball, I mean, girlfriends could *play!*

This past May, UCLA got to the Women's College World Series by beating the Bulldogs 6–1, and then they were eliminated by Stanford. The Bruins were Cody's jam, his "neighborhood fave," but he liked different teams for different reasons. The Lady Vols had that super tall (and super cute) pitcher Karlyn Pickens who could throw over 75 mph from inside the circle, equal to 105 mph with a hardball at MLB distance, and the Gators had shortstop Skyler Wallace, whose workout regimen looked like something Marines would be scared of. The Sooners featured Alyssa Brito, scary bat, undying spunk, and Cody's overall choice for woman of the century was Mizzou's acrobatic blonde and beautiful all-star left fielder Casidy Chaumont, who, before graduating in 2022, had been featured three times on ESPN for her signature circus catches flying through the air like a superhero.

Cody froze for a second. He was sitting at the computer, gazing absently at his Facebook feed, and he put the cereal box down and looked around for something to wipe off his hands. Of course. The Professor's ex-wife was still in the picture, and she still cared for him; why else would she scold him so and involve herself in his business this way?

Oh, Cody didn't have to "do" anything to the Mod Goddess except make her grudging, resentful, envious, and jealous. So ... who could the Professor take on as a lover that would drive his ex-wife absolutely batshit?

Cody smiled, almost embarrassed that he would even be thinking this.

How about a female college student? No, not a freshman, too creepy, and Cody wasn't thinking sophomore or junior either. Though they'd all be technically legal, it wouldn't read as believable. From what Cody knew of the Professor, the old dude played things by the book, hands-off, mentor only when it came to his students, as if he'd taken an oath written in blood or some such shit.

What about a twenty-five-year-old senior who had taken a couple of gap years in the middle of her studies to feed the poor in El Salvador or something ... a tall blonde starting left fielder for the college softball team who had never passed Comp 101? What if she had old buried daddy issues and the old Prof somehow struck a chord in her, the both of them vibing immediately, talking after class, out in the hall, on the walkway between the Student Union and the Quad, and one thing led to another and she finally said to him privately and oh-so "openly" that she was a grown woman now, ready to experiment, to explore and offer him her virginity, as long as he was … gentle?

Cody brought both hands to his mouth and giggled into them. Oh, *man,* talk about making the ex-wife explode!

He started making notes. He wasn't a "writer," but if he was, he would have called this a "character sketch" or something like that.

Name: Cassidy Clayborne

Height: 6´2˝

Hair: Long, honey blonde, usually kept loose and fancy free or in crown braids, faux hawk braids, or French braids with a high genie ponytail

Facial distinctions: Small mole at the outer edge of the left eye

Eyes: Sparkling

Nose: Button

Smile: Playful

Bra Size: B cup

Ass: Hello

Arms: Toned

Legs: Sculpted like a model on a poster in a repair shop, posing with a motorcycle, speedboat, or power tool

Attitude: Strong loyalty; loving and trusting to those good to her

Temper: Chooses to smile. She would rather walk around you than through you.

Realist or Idealist: Dreamer

Position: Left field

Batting Average: .690

*

The Professor looked up at the clock and registered that it was 3:51 A.M. He usually got up at 5 A.M., so there was no point heading back to bed. He was old school, of course, so he wasn't typing into his phone. He wasn't even in front of his PC. He was sitting at the kitchen table with a box of Post Honey Ohs cereal, a jumbo package of raisins, and a gallon of two percent, eating and refilling into his jumbo coffee cup that he got in New Orleans, the black one with the skeletons on it. He was happy. He was tired. He felt as if he was in college again, and he had been writing longhand fast and furious into the pocket notebook he kept by the coffee maker, and now, for more intricate specifics, he was jotting stuff on color-coded Post-It notes, the ones he kept in the junk drawer to stick on the fridge to remind himself that he needed bath soap, purple onions, Scotch tape or whatnot.

God *damn*, she was sexy, but it had been a chore visualizing her at first. It was the idea of a "Candi" that sort of gunked up the works, first because the image of the heart-shaped hips and tattooed eye wings were sort of baked into the equation, and the Professor had a sneaking suspicion that the actual woman was "Candi's" opposite. Since the Professor's ex, Margaret, had deeply resented any representation of herself in his horror stories, he had bent over backwards to make his female characters as dissimilar to her as humanly possible, while of course she always seemed to see herself in his creations, especially the women who happened to be the antagonists.

So, since Candi was tall, the real wife was short. Candi had exotic eyes, so the real wife wore glasses. Candi had long blond hair, and so Mrs. Kennedy had short hair, dusty-brown, limp and gimpy, a Goth follower with heavy black eye makeup and black lipstick, kind of sullen and forlorn, not at all clingy, but more than a bit needy, a lover of metal who had finally admitted at long last to herself that her husband's big dream was going to remain forever unrealized. Now all that was left was the two of them, he a music store manager and she … let's say a tattoo artist in a dark parlor on the second floor of a place that had Chinese takeout.

Of course, recreating a "Candi" for real and having her show up on Cody's doorstep would be a colorful combination of sick hilarity and weird poetic justice, but the Professor wanted ownership of this. And the first thing he had thought of in terms of driving the real Mrs. Kennedy straight off her rocker was that Cody had fallen for an older woman.

So, first of all, how old was Cody? The Professor couldn't recall exactly, but brutha-man had said he wasn't born yet in the '80s. He was a '90s kid, like the Professor's son Max, and so Cody was probably somewhere between twenty-seven and thirty years old.

That was when the Professor's writing went wild, his smile branded on his face, his wrist starting to ache, which he happily ignored.

Cody's homewrecker would be forty-eight years young at this point, name: Liza Nicolescu, her parents Vladimir and Elena, both champion gymnasts, Romanians initially living in Kolomna, Russia, southeast of Moscow. As a result of lingering prejudice and inevitable lifetime persecution, they fled to America in 1982 with their six-year-old Liza, and in an effort to distance themselves from a lifestyle so structured and controlled by an authority trying to reshape their history and identity that they put aside their love of tumbling to be their own bosses, starting their own herbal tea company, first working out of a garage in Cold Spring, New York, then a small rented warehouse in Brooklyn, a factory in the Bronx, and finally a plant in Hoboken, New Jersey, with multiple buildings taking up more than two city blocks.

And what a "Hallmark card" of a little family they were … the ultimate storybook contradiction, both parents free-spirited and strict, artistic yet regimented, and so it was no surprise that by age seven, Liza had made it clear that she wanted to dance balletically, eventually professionally, and her parents encouraged her, well aware of her natural skills and her thirst for perfection at such a young age.

Liza started dance lessons later that month, small group at first and soon private, and since she also had an early fascination with rhythmic gymnastics, they got her signed up with Manhattan Rhythmics, where she absolutely shined with ball, clubs, ribbon, rope, and especially hoops. At age nine, she made the juniors national team, winning a silver medal in Minneapolis, and at age ten, she took home bronze at the World competition in Tokyo. Shrewd and savvy even as a tween, but she passed on the Olympics, doubtful of any sort of future after a year of endorsements and getting her picture on a box of Wheaties, and that was only if she medaled. So, free then to focus more on classical ballet, she graduated from Juilliard at age seventeen with a BFA in dance, and at nineteen she became a premier performer for the New York City Ballet.

Still, when the artistic director and, eventually, the ballet master in chief both refused to let her choreograph her own routines, she joined Cirque du Soleil as the Mistress of Hoops, performing balletic dance sequences with hula-hoop-sized steel rings under feathery lights with energetic and sometimes dramatic and ominous mood music. She had long, jet-black hair that she kept in a tight bun most of the time, or pulled back hard into a long ponytail, sometimes with an added braid, oftentimes dyed with streaks of ghost-white or lavender. Movement altogether to her was an art, and even crossing the street was an action that required strict aesthetic precision and grace in line and in form.

On stage, she was dazzling in the spotlight, her features regal and severe like a fairy tale's queen, and even today, she was breathtaking in a leotard, a bikini, you name it, showing off every nip, tuck, and curve.

Oh, she was perfect for this.

She was familiar with the circus as was Cody, and now at age forty-eight her dance studio and etiquette academy would be built above his music shop in downtown L.A., that's how they would meet, and she would be in charge of training young girls to master ballet featuring a strict code of ladylike behavior, balance, adjustment, and flexibility.

God damn, Cody's wife was going to be beside herself!

The Professor's Post-It notes were filled with other, more personal particulars:

Lime-Green: Physical / Factual
Height: 5′ 9″
Weight: 111
Physical Characteristics: Face long, cheekbones high, eyes blue, chin

proud and often raised ever so slightly in cynical scrutiny

<u>Tits</u>: Small

<u>Hips</u>: Narrow

<u>Ass</u>: Petite

<u>Legs</u>: Olympic

<u>Fingers</u>: Long, expressive, feminine, and artistic

Amethyst Purple: Personality

Workaholic, rarely smiles, never jokes, always grounded. Critical but loyal. Loving and overprotective. A realist who opens her heart to few, but inside has rivers and oceans to share. Rarely lies. Extremely humble when discussing her talents.

Hot Pink: Secrets and Fetishes

Heterosexual. Strongly desires oral sex, both giving and receiving. Will not perform anal, but appreciates inventive positioning. Does not believe in threesomes, filming, or anything involving any sort of pain. Lost her virginity at age twenty. Appreciates all body types and will never speak again to anyone who body-shames another. A must from a lover: creativity; a mandatory characteristic: stamina. Lots of stamina.

*

The doorbell rang downstairs, and Cody was startled out of his brainstorming activity. He was still at his PC in the den, wearing his XXL Nightwish Live at Wacken tee and silk black gym shorts. He felt as if he'd been woken from a dream; he'd pulled an all-nighter. Was it really "tomorrow" already? Well … clocks didn't lie, and it was 7:12 A.M., and who the heck would be ringing his doorbell so early on a Saturday morning?

He made his way downstairs, thoughts a bit sluggish, trying to catch up, and by the time he had reasoned that it was probably more responsible to have thrown on some fresh clothes, he was already opening the door.

Out on the stoop was a woman, sparkling eyes, tall as fuck, long honey blonde hair in French braids twisted into a high genie ponytail. She was wearing the UCLA Bruins softball uniform, the one that was blue with Westwood gold lettering.

A coincidence. Had to be.

She looked him up and down, then folded her arms and put her weight on the back foot.

"You're telling me you're not ready?" she said.

God damn, even her voice was pretty …

"Um, uh … " he managed. "What can I do for you?"

She looked upward for a second, sort of like rolling her eyes, but not quite so emphatic, and Cody was telling himself, *Focus on her face, don't steal a look at the rockin' bod, don't fall for the hype, keep 'em up, keep 'em up.* She lowered her glance and glowered at him.

"You promised," she said.

"I did?"

She stared a second, looked off to the side, then slowly put her hands behind her back, clasping them, leaning in toward him like a co-conspirator.

"You're not married, are you?"

Cody slipped out and gently pulled the door shut behind him, his voice almost down to a whisper.

"Uh, no, no, I'm not … of course not."

He felt himself blinking, knowing that was a sure sign of a liar, and he made himself stop, and Lord God, he was close enough to smell her perfume or body lotion or whatever it was, and it was heavenly, almost making him swoon like a character in *Pirates of the Carribean,* having a corset pulled too damned tight.

"Well, get a move on," she said. "We only have the field for an hour."

"Field?"

She was already turning to go.

"Yes, the field," she said. "Easton Stadium. Where my UCLA women's college softball team plays. Make it snappy, I'm double-parked."

"But wait," he said, and she stopped there at the bottom of the steps.

"Yes?"

"Is this for real?"

She looked at him up and down. "What do you think?"

"Right," Cody said. He made to turn and rush inside to put on a pair of socks and sneaks, dig around for a baseball cap, and find his old glove, but he paused.

"Uh, aren't you … I mean … weren't you supposed to tempt and seduce the Professor?"

She flipped the long ponytail over the other shoulder and smiled.

"Surprise …"

*

The doorbell rang, and the Professor came up out of his notes, giving his head a shake, reaching back, and stretching to the point where he vocalized the sort of primal grunt that was ultimately satisfying. He looked at the clock: 10:12 A.M., shit man, the day was already running and gunning full speed ahead.

Another ring. The Professor pushed to his feet, muscles tight, and the kitchen table was a mess with his scatter of notes and breakfast cereal, milk, and other things he'd brought over without really noticing.

He laughed to himself, thinking that when he had written the Dark Doppelgänger chapter-segment, he had depicted it as a frightening experience to answer the bell after dark, but here in the daylight everything seemed normal and grounded. It was a registered letter requiring his signature, or maybe something about his dad's living will, or it was the Prevagen he had ordered from Amazon, or just a "howdy" from the lawn guy to let the Professor know that the handwritten monthly bill was there in the mailbox.

He opened the door, and there was that nearly inaudible *whoosh* as the air switched places with itself.

It was a woman there on the stoop, around 5′ 11″, perfect posture, shoulders back, cheekbones high, chin slightly raised. Her eyes were accented with fierce purple eyeshadow and the kind of dramatic liner underneath that was worn by professional dancers and stage performers. She had on a sequin performance shift dress that presented like a miniskirt and matched her eyes. Her jet-black hair was pulled back into a long, flowing ponytail with a side braid in it that had a tinge of ghost-white and lavender.

There was nothing to say except the nonsensical, but the Professor gave it a whirl.

"I created you for another," he said.

"Yes, but I am here exclusively for you." She had a slight accent, Russian, it seemed. At her feet was a suitcase.

"May I come in?" she said.

"Of course," said the Professor, heart thudding in his chest. "Of course."

PART 2

Chapter 17

The field was a bit awe-inspiring, with its fine dirt infield, no chalk lines today, of course, and the green outfield grass cropped short and neat all the way to the checkerboard blue fencing with the Bruins logo every other square. The dugouts were painted a matching blue. Cody had attended a game last year against the Oklahoma State Cowgirls, his seat on the left field side just past the visitors' dugout in section 106B. The Bruins wound up winning by two runs. He had caught a foul ball and handed it to a little girl who was there with her grandpa. She hadn't thanked Cody; she was shy, but she smiled, sort of squinting up into the sun at him. It was a good day, for sure.

Here in the here and now, the ride up had been odd. He had wanted to ask a million questions, but Cassidy didn't seem interested. Also, she was the one doing the talking, and there was something about her demeanor that made Cody keep quiet, playing the listener. She did not discuss the fact that it was more than obvious that Cody was monstrously attracted to her. She did not mention that she had caught him twice staring at her legs, and she didn't give one damned clue as to whether she felt the same about him, or where the fuck she came from, or what the fuck they were doing, driving along Bellagio Road looking for parking closest to UCLA's Easton Softball field.

Instead, she was briefing him on the two girls who were evidently waiting there for them. Neither were names he was familiar with. He couldn't recall who the starting catcher was for UCLA this year, but he knew it wasn't "Kristen Lewis," the supposed senior engineering major and math wizard who basically did all their analytics in this weird sort of hand drawn homemade fashion, all equations and pictures offering defensive positioning as well as hitting and bunting probabilities, like down to the millimeter. Then, in terms of the pitcher "Missy Torrence," who had evidently hit 81 mph on a speed gun last week (yeah, right), Cody was quite sure she hadn't really thrown for the UCLA Bruins, not in 2024 at least. The two big guns had been Taylor Tinsley and Kaitlyn Terry, and so, he figured, why not? He had invented a lover meant to make the Professor's ex-wife jealous, while in "reality", he had brainstormed his own fantasy woman who had called on him to "practice" with two made-up players who possessed skills so far above the norm that being in their presence was going to be like meeting Jesus or something.

They made their way through the gate, and Cody realized that he had left his hat and glove on the front seat of Cassidy's car. Fuck, man! I mean, he wanted to disappoint this tall blonde enchantress about as much as sticking his dick in a blender. Plus, he hadn't paid attention to where they had parked, and what if she asked him? What if he inconvenienced her, frustrated her, made her give up on him so early in this strange game?

Wouldn't be the first time ...

Yeah, his life story.

Missy Torrence, the hurler, and Kristin Lewis, the catcher, were standing together where the pitcher's circle would be, Missy being the smaller one, as Cassidy had prepped him to expect. Small hell, she was absolutely tiny, maybe four feet and a couple of inches. She was African American and had the face of a beautiful porcelain doll or royalty or something. She also had long fingers, and Cody wasn't so green that he couldn't put it together that more finger length meant more surface control of the ball and the ability to manipulate it. Kristin was super lanky and boyish with eyebrows that angled down in such a way as to make her seem gleefully devilish. Both girls were in uniform, both wearing visors, their hair in simple long ponytails going down the back. They waved. He mirrored the gesture, feeling silly doing it, and he and Cassidy broke into a slow jog.

"Cassidy Claybourne!" Missy said on their approach. "What's with the fancy braids?"

"Gotta look good to play good, girlfriend."

The three of them laughed, and they shared a round of double high-fives. Cody stood at the edge of the circle, wondering what to do with his hands. Kristin eyed him and gave her chin that slight jerk upward, like *Pay attention, I'm about to address you.*

"Hey, Cody-kid," she said. "You seem sad lately."

"Morose," said Cassidy.

"Churlish even," Missy added.

"Yeah," Cody managed. "Thank you, I guess."

Kirstin's eyes twinkled with fun.

"We thought," she said, "that you would get a thrill doing some softball stuff on the big-girl field. Look at the gift we got for you behind the plate."

Cody glanced back. It was a white plastic pickle barrel turned upside-down.

"Your throne, my Lord," said Missy. Cassidy smiled wryly.

"We thought you would like that better than popping a squat."

"Thanks."

"Warm me up, Cody?" Missy said. She had a softball in her hand.

"Really?"

"Really," said Kristin, handing over her catcher's mitt.

Cody was no longer regretting that he'd failed to bring his undersized middle school glove from the car. He took Kristen's mitt and slid in his fingers, amazed that something as simple as the touch of this smooth, worn leather could kick off such feelings in him. It was a good glove, totally broken in, responding to his hand like a faithful horse carrying a familiar rider without a saddle.

"Only fastballs," he said, still looking at the glove.

"No tricky stuff, promise," said Missy. "And I call mine a rise ball."

He looked up at her rather shyly, like the girl in the stands he gave the ball to last year.

"Half-speed?"

"Three-quarters, and I'll build up to it."

"Deal."

He walked back to the plate area and sat on the bucket. Missy was waiting across there on the rubber, the UCLA scoreboard parked just above her right shoulder like a picture or a postcard.

"All right," he said. "Let's see it."

She stood dead-still for a moment, and Ben was amazed at how small she looked in this context, a figurine, a dolly-doll forty-three feet from him. After her windmill, however, the ball exploded out of her hand, growing suddenly and alarmingly huge, a planet, the world, and it *thwacked* into his glove with authority.

The girls applauded.

"Nice grab, Cody-kid!"

"Way to frame it."

"A born catcher, for sure!"

He laughed.

"My life just flashed before my eyes," he said. He threw it back and got up to move the plastic pickle barrel to the side, much to the delight of the girls, who whoop-whooped him and whistled at him like lewd construction workers.

Love it.

Bring it on, and he hunkered down on his haunches behind the plate, and he suddenly didn't see Missy Torrence in the circle. He saw his eleven-year-old pal from the Metro Energy Athletics back in South Boston, Willy Barnes, with the long face and the crazy hair, always wearing sunglasses even on the gray days, all knees and elbows with his windup, coming right at you like a shit-bucket car with the wheels flying off, and he saw Lee Zatz, the pixie freckle-faced redhead who always worked from the stretch and threw it a million miles an hour.

"Let's hit the corners," Cody said, putting the glove high and outside. In his head, he'd actually just said, *Let's hit the corners, Willy-B,* and he was amazed at how distinctly he could live in two worlds simultaneously.

Missy hit the spot, and the sound in the mitt was like the report of a rifle. Everywhere Cody put the glove, she hit the glove, and as the pitches gained velocity, Ben found that catching them made him bend his hand back more and more. The ball was starting to look like a dart, a bright streak in the bright morning light, and he stood up, tossing it back.

"Too much pepper for me at this point," he said. "In fact, forget pepper. That's Crystal Louisiana Hot Sauce, and if that's three-quarter speed, I really do pity the batters."

Missy smiled. "Let's make it interesting then," she said. "Take a turn in the box and try to make contact. At full speed, including all my pitches."

From the side, Kristin approached. She'd put on her catcher's gear in the dugout, and she exchanged fo   ᵒr her glove a UCLA Bruins batting helmet and an Easton composite bat.

"You're kidding," Cody said.

"Nope."

"I'm rooting for you, Cody!" Cassidy called. She was standing in the second base position, but close up where the infield grass would be on a baseball field.

"Really?" said Cody. She grinned at him.

"No way you're going to get around on Missy good enough to pull it, Cody-kid. Gotta be realistic about things."

"You're not wearing your glove."

"You really think I'm gonna need it?" She bent forward and clapped her hands. "Okay, then, teach it to me, baby. Teach me a lesson." She'd growled the last word, and Cody laughed to himself. He put on the helmet and stepped into the box. Missy was a pristine little statue on the rubber, one foot balanced up on the toe in a ready position.

"Hey, kid," she said airily. "You're crowding the plate, naughty boy. I am going to have to show you what I do when I have to correct that kind of behavior."

He was going to back off a few inches, but she went into her windup too quickly for that.

From behind, Kristin muttered, "She's killed people, you know."

On Missy's downswing just before the release, there was another sound from behind that made Cody jerk in place. God DAMN, did Kristin just pop her glove with her fist? The ball shot out of Missy's hand and soared straight at him. It looked like a missile, and he'd never seen something jump on him this fast. He bailed back, feeling like a loose beachball, bat flying out of his hands, and when he landed flat on his ass, he saw the ball above him jerk with sharp, late movement away toward the plate. It wouldn't have hit him. It hissed past about an inch away from where his shoulder had just been, making a mighty *Ka-Pow!* in the glove.

"Lord holy mother of GOD!" he said. He shakily pushed back to his feet, grabbed the bat, and put the top-side to the dirt. He bent and leaned on it; he was almost breathless.

"You dance nice to Missy's chin-music!" Cassidy called. "If she goes there again, turn away, take one for the team, just don't rub it!"

"Yeah, you got this, kid," said Missy, ever so sweetly. "I do admire your flexibility."

She caught the ball thrown back to her like an afterthought.

Cody turned back to Kristin. "You always talk to batters like that?"

"Oh, I'm the sociable type."

"Did you pop your glove right before the release just to mess with me?"

"Sure did."

"Well, it worked."

"Glad you enjoyed it. Now get back in the box, and this time you show us a thing or two."

After only the briefest hesitation, Cody got back in the box, trustingly, yes, but five inches back from where he had been. In quick succession, then, he saw all Missy's pitches, and it was the most thrilling thing he'd ever done sports-wise as a real participant. Her rise ball was so fast, he felt he lost sight of it in the last ten feet or so, and her breaking stuff was pure magic. The only way to describe it was that she made the ball jump on the air. Like a live thing. Cody looked at some of the pitches, and he swung at most, coming close but no cigar. Finally, he went all-in on a rise ball, committing so early it felt ridiculous, and he made contact off the end of the bat with a dull *thud* that stung his hands all the way to the elbows.

The ball bounced lazily toward Cassidy, and she watched it dribble past her a couple of feet.

"You got wood!" Missy said.

"Nice poke," said Kristin.

"Way to go, kid," Cassidy said, still looking back at the ball coming to a stop a few yards into the outfield grass.

A few pitches later, Cody hit a hard liner to left center, and two pitches after that, he guessed right on Missy's screwball and bashed one up into the sky, a moonshot for sure, and it went over the fence dead center and disappeared into the tree line.

Cassidy was circling her arm in "c'mon-c'mon" motions, and Cody took his victory lap around the bases. The girls were clapping and hooting and cheering for him.

They met him at the plate, and he was the one getting the double high-fives, and they even did the thing where you hold hands up top and bring it down in the shape of parentheses.

And he sure as hell was no longer "morose."

Still grinning, Cassidy motioned for him to give up the bat and the helmet.

"Thanks, Cody-kid," she said. "Now you've got me feeling it, but do me a favor? I'm going to take a few hacks myself, but I have to protect my front ankle, already bruised from fouling off so many straight down, you know? How about you go to the storage chest behind the fence there and get me the batter's leg guard? Oh, and I'm a leftie, so I don't want the scuffed-up black Nike. It's the light blue EvoShield."

"Right!" Cody said. He jogged to the gate by the dugout, pushed in, and made his way along the narrow walkway in front of the stands to the area behind home plate. There, bolted to the backstop fence, was the storage chest. It said "KNAAK" on it, and the thing was huge, at least six feet long and five feet high. He laughed to himself. He wasn't the tallest kid on the block, topping off at a whopping five foot eight, and he was grateful that they had put a mini stepping-stool ladder there to the side.

He moved it in place, stepped up to the top stair, and pulled the lid of the box open, pushing it back to the fencing.

The first thing that hit was the smell, like bad pork and sewage swirled in a spread of expired duck sauce and garbage. Cody gasped, almost gagged. It was a naked dead body, lying amidst a toss of catching equipment, batting helmets, old gloves, and Gatorade bottles. It looked like a man, face covered in lime used for the baselines, giving him an eerie kind of scary-mime whiteface. His eyes were open, limed over, and his body was in the "gummy" phase of decomposition, colored sickly yellow and brown and crawling with maggots.

Someone pushed Cody from behind, and he was so surprised that he didn't even windmill his arms in an effort for balance. He tumbled into the storage chest and, landing on his side, had a flash of sightline looking back up the way he had come. Out there was Cassidy Claybourne shutting the lid on him.

Steel met steel, the *BOOM!* echoless and atonal. The darkness was complete, the odor a rape in his lungs, violating him all the way down to the tailbone, the body beneath him molding along the contours of his shoulder, hip, and leg like Play-Doh mixed with gelatin. He reached up to push up the lid, and it was stuck fast. He pounded it with his fist, and there was something "dead" about the feel of it. It was Cassidy. She was sitting on it out there.

"Cody-kid," he heard her say, "you messed up, so tell me, what did you learn?"

"What?" he shouted back. "Let me the fuck out of here! Oh, my fucking God."

"No, kid," she said. "No cussing. That'll cost you another two seconds you'll have to stay in there if I hear it again. I am asking you what you have learned. This is a simulation of what the Professor's first character, the Red Headmaster, would probably dream up and try to execute. You fell for it. He set you up with an emotional feel-good, making you warm, fuzzy, unprepared, and susceptible. You see what I'm saying?"

"Let me out!"

"Not yet, kid. If one of your creations is going to win the battle of Murdertown, you first have to realize that it isn't going to be every man or woman for themselves. It will be your characters versus the Professor's, at least at first, and so tell me how can you possibly write yourself to victory if your Cody the Clown, Rock Reaper, Wolf Shadow, or Ghost falls for this lame kind of stunt?"

"They're CRAWLING on me in here, Cassidy, I can feel them, please!"

"Roger that," Cassidy said. There was a soft sound, movement out there, and the lid came open. Air! Cody pushed up, hand sinking a couple of inches into what he could only guess was a partially decomposed intestinal area, and he hauled himself the hell out of there.

"Douse him," Cassidy said the second his feet hit the ground. Missy and Kristen turned their hoses on him, the water cold and furious. Ripping off his clothes in absolute disgust, Cody thanked Christ that first they were near a water source and second these weren't just garden hoses, maybe not firetruck material, but certainly "industrial grade."

They had him turn a few slow 360s, and he was so in a place of shock and revulsion that he let them totally baptize him, arms up, arms down, bent over like a prison move, every nook, every cranny.

Who cared if some college students happen to amble on by, right? Chances were that everyone would be the butt of some kind of meme at some point. It was like the modern version of the "fifteen minutes of fame" thing.

Right?

Ten minutes later, he was sitting in the visitor's dugout with Cassidy sitting next to him on the bench. He was wearing a blanket she had given him. He was still shaking as if it was subzero out here. She had on a blue windbreaker that on the back of it said, "LA Police."

"So," Cody said, "you are a figment of my imagination, delivered to me to train me so my characters can go up against the Professor's characters, who will all flock together at first as a team, sort of like the better warrior kids ganging up on the weaker ones at the start of *The Hunger Games*."

"You catch on fast."

"And you're really a cop."

"Yes."

Cody chewed at the inside of his cheek for a second.

"But," he said, "the Red Headmaster is supposed to be smart, a retired schoolteacher who thinks up these awesome tableaux. This wasn't awesome. It was a nine-year-old's trick, pushing me from behind. Did this 'simulated' vigilante villain think I was going to take the rap because I was the one caught in the box with the corpse?"

She looked at him for a second, her right hand up by her ear, the thumb moving across the fingers one by one, cracking the knuckles.

"Yes," she said.

"Because my DNA would be on the body."

"Yes."

"And that would work?"

She closed her eyes for a second, laughing to herself.

"No," she said. "And that's the point. The Red Headmaster is weak because the Professor never thought up any good tableaux except the monkey house in his query letter. He rushed it in conceit and arrogance, leaving his 'champion' vulnerable and transparent … stupid actually, and in my line of work this is the norm. Criminals are generally featherbrained, desperate, and therefore predictable. My job is figuring out which level of stupid I have to travel down to help my fellow officers get an arrest when they ask me to walk a crime scene. In this case, the Red Headmaster is nothing more than a regular guy, and in terms of how much experience he has with criminality, the closest he's ever gotten to exciting murderous tableaux was watching *Dexter,* Season Six."

Cody hung his head. "And I fell for it."

She reached out, put her hand on his shoulder, and gave it a little rub through the blanket.

"No worries," she said. "When it comes to the Red Headmaster, you will have to have your characters go in prepared. Look for things out of the ordinary. He prefers to place you in a scenario where you feel the most comfortable, where your emotions take over, like when you got to play ball. As for today, kid … when have you ever seen a backstop storage container so tall that it needed a stepladder to get into? The imaginary Red Headmaster here needed that feature so you could be more easily pushed over the lip. Have your characters be ready to find the oddball aspect of the puzzle so they don't fall for his idiot-tricks. Then he is just a retired schoolteacher who hopefully soon will be begging for his life."

Cody pulled the blanket tighter around him. Sullenly, he said,

"You could have just told me all this. You didn't have to push me in with the stiff."

"But now it's ingrained in you, part of you," she said. "It's more than just information. It's muscle memory."

"It was mean."

She put her hand on his shoulder again. She leaned in, close, right up to his ear.

"I'll make it up to you," she said softly. "I promise."

Chapter 18

The Professor followed Eliza into the kitchen, as she had walked past him rather abruptly, saying something about the best place to get to know a man. She had stopped a step or two in, put her suitcase on the floor by the pot rack, and walked over to the corner shelving with the microwave that was otherwise filled with Margaret's old cookbooks. The Professor paused in the archway.

"I, uh, wasn't expecting you, or, you know ... company but—"

She slipped out the book titled *Fuel Your Body: How to Cook and Eat for Peak Performance.*

"No apologies."

"But, madam ... "

"Eliza, please," she said, handing over the book. "This one will do for now."

"Right," he said, "Eliza. I feel silly saying this, but I created you for Cody."

"No," she said offhandedly. "You created me for yourself. Do not lie."

She moved to the middle of the room and turned slowly, the panorama thing, taking in the sink with his tea cup half filled, a bread plate, the small beechwood cutting board ... the fridge with all the magnets and the age stains shadowed up the side ... the old cabinets, the utensil drawer not seated quite properly anymore ... the rolling bar with a few unfolded towels on it, a smudged wine glass half full from two nights ago, and the toaster and air fryer, because there was no better place for them.

"I, uh, would have straightened up ..." he tried, his voice trailing off awkwardly, showing the glaring contrast between the two of them. She

116

wasn't looking at him. She was looking at the table now with his notes, and paper scraps, and empty milk jug, and the Disney Mickey Mouse coffee cup for the coffee and the black "Big Easy" mug for the Honey Ohs, and the cereal box that had fallen face down, dear Lord the crumbs, and the salt shaker that was almost empty next to the pepper and a small container of dill he hadn't returned to the spice rack after adding it to the tuna salad he made last week. She stepped in and picked up the pocket notebook, flipped a few pages. She looked at a few of the Post-It Notes.

"You flatter me," she said.

The Professor folded his arms with his shoulders up high, cresting toward his ears.

"I, uh, was just … "

She turned and slid gracefully to him, close enough to whisper. She had the soft fragrance of violets or some kind of flower meant for open fields in full bloom in kingdoms in fairy tales.

"Do you want to touch me?" she said.

He nodded, too quickly, but there was no saving face now. He had been turned to a wobbling mess of quivering jelly. She put her palm to his chest, warm, fingers splayed, and it felt as if she was playing his heartbeat like some kind of harp.

"I am here," she said, leaning so close he could feel her sweet breath. "I am here because your characters are going to go up against Cody's characters first, not counting the—how do you say?—*wild cards* belonging to neither of you, like Savage Alice. You have to think like a fighter to write like one. This is training, and it will be hard, but there are rewards. Just use your imagination and picture me in your arms."

He wanted to grab her shoulders, pull her in, and drown her with one long kiss ebbing into the next. He just stood there.

"What am I to do then?" he said finally.

She backed away. *God,* her movements were so fucking girly!

"For me," she said, "I am going to clean this kitchen, reorganize things. You, my love, will walk the stairs to the second floor."

He smiled, blinking. "Really? Why? What then?"

"You will walk back down the stairs."

He stared a second, thought about his paunch.

"Yeah," he said. "Okay, I get it. How many repetitions?"

"Until I tell you to stop. Do not change into workout clothing. You will proceed as you are. Work up a sweat so you no longer feel stiff. Remember posture. Shoulders back, but not so much that you push out your belly. Lift the legs high until your thighs are parallel to the flat of the stair. No trudging."

He swallowed, and it actually made a clicking sound. His Adam's apple felt like a yo-yo on a stick.

"And then I can touch you?"

She did not smile, but her eyes did ever so slightly.

"Yes, but just know that I will demand far more from you than a short flight of stairs."

Chapter 19

For Cody, the concept of time had gone wacko. While it seemed just a moment ago that he had been sitting, shivering, and wearing a blanket in the visitor's dugout at UCLA's Easton Softball Stadium, he had memories of more recently running through other scenarios initiated by the lovely Police Officer Cassidy Claybourne, difficult ones through which failure meant a shitload of shame, a major gross-out, wicked-bad pain, and a ton of embarrassment.

Before these, however, following the dugout pep-talk and during the ride back to her place, they had discussed the settings for the "scenarios," and how a softball field wasn't anything like the "abandoned tenements" that the Professor had originally proposed. Cassidy's response was that they needed to overprepare. The Professor could not be trusted, especially with his habit of switching up the rules when it was most convenient for him, and considering this, Cody had agreed that if the Professor lost a battle, say, in an abandoned warehouse, it would be no surprise if the next confrontation was in a funhouse, or a hot air balloon, or on top of a speeding train.

Done deal. They went forward with Cassidy's scenarios as she had planned them, and though these simulations had been against an imaginary Red Headmaster, Cassidy had explained that they were actually morphing the former with the Dark Doppelgänger, since both were the closest projections of the Professor's true self, both with similar skill sets. After a brief discussion, they decided to go with Cassidy's initial determination that the Dark Doppelgänger was actually the more dominant of the two. After all, the Professor had never worked out any future tableaux for the ex-high school English teacher, and even if he had, they were an "after-the-fact" kind of condiment and rather useless in what would be the actual kill-space during kill-time. And so, the Dark Doppelgänger's booby-traps were the most likely mode of attack to rehearse for, with Cody's defenses varying according to which of his own characters was being challenged.

For scenario number one against the Red Headmaster and Doppelgänger combo (following the test-run at the softball field, of course), Cody had entered a circus trailer now as Cody the Clown, and as he had done as a little boy in his family's traveling show, the wagon he was in love with was that of the lion tamer, the equipment van that had the black coachman's top hats, the red ringmaster tailcoats, the black riding breeches, and the knee-high black leather show boots, and there were stools stacked in the corner, used to confuse the lions by dividing their focus amongst the four legs, and finally there were the tantalizing whips: the stock whip, the bull, the snake, the cow, the signal, the fire, the bullock, and the performance hybrid.

It was like coming home, for sure, and of course their trailer camp outside had smelled vaguely of horse poop, pungent yet somehow lovingly familiar like wet mown hay or old damp canvas, and whether he passed a tumbler, fire-breather, or cycler, they were all busy talking to themselves, going over the choreography and stunts in their minds move for move, and once inside the lion tamer's trailer the aroma was that of gorgeous dark leather and after-shave lotion, and the unit was lovely and shadowed with silky veils covering the lighting, because a female tamer named Andrea Becht had recently joined their company and she insisted on "ambiance," and Cody went to the footlocker where they kept all the circus whips, to try them out right here and now, every one of them, seeing if he could go seven for seven making them *snap*.

He paused; something was wrong. It was the storage chest, an heirloom in itself, a pirate's treasure chest made of fancy wood, maybe teak or mango, ornate with decorative iron overlays. Still, something was off, and Cody stood there in momentary indecision.

Storage chest …

Right. I mean, wasn't it just yesterday (or a moment ago, as again, time was "funny" nowadays) that Cassidy tricked him into opening a booby-trapped storage chest? Wasn't this "double jeopardy" or whatever it was that determined going to the same well twice? Dang, he couldn't remember whether it was the law in court that made it so you couldn't be tried again for the same crime or the way a pitcher went back to the same pitch again, hoping the batter expected variety.

Either way, he wasn't opening the fucking thing without some safe cushion-space. Was it a bomb, maybe? No, too impersonal. Also, there was no foreshadowing that the Professor knew anything about explosives.

Hmm …

He was supposed to look for clues, right? Keeping his distance, he walked slowly around it, and on the second rotation, he stopped.

Wait.

Well, looky here …

On the left side panel near the top were three small holes about a quarter-inch in diameter. He crept around to the opposite side and noticed the same. And he would have bet a million dollars that, on closer inspection, you would see a fine mesh on the inner side of each of the openings.

They were air holes.

Cody backed off and looked around. Leaning up against some lockers was a lion tamer's fixed pole spear with a steel comb attachment on the end of it. He took it and stepped slowly back toward the chest, readying himself and reaching it across in slow motion, like a swordsman making a slow-motion thrust.

He edged the flat comb attachment under the hasp and nudged it up over the empty loop that normally held the padlock, next pulling back the stick, unscrewing the comb, and re-aiming it. He bent his knee, thrusting in slowly like Zorro, and he worked the tip into a deep depression in the lid handle, oh yeah, and he shoved it upward and back.

He instinctively jumped backward a few feet, and there was a sound from the chest, oily, yet at the same time sort of "whispy," like a cold wind across your shoulders. He climbed onto a barrel with circus colors back by the costume rack and went up on his toes.

It was snakes, at least fifty of them, all black mambas, all slithering over one another. He knew they were black mambas and knew they were deadly for the same reason the Professor did. On one of their music reaction videos two years ago, they'd discussed the Professor's absolute love and obsession with Quentin Tarantino, especially the *Kill Bill* series and, in particular, number two and the amazing scene with Daryl Hannah, code name "California Mountain Snake," killing Budd with a black mamba in a suitcase, which would next lead to her getting her second eye pulled out by Uma Thurman at the conclusion of a glorious Samurai sword fight.

Immediately then, he was back in Cassidy's apartment, the two of them in bed, she in her bra and cotton undies sitting up against the headboard and Cody positioned lower, cheek to her upper chest, all snuggled in with her arm around his back. She was smoking a cigar, and ironically, he hadn't vaped up in here even once. Seemed it would be impolite somehow, though Cassidy always smoked a cigar after sex, claiming that he would get to love the secondary smoke the same way he loved the smell of horse poop, wet mown hay, and damp canvas. Hey, to hell with the vape pipe. She was giving him sensory overload that made him feel like a God. Or maybe a porn star. Or maybe just some dumbass that got lucky.

She was so pretty and pure, but buckle in, bucco, she believed in telling the truth, the whole truth, and everything about it all the way down to the bottom and out to the periphery. She had told Cody that she wasn't a virgin as his brainstorming had indicated, too Disney to be believed, yet along those same lines she had only been with two other men in her life, the first a soldier who died in Afghanistan and the other, ironically, her professor senior year, but he was not her English instructor. It was a class in behavioral psychology that focused on pathological killers, taught by the US Army Cadet Commander who ran the campus ROTC. It was only one night, and it was rather … formulaic, her exact word.

The intimacy between them, after Cody successfully discovered the black mambas, had been anything but formulaic, featuring Cassidy on top most of the time, pumping up and down in hard rhythmic breakers and rip currents, her chin jutted out, eyes closed, her neck cords up. Cody had specified that he wanted to have his hands on her ass as much as possible, like a trigger for him, and they had laughed together like old friends in a dive bar when she said that his obsession was good with her as long as he understood that she had tattoos back there, one on each cheek saying "Exit" and "Only."

When they were spent, she orchestrated a slowdown that, at least to Cody, seemed better than even the best of the fadeouts in classic rock outros: the two of them, pressing their lips together, altering the relative pressures and duration, and running their fingers through each other's hair. Then they were face to face, sharing breaths, with a kiss on the end of his nose like a cutie-pie emoji.

It already felt like home here, the apartment neat in a militaristic sort of way, with lots of glass, chrome, and leather, some high school volleyball and soccer trophies on the mantel, and a collection of rare hunting knives on the opposite side of the apartment in the nook area on the inlaid shelving. Still, the place was also cluttered with other stuff still in the boxes, on the living room coffee table, on the bar separating the den area from the kitchen, and along the wall by the elliptical, as if she worked for a living and lived for working, always at the station or on the streets of L.A. with little time to enjoy the small comforts she'd earned.

Why they never spent time at Cody's place was something he avoided, and she had seemingly accepted. When they talked about her job, she always went monotone, sounding very much like a doctor delivering a baby, giving blunt orders to both nurse and patient, and ignoring the latter's obvious pain, because to her, *the screams are not important …* now where the fuck had he heard that before? A movie? A book from high school? Maybe it was J. D. Salinger or Hemingway or any of the others that all sounded the same to him, except for that line, because he'd actually remembered the fucker.

"What's your favorite cop show?" he said.

"They're all the same."

"How so?"

She took a draw on the cigar, savored the flavor a second, and blew it up at the ceiling.

"You ever see the Netflix show *The Derry Girls*, kid?"

"No."

"It's good. You'd like it. The plot is all over the place, but it's about a group of friends in high school, Catholic school in Ireland in the '90s, and they have situations, you know, adventures that play as real and at the same time humorous."

Cody was tracing the back of his index finger along the side of her throat.

"You have a nice neck," he said. "Long and supple."

"Yeah?' she said, looking down to him, smirking. "Sounds like you're describing a tree branch."

"I like climbing trees."

"Promises, promises," she said. "Anyhoo, about the Derry Girls, the one in charge of the school is this nun who's the best character in the series, down to earth, no nonsense and sarcastic as hell, and they have a scene where she's on a bus reading *The Exorcist,* and she's laughing to herself, kind of like, *'Oh, that's so cute'* and at the same time *'Oh, how fucking ridiculous.'"*

She put out the cigar in the ashtray on the nightstand and shimmied back down under the covers. She tucked his hair behind the rim of his ear.

"So that's what I think of the cop shows, like *Law and Order, Blue Bloods, 9-1-1,* all the *CSI* versions. They glorify the violence and ignore the busywork and red tape, the logging in of everything you do, all the procedures and processes."

"You ever have to kill anyone?" Cody said.

She went cold, deadpan.

"Excuse," she said, releasing herself from the embrace, turning her back to him, and pushing up and out of bed. Cody was so stunned that he didn't say anything, watching her leave the room, her body and demeanor like some warrior queen who'd been told her swordsmen had been beaten back, sacrificing a bridge or some mountain stronghold. Before he could even think of cooking up an apology, however, she came back into the bedroom with, of all things, a Taylor Swift doll that was dressed in the superstar's Eras Tour costume, the one with the sparkly pink and blue body suit with matching glitter-boots.

It was so "cutsie," Cody nearly laughed outright, almost going from being hopefully presumed innocent for his question to the ugly conviction of a pillow-talk felony; yet when she pulled up the covers, slid in, and retained her sitting position up against the headboard, he saw it was a foam rubber stress doll that she was obviously going to squeeze the living shit out of while she confessed why discharging her firearm was such a hot topic.

He propped himself up on his elbow. "What happened?" he said.

She squeezed the stress doll, twisting the head like a screw cap on a bottle of Mad Dog 20/20.

"I was working vice," she began, "with my uncle Kenny, my favorite uncle, my dad's side, the one who lived with us since his divorce and of course the one I idolized my whole life, always there for me, helping me learn the basics I would need for the Law Enforcement Exam long before I had to take it, you know, all the stuff we talked about and revered, sort of like singing the National Anthem or saying grace, like conduct of search and seizure, patrol operations, elements of proof, all the good stuff. He was my sounding board as I followed Dad's wishes, playing softball for UCLA and studying hard. When I got my bachelor's, I had a 3.8 cum in Criminal Justice, and then I came up through the academy just to become the luckiest rookie in L.A. when I got assigned to Uncle Kenny's precinct, eventually paired up with him and working the streets where it counted."

She was digging her thumbnail deep into Taylor Swift's forehead now, making the pop singer's clever grin more exaggerated as if the doll was laughing without a face.

"Anyhow," Cassidy continued, "we were on patrol in the Wholesale District, you know, Skid Row, and Uncle Kenny had just filled the tank at the ARCO. And there on pump number two, he got a visual on one Fernanda Flores, first assistant to the drug baron Diego Pineda of the Sandoval cartel. Her picture was on every precinct wall on the West Coast, the fifty most wanted and all that noise. I mean, I even recognized her, and I had only been on the force a few weeks. We had struck gold. We were going to get the collar of the year, and we were smiling, pure adrenaline, almost laughing out loud with it, because she was driving this tiny car, a 2021 Chevy Spark, and it was oxymoronic and funny to have spotted this big drug lord in a little car, kind of like that old school *Tommy Boy* movie, when he sings *'Fat guy in a little coat.'*"

Taylor Swift was now bent double on herself, and Cody couldn't help but think of the old joke about being in an airplane in a nose-dive and assuming the position the flight attendants taught you where your head went between your knees, and you could kiss your sweet ass goodbye.

Cassidy took in a deep breath and went on, her bottom lip starting to tremble.

"We tailed her," she went on, "but we were in a police cruiser, not an unmarked vehicle, and she picked up on it pretty fast. We were at the corner of Fifth and Crocker Streets, where there's that billboard that says *'There is Hope on Skid Row,'* and she bangs a hard left between an abandoned warehouse and the tool and die factory. It was a dead end, the opening back there blocked by the back side of a cardboard recycling dumpster. We knew this because, two months before, we had arrested three prostitutes hiding from us back in there. Therefore, we also knew that the alley was narrow as fuck, and that the cruiser wasn't going to fit."

She smiled sadly.

"There was screeching of the brakes, and Uncle Kenny parked crossways, blocking the only exit for her; we had her dead to rights. We proceeded on foot, both of us with our service revolvers drawn, advancing down the right-side edge of the alley, guns in close-ready position. The light was different, darker, and her car was sitting there, brake lights on, exhaust visible in the partially enclosed area, making it seem mystical and strange, like a movie."

Cody almost jerked in reaction to the tear that suddenly came down Cassidy's face, left eye, then another, same eye. How could she keep talking without her voice changing? I mean, it was totally creepy and behaviorally odd, as he knew from experience that if he ever tried to speak while tearing up, he had voice tremors, a higher tone almost in falsetto, and the need to take major rest stops. Cassidy continued robotically, like giving a report now, an official statement.

"We slowed coming near the back of the car. Fernanda Flores was a dangerous criminal, resourceful and merciless. A decade back, she had killed two undercover FBI agents in the courtyard dining area in front of the Burger King in a bus depot in New Mexico. She did it with an acetate hairpin she stabbed to the hilt through their ears, methodically, quickly, the second victim barely having the time to reach for his holster, let alone get a hold of his weapon. She had assassinated five men in competing cartels with her compact custom pearl-handled .32 Smith & Wesson pistol, a big business kingpin in the US beef industry in one of his slaughterhouses with a meat hammer and a ten-inch cleaver, and the latest, a border agent in the men's room in a bar close to a Del Rio tent city, gutting him with a jackknife and a pair of sewing scissors she kept in her knitting bag."

"Jesus," Cory said.

"Yeah," she said. "Scary bitch. So I had just enough space to flank the right side of the vehicle, and Uncle Kenny tried to cover the left. But it was darker on that side, and there wasn't as much room as it had seemed on approach there in the cross-shadows, and just when I drew even with the passenger side window, which was open, Uncle Kenny was coming back across to my side of the alley." She rubbed her nose. "It was all so fast then. I aimed my weapon, loaded to the teeth with jacketed hollow points that would penetrate the size of a dime and come out the size of a basketball, and I stared in at her pointing that pearl-handled Smith & Wesson right back at my face. It was a no-brainer. Lethal force was justifiable, my life was in danger, I should have taken my shot, right then, done deal, but I didn't. I saw out of the corner of my eye a kid in a car seat in back. I paused, and she hit the gas in reverse, screeching the tires. Uncle Kenny was ten feet behind her. He knew when he started coming back to my side of the alley that it was a risk. One of the first things they teach you back at the academy is never to take a position of jeopardy in front of or behind a vehicle that can be used as a weapon against you." She sighed, staring dejectedly at Taylor, who was looking back up at her with that paper doll smile.

"When she hit my uncle, the sound was literally sickening, like taking a Louisville Slugger to a soaking wet duffel bag filled with wood shavings and eggshells. He was flipped up and over the roof of the car like a pinwheel, feet clunking down on the front hood like a puppet off the strings as she raced out from under him, and he spun to the asphalt at the foot of the dumpster."

Cody's mouth was ajar. He had nothing here. She went on tonelessly, as if she'd cried about this so many times by now that she was actually starting to go dry.

"I did the right thing next," she said. "I went to my uncle, assessed that he was still alive, and I called in for an ambulance and backup. It is a policeman's duty to attend to the injured before further pursuing a suspect, and hearing Fernanda Flores bashing into the cruiser blocking the exit space over and again until she finally got clear and sped away sounded to me like a faraway echo, a bad dream, insignificant."

Cassidy was sitting Indian style now, legs folded under the comforter, her hands in her lap, lying limp on either side of Taylor Swift like dead wildlife.

"He lived," she went on, "and he never allowed me to apologize. He had broken his femur, his hip badly fractured, and he never walked the same again. Uses a cane to this day, and he went gray and then lost all his hair all in one year." She laughed, and it sounded rough and abrupt. "Turns out I have hoplophobia, fear of firing guns to the point of near paralysis. Funny, how I was the best marksman at the station besides only Deputy Chief Lundy and Lieutenant Barnaby, but the range isn't a back alley, and a person is no paper target."

She looked at Cody for the first time since starting this God-awful story, and said without sarcasm or malice,

"So, no, Cody-kid. I never killed anyone. I hold the rank of 'Uniformed Officer' and I am proud of it. I don't have a 'beat' for obvious reasons, but there is no one at the station that works the Complaint and Information desk like me. I organize and maintain the Property and Evidence Storage Area, and I can even jump in and play dispatcher. I also have a good feel for interpreting crime scenes, and there are four of our detectives, two ballistic experts, and our best blood splatter analyst, who often bring me along to bend under the caution tape, so to speak. As for my Uncle Kenny, he took a pay cut and was moved to Desk Sergeant as soon as he got out of the hospital and was fully rehabbed. He's a good in-house cop. Strong. Dependable. Fair. He forgives me with his eyes every day, and I honestly don't know what feelings in me are stronger: those that thank God he's alive and that I can still see him every day, or those that torch my insides with shame every time I see him limp by."

Cody pushed up so they were sitting at an equal level, and being that she was all legs all damned day, their relative height was even-Steven. Words didn't matter here. He put his arms around her, embraced her, and their heads fell to each other's shoulders. She sniffed like getting over the sniffles, but her voice was the usual reinforced steel.

"Don't you go getting soft on me, kid," she said.

"I won't," he said.

"This is a nice hug. Can't last forever, though."

He gently came away in looked her in the eye. "I wish it could."

She looked at him with open frankness, all business.

"No time," she said. "You've proven that Cody the Clown can survive the Red Headmaster's and Dark Doppelgänger's booby-trap, but now you have to go in as Tito Quiñones, the Rock Reaper. Since this character has no clear and present 'Cody' in him besides common knowledge of heavy music, you will not be alone in the body and mind. He steers the ship, big time. He will not know you're there, but you can give input. And if you do, give it with force, Cody, make him obey. He is a strong personality, an Alpha male if there ever was one, and you don't want to end up on the wrong side of this particular stratagem cooked up by the Red Headmaster/Dark Doppelgänger hybrid."

"Thanks for the advice," Cody said, his smile a bit sideways.

"Goodbye," she said.

Cody had just enough time to wonder why this sounded so final when he was transported, hurtling into the dark.

Chapter 20

It was ultimately ironic the way this turned out, and not just because the time continuum had been fucked with to the point that the Professor didn't know what day it was, let alone the week. He felt as if he had been in intensive military training for months, and it wasn't something just "in his head." His body was different. He'd lost twelve pounds. He could do fifty pushups, and he could whip off thirty-seven perfect pullups, the kind going all the way down till there was no bend in the elbows. That said, he could advance up and down the stairs in perfect form like a Marine marching for an hour at a time without stopping, and he could dive over seven barrels set up in a line, next rolling and coming back up to a fighter's stance.

Eliza had him on a strict regimen: 7:00 to 7:30 A.M. for breakfast, all fruit. 7:30 to 8:30 for balletic stretching. After a half-hour breather by means of meditation, it was back to work from 9:00 A.M. to 11 A.M. with a focus on legs, squatting with free weights, calf lifts with bungee cords, and thigh spreaders with high tension elastic bands. 11 A.M. to 12 P.M. was dedicated solely to arms: pullups and pushups as before indicated along with dumbbell work for biceps (every other day like the squatting) and what she called "hatchet hacking," through which he was to do pull-downs from back over the shoulder using baseball pitcher's J-bands affixed to the wall, both sides left then right, hard and deep, as if chopping wood in slow motion. Lunch was all vegetables, nuts, and different salad combinations without dressing, Eliza's special formula smoothies, and the rest period, 12 P.M. to 1 P.M., always seemed too damned short.

Well ... it was easier lately. He wasn't just in good shape; he was in the best shape of his life, even better than he'd been during his weight-lifting addiction as a sophomore undergrad at Temple University through the spring semester and deep into the summer. Here, there was more cardio, stuff that he had always thought too much a pain in the ass, and the early to midafternoon in this "boot-camp" was allocated for running, he and Eliza currently on the verge of ten miles, final goal twelve. Preceding a high-protein dinner, 4 P.M. to 5 P.M., was for talking, planning, strategizing, and this is where the irony proved the biggest and brightest.

He had invented Eliza to seduce Cody, with the purpose of sticking it to the guy's wife, making her jealous ... in other words, fucking over the Mod Goddess, and according to Eliza, this mysterious character was hands-off, at least as far as the planning went for whom they were preparing to confront. The Mod Goddess had control of Savage Alice, a dangerous spirit that made weight-lifting and stretching rather pointless. Same with Cody's other supernatural pawns, Ghost and Wolf Shadow, at least in terms of "hands off" in the part of the war-scheme requiring physical preparation. First of all, they couldn't be killed, and secondly, Eliza was pretty sure the Professor could handle Ralph. They had been friends, after all, and the guy was all about "love." It was a riddle she thought best to leave to fate ... choosing the right hills to die on and all that. And as for Wolf Shadow, Eliza strongly felt that since the one to expose the logo on the drum head had power over the beast, the target wasn't actually Wolf Shadow. It was Cody the Clown, since that was the closest thing to Cody the actual person, who had the drum set downstairs that the Professor needed to get to before him if one of his characters was thrust into that scenario.

Consequently, the field to prepare for was actually quite small. The Professor's Beekeeper and Lucifer's Gal seemed untouchable if pitted against Cody's Clown character and his Rock Reaper. Wolf Shadow and Ghost, as said, drew at least even with their aforementioned supernatural "others" on the Professor's side of the ticket, so the ones to prepare the hardest for were the mortals: Cody the Clown and the Rock Reaper, both of whom seemed at first glance to be physically superior to the Professor's Red Headmaster and Dark Doppelgänger.

All this considered, it was the one character they had mentioned the least that Eliza finally admitted was the one she most feared, and that was the Soldier. To her, he was the X factor because he didn't fit quite right in the puzzle. The Professor's four characters matched up evenly with Cody's, at least relatively when you considered this training regimen and the way the Professor was getting to the point that he was learning enough about the body, by muscle memory, to form the ability to write himself into at least calling a draw with Cody's mortals, the entire eight from both sides first going for the other guy's inventions as if competitive teams. There was a balance there. As far as Savage Alice and her creator were concerned, they were as much a threat to Cody's clan as to that of the Professor.

Altogether, then, in terms of the supernatural beasts on both teams, they all had weaknesses in their makeup, their DNA, so to speak. The Beekeeper wanted to play Metallica solos in his garage. Lucifer's Gal wanted to play guitar in arenas. Wolf Shadow wanted to fuck like there was no tomorrow, and Ghost wanted to spread peace and love as if he were Christ. The Mod Goddess was no threat without Savage Alice, and Alice wanted to get revenge on rapists; in fact, if you threw open the hood of your pickup, she'd probably transform into her human form to help you get back a charge and turn over the engine.

But the Soldier ... *this* fucker was keeping Eliza up nights. He couldn't be reasoned with, because he felt murder was his patriotic duty, and he would be difficult to overtake because he better knew the chessboard, the mountain, the tunnel, the hill ... let alone abandoned tenements where he'd thrive like a spider in the shadows trapping house flies.

The Professor and Eliza had been making love every night, but tonight, when he walked into the bedroom, she was not dressed in seductive silks, as was her preference. She was wearing a Karate Gi with a black sash. She was barefoot. She was holding in her right hand a sword.

"This is a war saber," she said. "I will teach you the eight angles of attack, how to counter cut, thrust, feint, and parry. For now, do not just chop down as we have done with the baseball pitcher's J-bands. Be careful not to overplay your move, or the curve in the blade will betray you. Subtlety is key, poise and balance, your friends. This will be the first of many weapons we will master together, and the Soldier will be surprised to be met with such enthusiasm, I assure you."

She pointed the end of the blade at the bed. On it was another Gi and a saber for the Professor.

"Suit up," she said. "And in the words of Laurence Fishburne in the film you referenced earlier in this saga, hit me … if you can."

Chapter 21

The transfer in the dark to the simulation starring Cody as a passenger inside the Rock Reaper–Tito Quinones took only a few seconds, almost instantaneous, but thoughts came to you in the wink of an eye as well, and Cody had a few of them. Questions actually. Scary questions he should have thought of before.

I mean, first of all, what was "before" anymore anyhow, considering that this "training camp" seemed as quick as the wink of an eye in itself? His memories were stacked with what seemed like days upon days, but he also knew he'd hardly been here more than a moment. Kind of.

Sort of.

Still, it was pretty important to get a handle on this time-thing, because, hello, the fucking Mod Goddess had given them twenty-four hours to bail on the whole project or else she was sending down Savage Alice to torch their asses. Cartoonish, sure, but the scarier, more authentic version would be that some sicko man or woman posing as the Mod Goddess was to show up at Cody's bungalow and the Prof's house, throwing Molotov cocktails through their living-room windows. But. Uh. Naw. It had to be, as Cody first suspected, that the Professor's ex-wife was having a sadistic kind of fun with them, inventing the Goddess, the Soldier, and Savage Alice to throw wrenches in the gears, confuse them, fuck up their podcast.

A sudden and creepy analogy came to Cody.

If he figured the Mod Goddess was the Professor's ex-wife, and therefore Cody created Cassidy Claybourne to make the intrusive witch insane with jealousy, would it not make sense that the Professor had denied to himself that his ex could be to blame and had flipped the script, coming up with the same scheme to make Cody's "wife" the aggressor, therefore inventing his own fantasy girl who wound up being his trainer as if that was the way it was supposed to be all along? How was the old guy being prepared? Was it similar to what Cody was doing?

He felt his stomach drop, a mere nanosecond in itself, but the thing that had been nagging at the back of his mind as a blur was suddenly glaring in bright fucking neon. It was a simple number. Eleven. There were supposed to be twelve contestants in *The Kill or Be Killed Project,* and they were one short: four created by Cody, four by the Professor, and the three wild cards that the Professor denied constructing himself: the Soldier, Savage Alice, and the Mod Goddess. What the fuck? This threw everything off. They were training too soon, it made no sense, unless it was …

Real maybe? Really real, because "real" was never perfect, always messy, and that's why life was such a shitshow sometimes?

Cody was no longer in the dark. He was in an arena with eighteen thousand empty seats rising up on all sides like some Greek amphitheater. There were sounds, drills buzzing, electric ratchets clackety-clacking, hammers hitting home with an echo, with authority. The stage was humongous, one hundred forty feet by two hundred and seventy, and the opening band, an Eclipse Records project called Sifting, were all waiting with their roadies off to the side with their gear. The house sound system was going to be the best Tito had ever played through, hanging thirty feet high above the left and right front corners of the stage space: two flown arrays of three-way full-range enclosures, plus four arrays of speaker clusters in addition to subwoofers flown in an end-fire configuration. From the rear of the stage up to about the three-quarter mark, Saint Diablo's majestic instrumental set-up looked like a steel fortress; in fact, they had brought all their equipment, the heavy stuff, too many amps really, and Justin and Zach had had a minor disagreement about stage volume, finally concurring to flip on just two cabinets each, leaving the rest of the Marshalls on standby for show, a visual wall of sound kind of deal.

Tito felt good. He felt strong, and Cody was amazed at this guy's inner hype-flow. It felt like an engine too big for its chassis, but fuck it, man, it seemed Tito's frame was cut out of rough granite itself. And the dude was jacked, thinking a million things about the venue, the sightlines, the way it would sound up in the seats closest to the rafters where there were NBA team banners and a monster four-sided scoreboard. He was thinking about the width of the pit and the extra security that would be standing there, the pyrotechnics, the flame throwers inset at stage level so the boys wouldn't trip over them, his family and friends who had specialty guest passes and those he'd been forced to overlook, the gear van, the smaller of the two that they had nicknamed "Cerdito" (Little Piglet), and that Richie had forgotten to gas up, so after the show the caravan would have to stop and wait, and he was practicing the lyrics to the songs off the new record *The Reckoning,* and considering the fact that they had positioned those tunes alternately at the beginning of the show so they could climax with the good ole shit from *Devil Horns and Halos.* His voice was good tonight, a bit rough, so lubricate, lubricate, bitches, let's go!

Time to sound-check. Tito climbed the stairs behind the stage, slapping a few techies five as he passed. When he mounted the platform, Cody was amazed at how fucking high it felt, as if you'd be a God over the sea of followers, and suddenly he got paranoid. He willed Tito to look above, and while the singer complied, admiring the rack lighting, the raw quantity of adjustable quad-color heads, the floods, and the steel nests for the follow spots and their operators, Cody got vertigo or its inverse, so bad he thought he was going to heave, if that was at all possible in this state of being. The lights, man, the lights! That was what Cody's instinct was telling him. One of those heavy motherfuckers was going to pop loose, hurtle down through the air, and crush Tito's skull mid-performance. Since he wore fake blood on his chrome-dome anyway, the crowd was going to think it a stunt, cheering it, then slowly falling off to dead silence when they realized Tito wasn't moving.

Tito must have felt something too, because he stopped looking up and shook it off, inwardly shaming himself for this temporary moment of nerves. Cody tried talking sense to him in a calm and rational voice, but as Cassidy had predicted, Cody had no voice, and Tito was a tough nut to crack.

Delgado, the stage manager, called Tito over, and in the singer's mind, any lingering thoughts about the lighting were banished. He gave a pert nod and ambled over. Delgado had on a headset, a collared shirt unbuttoned top three, and loose, comfy khakis. He had long, wavy California hair and wire-framed glasses.

"Sweetheart," he said, "Tito, before you sound-check, I want you to memorize your landing spot for when you first come on stage in a few hours. The space will be dimly lit with only the soft glow of a couple of footlights, so baby-doll, when you approach, your color is red, remember red. That's the color of the duct tape that will be in the shape of an X. You stand right on it to begin."

Delgado started walking to the mark, gazing down at his laptop as if planning to move to the next thing on the list after absently playing chaperone to Tito's practice stroll, and he paused to look back at Tito as if one of them had missed something.

"Well?" he said.

Tito's expression was flat. "I see it, boss. It's right over there. Now what?"

Delgado grinned like a greasy politician. "Babe," he said. "Walk the walk. Practice the blocking. It's procedure, company rules, liability, and all that."

"No thanks," Tito said. "I got it. Now, Pops, we've never headlined a place this big, and Edu over there with the Sifting guys is one of my favorite homies. Let's fire up the instruments, sound-check, and get the fuck out of their way, right? They're the opener, but they need time too."

God, I love this guy, Cody thought. And then he got it, the hint, the clue, the thing out of place. It was the red duct tape. X marks the spot, and Cody somehow had to convince Tito to change his mind, to walk the walk and actually stand on that X.

But how to communicate with the mother ship when you were but a silent passenger?

Scream.

Yes, he would do that, go through the motions, even though he was like the wisp of a dream disconnected from any sort of body part. God, Cody hated this shit, when the rules weren't clear, when movies and stories like this had parameters impossible to measure and translate, so it gave license to the author to manipulate them any way he or she wanted.

Stunned, Cody realized that he sounded like the Professor just now, and it was the same as taking a big bite of your corned beef special and getting a whopping mouthful of shit sandwich.

Oh, Cody screamed. If he had had possession of a face, it would have turned scarlet with it. Tito paused, turned, and looked back past Delgado, then made his way toward him and around him to that fucking red X on the stage. On approach, the presentation looked uneven, bumpy, as if the surface beneath it wasn't quite flat and sure, and then he saw it. The X wasn't taped down over a safe space. It was pressed across the area holding one of the inset gas-powered flame throwers.

The big intro would have been Tito's last. He would have burned like a fucking witch, and instead of maybe two hundred and fifty jeering townspeople, it would have been eighteen thousand fans witnessing first-hand the cruelest assassination of a rock star since Dimebag Darrell of Pantera.

Cody was in the dark again, flying hard, and when he emerged, or rather, popped back into Cassidy's bedroom, she didn't look happy. In fact, she was absolutely miserable, her face warped into a frown like a Greek tragedy drama face. She was sitting on the edge of the bed, wearing her police windbreaker, a gray tee, black leggings, and off-white New Balance low-tops. When she spoke, she didn't look at him, and her voice was hollow and dry, like a ghost town with tumbleweeds.

"We have to talk," she said. "Things have changed: there's a new wrinkle."

"Spill," Cody said. "Please."

She looked at him and patted the space next to her on the bed.

"Sit," she said. "There's something I have to show you."

Chapter 22

The Professor walked into the kitchen, and Eliza was at the table weeping, right elbow down, hand in a fist, knuckles against the forehead. Her shoulders were shaking. Her hair was in a long, loose ponytail in what seemed an effort to keep it clear of the waterworks.

He pulled around the other chair and sat next to her. "Hey," he said.

She squeezed her eyes shut. "It is all so tragic," she said.

"What is?"

"Everything!"

She sat back, straightened, and dabbed under her eyes with her fancy handkerchief, the soft cotton one with the ritzy signature sewn into the corner that the Professor had never actually asked about.

"I watched the news," she said, "while you were in the bathroom for your shower."

"Well, that's your first mistake," the Professor said, immediately regretting his cavalier tone. "What channel? CNN? Fox?"

"Channel Six."

Her hands went to her lap, and she gazed at them.

"There is nothing but shootings, poverty, bad housing, hunger, and war," she said. "And why are politicians allowed to lie as long as they call it 'political speech'? Is that not slander? Why are not children all equally educated? Why does the color of your skin determine the weather of your journey? Why is bullying never to be solved? Why do some people promote the idea that hate is stronger than love, that greed is better than brains, and that ambition must be defined by a power hierarchy based on wealth?"

The Professor didn't respond. He wanted to say, *You said it, sister,* but again, this was no laughing matter. The tears were real, and besides the oddball idea that this creature or woman, or apparition or whatever she was, conveniently "just discovered" these things, there was the strange contradiction in her reaction to world violence and lawlessness, when she was training him to fight and to kill, at least in the writing of it.

He leaned back, and in doing so, he saw something at the corner of his eye. Her suitcase by the pot rack.

"Is that packed?" he said, thinking that he was the one about to choke up. She stood, dabbed at her eyes again, and looked at him. He started getting up to go to her, but she put up her hand: stop where you are.

"Please," she said. "Sit and listen. I won't be long."

He sat. Her shoulders were back now, strong and proud.

"I have taught you well," she said. "You are in a performer's condition, an expert with the foil, rapier, cutlass and dirk, the long sword, the Viking, the scimitar, the gunto. You have mastered all the Soldier's hand-to-hand combat techniques, and you know your way around guns and explosives enough now to at least figure out where the safety is and how to detonate nitroglycerin, TNT, and cordite in a variety of conditions. You have learned strategies to defeat any of the other characters in this game mentally and physically, at least those within reason, and it is time for me to be on my way. I am a showgirl, after all, and I miss the family and camaraderie of the big tent. I miss being on the brighter side of the light. I miss being on tour with only one day off a week, the rehearsals, TV shows, promotional events, and interviews. I miss listening to my body, my inner-me, and I miss my mentors watching me perform, thinking, hoping, and praying for me. I miss revealing to an audience the great secrets of the hoops, the snake-like movements that look like magic, and I miss being so committed to my art that I tell myself that I can sleep later, have fun later, vacation later, relax later."

"I am going to miss you," the Professor said. The silence pounded. True, it was sweet, but he wasn't begging her to stay either. She walked over to her suitcase, picked it up, and made to leave the room, pausing there in the archway and turning back toward him.

"Just so you know," she said, "there is a reason other than love for my craft that I leave you at this particular moment."

"And that is?"

She held the suitcase in both hands in front.

"I had a vision, a prediction of the future," she said. She took a moment to look around the kitchen, similar to the way she did on her arrival. "In this place," she continued, "you well know the rules of time have been altered in order to fit weeks and weeks into minutes and hours. Considering this, in the real world, it is a common belief that if you know the future, you can change it. In this case, and in this … place … I am not sure if one can twist fate in that way, but I need to tell you why I feel you have betrayed me."

The Professor was expressionless. So was Eliza.

"In the competition," she said, "in my vision, I saw the way you will defeat a superior, supernatural opponent. Writing as the Dark Doppelgänger, you will not only lift the cover of the Wolf Shadow logo on the bass drum so you can control the beast, but you will go on to fuck Candi Kennedy, in order to weaponize her for yourself."

Chapter 23

I have had a vision, a prediction of the future," said Cassidy. Beside her on the bed, Cody sat sulking, his forearms on his thighs, hands between the knees, fingers slightly curled inward. It felt like a fetal position, weak, blind, and helpless. And it was not as if being aware of this led to wearing a stronger mask. There would be no fake bravery here, as he was sure beyond sure that she was breaking up with him; he knew the drill, the shape of this kind of thing, all too well. She was about to tell him how important their time together had been, how she had grown as a person, and the way that he was unlike anyone else she'd ever known, so tender and honest and gentle and sweet. But … yeah, there was always the "but." It was the worst vocabulary word in the whole fucking universe, because no matter how much someone buttered you up on the front side, the "but" let you know that the latter part of the sentence was going to cut you right off at the knees.

"What's your prediction?" he muttered. "What do you have to show me?"

"I love you, Cody," she said.

He looked at her. She was looking straight forward, away.

"I, uh, love—" he said.

"No," she said. "Don't say it back." She stood and walked toward the mirror hanging on the back of the bedroom door. Briefly, she looked at herself and removed her police windbreaker, hanging it carefully, almost with reverence, on a wall hook. She moved back a few feet left and was looking at Cody in the reflection as he was studying her. The tight T-shirt and black leggings unapologetically yet modestly showed all her curves and cuts; she was stunning. She spoke to Cody's reflection.

"I never say 'I love you,'" she said, "and I wanted to try it. I never want to say goodbye ever again without saying 'I love you' first."

Cody's shoulders sagged, his head hanging down again.

"Then you are saying goodbye," he murmured.

"Not exactly," she said, "Not the way you are thinking." She turned, walked back over, and sat again on the bed next to him.

"Hey," she said, "I didn't just remove my jacket to better display my body. I already know you like my body. I did it because what I am about to do is against the law. You don't wear any part of the uniform unless you keep to the code."

"What do you have to show me?" Cody said.

"In a sec," she said. "Let me explain first. You see, the Beekeeper, your neighbor Bill Robbins, has quit the ***Kill or Be Killed Project***."

"What? Why?"

"He doesn't need the five million dollars."

"How could he not?"

"Because he understands that his newly found power makes him a god. Give me your hands." He complied. "I am about to show you what Bill Robbins intends to do. He wants a test-run of his power, the way he killed the dogs at the dump, and he has already bought his plane ticket to Philadelphia, to the Professor's hometown, so it will be personal to the both of you."

"What the fuck is he going to do?"

"You will be a passenger inside of him in this simulation, Cody, but this time you will be absolutely passive. You will see what he sees, hear his thoughts, and feel what he feels, but you will be unable to influence anything he does."

Cody had a million questions, but before he could ask even the first, the bedroom vanished around him.

It was ten degrees cooler, and he was in the mind of his neighbor Bill Robinson, the man's thoughts immediate, odd, rough, and rather singular in the way they were blunt and fully formed out of the chute without any democratic sort of reasoning behind them. He was hungry. He was excited. He was hopeful, and he embraced evil unconditionally. Where he fell short in cleverness, he gained ground with decisiveness. What he lacked intellectually, he made up for with a dark and low cunning.

He was smack in the middle of downtown Philadelphia. He wasn't looking at a street sign, but from his thoughts, Cody knew he was on "Broad Street," at the east corner of "Locust," primed and ready for his coming out party, his coming of age.

He stepped along the sidewalk due north, and a gentle wind was making the successive light pole banners advertising *Candide* and the rainbow colored "LGBTQ Pride" ribbons ripple like the sails of small, hearty schooners. The sky above was a pale blue canopy, and people were bustling around, most of them looking determined to get somewhere. Robinson passed a construction site to the right, and a firetruck moved off from behind a double-decker tour bus, yielding a sudden, clear view straight up Broad Street.

Ahead was City Hall in the middle of the thoroughfare three blocks north, a remarkably elaborate structure, constructed in a Victorian French Renaissance sort of way with turreted courtyard stair towers and monumental arched portals. From its center rose the mammoth clock tower, forty stories high and adorned with William Penn's statue above the observation deck, all of it centered between the frame of buildings leading up to it in what appeared to be some grand, imperial corridor.

Suddenly, in Robinson's mind, Cody picked up on an internal sound he was making, almost like humming, and out here, there were vibrations everyone was starting to react to. Robinson glanced back over his shoulder, and in front of the defunct University of the Arts building, a street drummer in a threadbare Eagles hoodie who'd been playing hard on a collection of plastic buckets by the entrance stopped what he was doing and gazed all around as if he were trying to figure out which way the wind was blowing. A few feet away in front of the Wawa, a woman in a trench coat and high leather boots lowered the cell phone she'd been gazing at and came to a halt.

Robinson looked back up along Broad Street; Cody could feel he was smiling like a madman mixing a potion. Many had stopped walking. A few who had been riding bicycles had braked and planted one foot to the street with the other up on a pedal, looking around, removing sunglasses and ear buds, one dude taking off his helmet and resting it on his hip. It was as if the world had paused, and people were looking out yonder, toward what would seem the direction of the trembling.

There was a more pronounced sound now, born of the vibrations, swelling like a siren from a distance with no tangible pitch or recognizable tone, like a stockpile of old television sets tuned to the same empty channel blasting high-pitched static and snow.

People were squinting, some covering their ears, and then they were pointing up at the City Hall clock tower where the sky was darkening. It was a cloud swirling high behind the structure, then taking a rolling pitch downward, and the stunning visual somehow "humanized" the monolith, making it look as if it had a massive scarf being whipped off its neck in slow motion, the black cloud fluid and saurian, nearly as wide as the city block it was about to consume.

The scene moved to darkness as Robinson had closed his eyes, concentrating, focusing his commands, and those eyes opened promptly, steely and bright.

Out front, Broad Street had utterly darkened three blocks north, the black cloud coming on in waves that churned and swirled into one another in barrel rolls, sounding like a million stadium airhorns ramped three octaves up, making the air pulsate and quiver while the concrete buzzed underfoot.

Ahead, up at Chestnut Street, people were running. Horns. Brakes screeching as the assailed looked like tiny stick figures falling down, running into traffic. The cloud advanced, and a block closer at Walnut Street the pedestrians looked like toy soldier-dolls, flashes of color, streaks and dashes quickly overwhelmed by the storm like scrap sifted into a factory vat of black grain, and then in the space before Locust Street the hurricane consumed every living and moving thing on the pavement with the sole exception of Bill Robinson.

The sound was incredible, and through what looked like the dust storm of the century, Cody saw cars crashing into one another, people pushing ahead in panic with their hands splayed out in front of them, others rolling in the streets, taking on dark and shimmering contours of likeness.

A big vehicle that looked like an army truck plowed down a "No Parking" sign and smashed into a newsstand in a burst of debris. The insects that had been covering everything short of the tires flew off in a wave, revealing that it was an ambulance. People were running for cover into the parking garage under the Sporting Club at the Bellevue, waving, swatting, pulling shirts over their heads, trampling over the fallen.

A blonde with a perky ponytail, a loose-fitting tank top, and yoga pants got consumed and ran into the waist-high railing in front of the basement entrance of the "Tavern on Broad." A shrouded SUV immediately hit her dead-on from behind, sawing her in half, and sending her upper body skidding down the stairwell. A tall balding dude in a purple dress shirt, slim jeans, and brown pointed shoes ran up the sidewalk flapping his arms and bobbing his head like an ostrich, only to be hit by a taxi that drove him straight back into the Plexiglas of the bus stop shelter in front of the PNC Bank building. More crashes, more horns, and screaming. There was a throaty *whoosh,* and a gushing that sounded like a fire hydrant ripped up from the concrete.

Robbins turned to look at the southwest corner back across Broad Street. A fire-red pickup truck with Yosemite Sam mud flaps was wrapped around a sign pole that was bent almost double. The white van that appeared to have swerved to avoid rear-ending him had jumped the curb and rammed over what looked like a pair of heavy aggregate trash receptacles that had the undercarriage propped off the ground now, front tires still spinning. The worker on the passenger side had been thrust out through the window and was hanging down over the rim like laundry, green fisherman's cap lying on the sidewalk below him and both arms covered with wasps as if he was wearing long and glistening evening gloves. There were at least twenty infested figures writhing on the sidewalk there, clawing at their faces. Others were in the street, quivering or just lying still. A man was flat on his stomach like a chalk line sketch in the middle of the intersection, head smashed flat to the asphalt in reddish-gray mush that was molded down by the tire marks running through it.

The mass of insects moved on, it was that quick, though some were still swarming the air in hovering clouds, others skittering over the corpses, a bunch of them clustered on the gas lamps on the façade of the Kimmel Center and hanging down off of them like long furry beards. There were sounds of aftermath, none of them human, something made of steel clunking to the street, a faint hissing, glass tinkling.

Cassidy's room rose up all around him, and Cody jumped off the bed, rubbing himself all over, similar to the way he felt in the KNAAK storage chest with the maggots. It was by far the worst thing he had ever experienced: the drone, the harsh voices of the wasps and their militaristic inhuman purpose, the screams of the victims, the violent visuals he would never be able to scrape from his brain, no matter how hard he would try to rationalize them back into the fog.

"Can't you arrest him?" he said.

"On what probable cause? A vision? Won't fly, Cody."

"What about the bee farm in his tree in the back yard?"

She pushed up off the bed.

"Lots of people hoard bees," she said. "In fact, it's considered a mainstay in the academic world. Take UCLA, for instance, with its 'Bruin Beekeepers' dedicated to bee education, research, and conservation. They manage beehives and various bee-related programs on campus and in the local community, so Robinson's little buzz-hotel wouldn't even move the needle a millimeter."

"But—"

"There's nothing I can do, Cody, at least with the levers available to me through the police department. Our hands are tied until he actually does something, and even then, linking it to him in any tangible way would be virtually impossible."

"So … "

"So it can't be me, Cody. I have anaphylaxis, leaving me vulnerable to severe allergic reactions to even one bee sting. It would be suicide."

Cody shook his head as if to clear it.

"So exactly what *'can't be you'?"* he said. "What exactly are you asking of me?"

She approached him, made to rub his arm, but seemed to think the better of it.

"All the police officers in the world are useless to us here," she said, "trust me. There is no justification I could come up with that would convince any of them to put at risk their badges, their pensions, their family security. I can't pass the vision to them, Cody, and my paraphrase would fall on deaf ears."

She looked him in the eye.

"So I'm saying that the drills and simulations are over. I'm saying that I am sending you back to a real place in real time with real risks and consequences, and that you need to take care of your neighbor."

She came closer and put her hand on his chest.

"Cody," she said, "I'm saying that it's time for you to go home. I'm saying that the game has turned real and that you need to take out Bill Robinson before he boards that plane to Philadelphia."

Chapter 24

The Professor knew to let it go to voicemail and then call her again, especially at this hour. On round two, he let it ring three times, almost hung up, and she answered her cell on ring number four.

"What's wrong, hon?" she said, sleepy and distant.

He was sitting at his kitchen table, and he shut his eyes and put the phone up against his forehead.

"Babe?" she said.

He put it back to his cheek. "Yeah."

Silence.

"Hey," she said, "You're the one who called me, right?" He thought he could hear her sitting up in bed, but he couldn't be sure. She sing-songed to him,

"I can hear you breathing ... "

"I miss you," he said.

She sighed. "Do you want me to tease you in the Candi Kennedy voice, all werewolf whorehouse growly and shit?"

"No."

"Do you want me to be the sexy Russian hula-hoop circus lady again?"

"Please no."

Her voice got small. "You want me to come over?"

That one hurt. "No, I don't think so," he said. "That's for absolute emergencies, we agreed."

"Is this an emergency?"

"No, I don't think so."

"You're a regular broken record. So what's wrong? I'm full awake now, and I'm actually curious. I'll hang on every word, I promise, as long as you don't start talking about your master's degree and teaching English and MLA citations and Oxford commas."

"I won't make that mistake again."

"You made that mistake for twenty years." She paused, seemingly to allow her voice to gain back its warmth. "I know," she said. "It wasn't your fault, wasn't anybody's. You're never too old to find the dream right in front of you."

The Professor was smiling wanly.

"I love it when you quote me back to me."

"It's a good one, a keeper. Too bad your dream was written in a language I couldn't understand."

"I couldn't stay at the restaurant."

"And now you can make people call you 'Professor.'"

"I'm proud of my teaching."

"It put us in debt, and it made you a stranger."

"Could we not do this now?" he said. "I'm feeling … shaky, stressed, hot and cold."

"You coming down with something? Take a Tylenol."

"I don't have any."

"How about some melatonin? You don't sleep enough. Is your throat scratchy? You got some Nyquil?"

"No. None of those."

"You don't know how to take care of yourself. You're such a boy."

"How come you never read my horror books?"

Gaping silence, except now he could hear *her* breathing.

"I'm serious," he said. "I know you didn't care for my first two novels when I was just cutting my teeth, but I've gotten better at it. Why wouldn't you at least be curious?"

"Ya sure you want to stop drinking that Kool-Aid, keeping you up in your ivory tower in arty-farty land?"

"Yeah, I'm sure, set me straight."

"For real, now?"

"Let's have it."

"I can't read your books, Professor, because you don't write stories. You write invitations for people to tell you how brilliant you are."

Now it was the Professor's turn to be at a loss for words. It was the best two-sentence criticism he had ever heard, and he felt as if his soul had been fractured.

"Why then," he said softly, "do you like talking about *The Kill or Be Killed* project so much?"

"Because it's funny."

"Funny as in weird or funny as in funny?"

"Both. Neither. I don't know. It seems for the first time in your life you gained a sense of humor, not taking yourself so seriously."

"So you think I'm writing comedy?"

"Of course! Aren't you? Isn't Cody?"

"I don't know, I never asked him."

"Well, the Professor character is a riot. He's conceited, annoying, and almost cute in the way he thinks he's writing such good stuff when you actually have him churning out, oh, I don't know ... hopeful, happy horseshit and nonsense. And Cody is a scream, playing grasshopper to the childish master. You are trying for that angle, aren't you?"

No response.

"Honey?"

Crickets.

"Oh ... " she said, voice low. "Well ... "

"No," said the Professor. "Don't hang up, please."

"Okay."

"I, uh, hadn't quite seen it through that lens, and I need to process—"

"Babe, there's no need to explain. People are going to enjoy this one, so let them. Nobody cares what you did at the Ford plant, they just want to drive home their new F-150."

"Yeah. So, how many shifts do you have this coming week?"

He grimaced while saying it. He hated changing the subject because it always sounded so much like you were uncomfortably changing the subject.

"Ten," she said, "three lunches, six dinners."

"That's a lot."

"Walter's short two servers."

"Is your back still killing you?"

"I have Dennis walking out the big serving trays for me. I just do drinks now."

"You pay him for that?"

"No, he does it from the kindness of his freakin' heart."

"Is Wentworth still being a dick?"

"Of course he is. But no one could ever fill your shoes."

"Stop."

"You know it's true," she said. You were the best maitre d' that Avante Bellas ever had. We both know that the restaurant business is like being on stage, and when you were in a place where you had to stick to the script, you were everything: charming, welcoming, clever, and fancy. You didn't try too hard because you were a natural. And you didn't have to be boastful, because the tux made you look and feel like royalty from the get-go."

"My students make me feel that way, sort of."

"But I don't work there."

"Yeah."

"Yeah." She paused. "So, not for nothing ... how are you going to solve the math problem you're having with the podcast to be?"

"What math problem?"

"The *Spinal Tap* problem."

"I love riddles and I love that movie, but I'm lost, help me out."

"Your murder-cast only goes to eleven."

"What?"

"At the beginning, you say you plan to get twelve contestants. You have eleven, and you seem to have moved on to another section or something. So who is the twelfth psychotic idiot going to be?"

He ran them off in his mind. Christ …

"Hon," he said. "I gotta go."

She laughed heartily.

"No," she said. "Really? Babe, how much of your own show don't you have a handle on? It's as if the idea itself has taken over on its own. Hey! Maybe that's part of the plot! Maybe the Professor is such a nincompoop that—"

He hung up. Fuck. The meta on meta on meta was fun, but in their zeal, they were just getting sloppy.

It was time to stop peeling back so many layers.

It was high time they slowed this runaway train.

Chapter 25

Every time Cody tried to talk sense to himself, that he couldn't possibly will himself to step out of the story and murder his neighbor in real life, he remembered so vividly the panic, the screams, the people clawing at their faces like hyped-up kids ripping open their presents. It had been no simulation, and it wasn't a dream. He remembered the taste in the air, like static and rich copper mixed to buzz your saliva and vibrate your eyes. He remembered so clearly the human head turned to gunk in the road with a tire mark molded through it, and he especially couldn't get out of his mind the image of the woman hit from behind and sawed in half by a waist-high steel railing. He only had the angle to see her torso bump down three or four stairs leading to the restaurant's basement level, but her entrails were exposed, chasing behind her like snakes.

This was real. It wasn't a story, it wasn't a podcast, and it certainly wasn't a softball storage container or a rock star's fucking flame thrower. It was the real deal, and it had to be taken care of. Yesterday. Of course, how this could have manifested itself from the bowels of the Professor's wild schemes and Cody's eager assistance was still a mystery. It also wasn't the point.

Bill Robinson had to be stopped.

It was four in the morning.

Cody had a hammer in his hand, palms slick, heart pounding, and he was picturing raising the weapon and bringing it down hard, no punking out, and he reminded himself of his sweaty palms and the fact that he had to keep hold of the handle tight like a kid grabbing the seat bar on a roller coaster.

He started down the path of uneven stones between their houses, and he couldn't help but envision what he looked like here in the semi-dark, thirty feet away from the dull glow of the nearest street lamp. He should have put the weapon in his waistband with his shirt over it, at least walking from the front door to this point. What if the weird guy across the street who always brought out his trash and recyclables in his bathrobe and rainbow-colored Croc clogs ... what if he took a mood pill that gave him dry mouth and, on the way to the kitchen for an orange juice, he had seen through the picture window Cody's hunched figure slipping into the shadows with the silhouette of the claw hammer hanging low by his side? What if the woman two doors down, a cleaning lady on the hospitality staff at the Sheraton Gateway, had found some extra work in private residences just after sun-up and was standing in the shade of the front doorway with that first cup of coffee and a smoke, because she loved the fresh morning air and didn't want her home smelling like tobacco?

Too late for that noise; he was already here, looking up the short incline adorned with the string of spiky yuccas and baby palms. He climbed the grassy slope in three strides and walked between the trees, amazed at himself for actually trespassing, for actually doing this.

Right. What the fuck was he thinking? The podcast was fake, the characters were fake, the stories were fake, and even the unspoken animosity between himself and the Professor was fake, fake, and more fake.

Overhead, some clouds blew past the moon, and the shadows changed, making it darker where there was a rectangular bare spot in the grass where Robbins must have been working on a car like a hobby at some point. It also brought into dim relief the back of the yard by the shed built like a log cabin and, beside it, the tree with the low-hanging branch.

No.

No. Fucking. Way.

There was a black hive bag on the sawed-off branch, looking at first glance like a lawn mower's grass-catcher.

The beehive bag was supposed to be a figment of the Professor's imagination.

Ralph had said that the game was getting away from them, that they had created something that had mutated, spreading like a disease, taking on a life of its own, and Cody was the one to know best the paraphrase, because God damn it, he wrote the original version! And so the figment of the Professor's imagination had come true, come to be in real life, in real time, because someone who was a figment of Cody's imagination had predicted it? What?

But there was no denying that the hive bag was there.

Cody started inching closer, thinking that he was putting his life in more and more jeopardy with every step, because if somehow fiction had bled into reality, the bees inside the bag would be on the lookout, wouldn't they? Like sentries at the gate?

The bag was empty. He ran his fingers through his hair, straight back, and he took a shaky breath that felt hot and splintered.

It should have relieved him, proving to him that there was no real threat, and therefore no reason to go through with this, but there was no relief in this whatsoever. He could still feel those vibrations at the base of his spine and behind his eyes as the thousands of bees swarmed the streets of downtown Philadelphia like a tornado, a plague. Plus, why would the real Robbins in the real world have a hive bag at all?

Wait a minute.

The Ralph character had also predicted that they were going to have an ending no one would expect, and Cody suddenly wondered when that end would actually occur. What if Robbins was waiting for him in the house with an AR-15? Cody had not considered the idea that he might lose this assassination attempt, bringing a hammer to a gunfight and all that.

But …

Cody had invented that prophecy almost like a one-liner, a cheap thrill, and regardless of its overall effect on future viewers or readers or whomever might be interested in this glorious disaster they'd created, it was Cody Kennedy who made this shit up in the first place. Talk about having your own words coming back to haunt you …

He made a sharp 180 to the left and walked to the steps leading up to his neighbor's back door. In his mind, he pictured himself having gone one more quarter-turn and walking back between the yuccas and baby palms, heading along the uneven pavers toward the front of his house to go inside and get some overdue shut-eye, but the reality was that whether he "believed" in this or not, he was going to follow it through. But then again, he just couldn't … he didn't have it in him … he didn't have the gumption to even *picture* himself bringing the clawhammer down hard enough to bash through another man's skull …

He climbed the steps and stood at the door now. There was a shade pulled down on the other side of the glass. He had been in this house only one other time, to ask if Robbins had gotten his mail by accident, but he felt pretty sure that this was the kitchen.

It couldn't be open, now, could it?

He put the hammer in his left hand and reached for the knob with his right, thinking that Robbins could be waiting right there three feet in, waiting for Cody to cross the threshold, because when someone broke into your house, you had the legal right to end them. Cody was damned sure he'd heard that somewhere. He turned the knob, thinking that the hammer should be in his dominant hand and not the other way around, and he was going to die or someday die a murderer, and he pushed the door open.

The wood was swelled or something, because the bottom of the door scraped on the floor, and worse, Robbins must have owned a dog at some point, because he'd left the strap with the doggie bells on the inside knob for when the mutt signaled to go outside. Cody clamped down his teeth in an angry grin. He may as well have pounded the front door with his fist and then used a brick.

He stepped inside. The kitchen overheads were off, but one or two rooms in, a light was on, pitching shadows, gray threads, and undercurrents. In the northside right corner by the stove was Bill Robbins.

He was barefoot in boxers, all that long frizzy hair loose of the ponytail like the Wicked Witch of the Weird. Seemed he'd jumped the hell out of bed when he heard someone breaking in before Cody just did it himself.

Southwest, in front of the cabinet with the plates and the plastic drinking cups, was something shaped like Cassidy Claybourne; Cody would know that bod anytime, any day, anywhere. She was covered with bees, the ones from the bag outside evidently, all except her eyes, which were wide open and terrified, and her mouth, which was ajar. She was holding her service revolver before her with both hands, pointing it at Bill Robbins, and even the gun was covered. In the semi-darkness, the many creatures shimmered like dark glitter.

It was a Mexican standoff. If Robbins gave the green light to his monsters, Cassidy would still be able to get off a shot. If Cassidy went first, he had probably ordered his "troops" to unleash the equivalent of a stabbing episode worse than anything in Julius Caesar's worst nightmares.

And she was just as allergic as she was phobic about discharging her weapon.

But Robbins didn't know either of those things, the latter the secret more precious than the former. Maybe Cody could use this somehow and get her out of it. Maybe he could—

"Cody," she said. "Remember I promised that from now on I was never going to say goodbye without saying ... the other thing?"

"Yes," Cody said. Then he shouted "NO!" at the top of his lungs. Beneath it, he heard Cassidy Claybourne say,

"I love you."

She fired her weapon and hit Robbins flat between the eyes, exploding the back of his head in a spray of blood and meat up the slant of the range hood, and like a mirror ball, Cassidy sparkled and shined, as more than a thousand baldfaced hornets rammed home their stingers, completing the equation and sending this good cop to glory.

Chapter 26

The Professor couldn't sleep because he was furious. This in itself wasn't so rare, as he often woke up in the middle of the night, thinking about shit someone pulled on him thirty years ago, or fifteen years ago, or last week at the Giant Supermarket, when this asshole with a gray ponytail and a Grateful Dead T-shirt barged into his space at the self-checkout, literally breathing on the back of his neck before the receipt had even printed.

Still, it wasn't as if the Professor had "anger issues," at least nothing major that he needed a pill for, since in the bright light of day he was such a sucker for a kind word, given or received, and he was without a doubt the world's greatest optimist. Though the rules he laid down for his college classes were firm, he granted extensions on papers and offered the opportunity for rewrites. He treasured student responses, student effort, and student growth, and he liked best the classes that turned into open discussions instead of straight lecture.

Moreover, he never lost his temper in front of a class, even if a student was toying with him, trying to get the lesson dumbed down by openly questioning its worth. He never blew a gasket if students whispered to each other a bit while he was talking; he handled it civilly with a short email, a Zoom, or even a gentle reminder right there during the lesson, of what constituted the sophisticated and delicate culture of the college classroom. And even these instances were extraordinarily rare. His classes tended to be well-behaved because he did his level best to keep them interesting, and he had an honest love for the written word, creative or expository. He was organized with a near military efficiency when it came to lesson planning, timed in-class writing, due dates, makeups, and reminder-warnings about absences. And man oh man, the Professor didn't just love teaching; he was head over heels *in love* with teaching, it was infectious, and *God*, did he dig spreading the word.

Still, it was those damned nights, especially when he felt someone otherwise had treated him unfairly or with a lack of respect. He despised injustice, even the petty stuff, and things ate him alive in the wee hours, his mind circling back and back and back to the insult itself, the inference, or the offhand comment that made him feel small.

In this case, it was Cody fucking Kennedy and his blatant disregard for the Professor's work … and his feelings, yes, his ever-loving, motherfucking feelings, though admitting that to himself even silently made him cringe as he conjured up in his mind vague images of self-help books, group therapy, and his overly protective mother back in the day making him talk about his sentiments and emotions at the kitchen table so she could dissect him like a biology frog.

But he couldn't deny what he felt as a result of this theft, this sin, this … murder.

Cody had no right to kill off the Beekeeper. Not only was it one of the best threads in the project, but it was a treasured part of an older unpublished work that the Professor had been saving. Back in 2018, he had hooked up with a popular Canadian online music magazine, and the guy who ran the publication had the Professor writing super hyped-up fan fiction based on the given band's press kit and forthcoming album. The deal was to offer it to the band for free (at first), and in return, the band would advertise the link on their socials. As for the process, the product, and its makeup, the Professor would study all the respective bands' YouTube videos to get down their mannerisms, expressions, and speech patterns, and he would next write a horror story starring them as the monsters themselves (rarely) or the ones defeating the evil (almost always).

It was a bit "comic book," but Anthrax and their publicist loved the novella the Professor wrote for them so much that the bass player, Frank

Bello, emailed over a short video thank you, as well as snail mailing a vinyl collector's set of all their albums. Slayer, however, didn't go for the sixty-page story the Professor concocted for them, so it got shelved. In it was the original Beekeeper, the junkyard scene and the Philadelphia Street disaster, easy to adapt to this podcast idea with only a few contextual adjustments.

And just like that … trashed, before the Professor could write new original stuff and develop this awesome, intriguing, fascinating specimen.

The Professor rolled over to the other side and balled the sheets in his fist up under his chin. Okay, okay, let's think about this, all sides. Had Cody's writing improved throughout this whole thing? Yes. Did his climactic scene in the backyard and the kitchen work? Double yes. Was the Professor jealous somehow? A categorical no. The Professor had nothing but admiration for Cody's work, that wasn't the point; in fact, it was Cody's idea to invent the lover who would make the other guy's wife insane, then switch it up so they ended up sleeping with their own creations.

But then again, there was a bit of a problem with it after all, and the Professor hadn't thought of it this way until now. It wasn't just the Beekeeper's death that was fueling this. It was the embarrassing, glaring contrast throughout the whole section with the Professor's Eliza versus Cody's Cassidy Claybourne.

Plainly, the sex scenes Cody created were better than the Professor's "off-camera" references, and not only better crafted; there was more quantity on Cody's side, more description in real time. And it wasn't just the humping and pumping. Cody also had moments of intimacy that seemed personal, real, and distinct. The Professor's Eliza was a cardboard character, interesting, yes, but believable? No. The reader couldn't feel her, taste her, experience a real human being, because there was almost no real on-stage contact, no warmth.

Cody had outdone the Professor.

Cody had gained exclusive control of this story.

The Professor rolled onto his back, staring up at the darkness. The problem here was an age thing, and he'd sort of been fucked before even starting to create Eliza Nicolescu. Though she was in her forties and believably alluring, the Professor was sixty-two in real life and in story life. He didn't want to change that, because it was embedded in the overall work far too deeply, too many sweater strands to pull loose, and the point was that a sixty-two-year-old "rocking the box" and "fucking like a beast" was rather disgusting, Christ, *he* didn't even want to read that, let alone would the audience Cody's age. There was a Stephen King story called "The Life of Chuck" where there was a guy in a band, a singer, rehearsing in the guitar player's rec room, and after practice, the guitarist's sister approached and said, "You sing like old people fuck." The Professor had found this to be hysterically funny, he'd actually laughed out loud, because it was so true, the idea putting a picture in your head both pathetic and grotesque: a pair of old farts huffing, puffing, and slobbering all over each other in a sad, bizarre montage featuring man-tits, sagging bellies, varicose veins, and arm flab like bat wings. Sure, it happened, sure, it was a truth, but it was better kept behind closed doors. With the lights off. And the walls soundproofed if at all possible.

Plus …

Hey. Wait just one goddamned minute …

Cody had pulled this off almost perfectly, outwriting and outclassing the Professor in his own arena, but he had never solved or answered for the one little plot issue of his own left dangling in the wind.

Where was Cody's wife in all this? He answered the door when Cassidy Claybourne was out on the stoop in her UCLA Bruins uniform, and when she asked if he was married, he slinked out to the step, carefully closing the door behind him, looking guilty as sin and solidifying the inference that there was someone else in that house, someone he didn't want to reveal. And now he gets to unload this incredible death scene and play Boy Scout, both as character and author?

No, sir.

Some shit was going to change. First of all, Cody was going to account for his wife as a part of the story, not only for the semantics, but the whole thing's relative structural integrity. In third-person limited voice, you were absolutely *not* allowed to hide things from the reader oh so conveniently. If there was a wife in that house, Cody would know it whether "thinking about it" or not, and therefore, so would we. You had to give the reader the protagonist's whole mind, not just the "easy" parts that would make your plot work. Hey, sure, for the sake of charity, the Professor would give him the first interaction out on the stoop, because that special "someone" inside was at least alluded to, but what about all the time they spent together without Cody worrying that he would be missed at home? Well, okay, all right, maybe it was only a day because "time was funny" in Cassidy-Claybourne-land, and gosh darn, the Professor had used the same questionable device for Eliza so that he could squeeze months of physical conditioning into the equivalent of a single night. But how about the way Cody so "cleverly" started the climactic death scene outside his house holding the hammer instead of inside, deciding on using it versus a chef's knife or a long-tine barbecue fork?

He did it so he could avoid having to "think" about the wife sleeping upstairs.

Fucking cheater.

There was going to be some heavy revising on Cody's end, and the second part of this was that they were going to write the Beekeeper back into the story. He belonged to the Professor in the first place, and he was more than glad to help re-caulk this leaky ship, soon taking it back for his own. And finally, aside from the adjustments he was going to ask for from Cody in the name of fair play and story-sense, there was the issue of omission in a more practical sense. Minus the Beekeeper, their cast of killers didn't even "go to eleven" anymore.

The television came on, volume cranked, all static and snow, and the Professor jolted up, spine to the headboard, sheets again in his fists up at his throat like a nineteenth-century flower girl who'd just seen a ghost.

The TV went dark and silent, and for a moment, the Professor thought it was blank. But wait. He lowered the sheets down away from his jaw, and an exact mimic was barely discernible on the screen, like a found-footage movie that needed better lighting. He looked around for a moment, wondering where the camera was that was filming this, making the Professor watch himself backward, right being left, and slightly off-center in third-person-like the shot they used for most Major League Baseball at-bats. No avail. It was like trying to look in the mirror and trim your hair, pitching the scissors or battery-operated beard trimmer with no depth perception front to back, and the wrong angle, no matter how many times you did what you thought the opposite of what your instincts told you.

On screen, something was sliding over the television from behind it, and it was difficult to discern a shape other than that it was a dark outline like a giant worm, slithering over the "hump" and gliding on the air toward the Professor figure facing it and parroting the real Professor's actual movements. He even raised his right hand to half-mast, queasily fascinated to see his replica do the same while being slowly approached by this shadowy aberration.

The television blared on, static loud, snowstorm fierce, and it illuminated the face of the beast from behind in spatters of shadows and light. It was a serpent-human hybrid, with a head from the nose up that was amphibian-like, the eyes a reptilian green with black devil's slits down the center, and from the nose down it was a woman with diamond-banded snake pigment tight to the cheekbones like plastic wrap.

The Professor couldn't move. He had not included snake charming in the defensive scheme he'd developed with Eliza, and as if on a raised flat platform, the thing slithered toward him, aimed for the middle of his face, its body making S-shapes behind in the air.

It was five inches from him, and on screen, a forked tongue darted from its mouth. The Professor felt it flicker on the tip of his nose.

Revolted, terrified, he rubbed at his face hard like it was on fire, and he flailed out with his hands in scratches and swim strokes as if drowning and dying. His eyes were closed, and he opened them. It was dark. There was a breeze and a smell in the air of deep forest and a hint of smoky autumn as if someone was burning leaves three meadows over.

Blood Red Meta

He was standing amidst the trees at night, and after turning a 360, he thought he saw a dull glimmer through the leaves toward the northwest, maybe a clearing or glen. He started walking toward it, trying not to fall to the ground in a panic and curl up shaking and wailing, and the low-hanging branches seemed to sneak up on him, and he was elbowing them away, scraping his forearms, and he started to run because the light was clearer, flickering through the foliage, and he burst from the woods and he was at the top of a short hill overlooking the backside of an abandoned drive-in movie theater, with two maintenance sheds before the back side of the gargantuan wooden viewing-screen framework, missing two big panels like the smile of a loser in a bare-knuckle brawl.

No way. No fucking …

The Professor jogged down the dirt hill. He didn't fall and get dirt down the back of his pants, and that convinced him, at least in a fragile and childish way, that this wasn't an ignored warning about to be played out in full, nor some prophecy written in stone. He had created this tale. He steered this ship. He was the one pulling the levers behind the curtain.

He got to the bottom of the hill and from behind he heard something … an engine vrooming, revving in a fanfare of screaming gears and exhaust. It was getting closer, and reflected off the sky were the licks and roils of flame, and then up at the top of the hill a path eating its way through the forest exploded, sending timber and debris flying over the Professor's head like fireworks, the stretch of trees twenty feet wide in front of him lighting up the night, the woman of flame blasting through it on her motorcycle and stopping at the crest of the hill with a dramatic skid in the dirt. It brought the Professor a side-view he could feel, like stumbling too close to a bonfire.

She pulled up on the handlebars with one hand, kicking up to a wheelie, and with the other hand, she raised the flaming chainsaw overhead like a war flag. Her face was long, broiling, and running into itself like liquid steel in a forge. Her black eyes were slanted, and her mouth undulated in that long side-oval, like Ghostface in all the *Scream* movies.

She said something. It was like an echo that didn't echo, but poured itself onto your soul like hot engine oil.

"Run, Mister," she said. "Now."

The Professor turned and ran. The snake was the Mod Goddess, of course it was, and she brought him to this place to behold Savage Alice, of course she did, but again, a lot of the initial threat had been tossed to the wayside. Where was the chorus of honking cars in the audience area? Why was he not fastened to the sheds, suspended between them in the air with handcuffs and chains?

He ran around the screen, and the moment he stepped to the cracked concrete parking and viewing area, the scene changed. He was no longer tasting the smoke of a forest fire at the back of his throat. It was no longer autumn, but more like the middle of summer.

He had been running, but now he was still.

He had been breathing heavily, and now he held it for a second.

He was standing before a building with boarded-up windows and doors, the concrete weather-stained like the underside of a bridge or highway overpass. The steps leading up to it were pockmarked with spots of old chewing gum and bird shit, and the sallow glow from the street lamp revealed that this building was the first of many shadowed down the avenue.

The Professor turned to run, and a familiar voice stopped him.

"I wouldn't do that, Professor."

He halted and spun back on his heel. From the alley between this first building and a check-cashing place next door to it came Cody Kennedy. He was bigger than the Professor had imagined from their Zooms, taller, broader. He was wearing a black Wolf Shadow T-shirt, loose jeans, and boat sneakers. He was not smiling.

"You run, you die," he said. "Watch this."

He bent down, picked up an empty soda bottle from the gutter, and tossed it toward the opposite side of the street where there were no buildings, just darkness. The projectile made it about twenty feet, and then it hit something, some force like an invisible wall, sparking, smoking, flashing with what looked like three or four lightning bolts making razor patterns along the surface, then fading to the darkness behind.

"What the fuck," said the Professor.

"It's your electric fence," Cody said. "Nice job, by the way."

"Don't mention it."

"Don't worry, I won't."

They faced each other. It felt as if they should shake hands, but it also did not, and they didn't.

"The set-up is over," said Cody. "Game starts here. We're contestants eleven and twelve, and so, Professor, welcome to Murdertown."

PART 3

Chapter 27

The smartest thing the Professor and Cody could have done would have been to stick together, hide in one of the buildings, and work up a battle plan. They were the creators, after all, the fiction-czars, but there was no denying that the Professor was thinking what Cody was clearly working through himself.

Aside from the three neutral players—the Soldier, Savage Alice, and the Mod Goddess—it's your characters against mine.

The Professor and Cody were the field generals. Did that mean they were less vulnerable to injury and death? Unknown. Did it mean that the one wiping out the other's gang quicker would gain some kind of advantage, like accumulating bonus points in a video game that would enable them to better challenge the supernatural characters, even their own?

Cody walked away. The Professor almost called after him, but he didn't. Right and wrong had flown out the window, and common sense seemed an antiquated fairy tale he'd long learned not to trust.

I can take him, the Professor thought.

He strode up the wide concrete steps of what had been a YMCA, the shapes of the long-removed letters shadowed above the double entrance doors in a soft arc, and he walked those stairs like Eliza had taught him, back straight, movements purposefully slow like a military march, holding that extra moment each time his thighs were parallel to the concrete beneath him. He hoped Cody was peering at him from behind a corner or the depths of a shadow, because the Professor knew he looked insane. He also looked formidably strong, and he opened the door.

Blood Red Meta

A YMCA would have interesting props, weapons, possibly bows and arrows for offense, a tool shop with power tools and box cutters, hacksaws, heat guns, and screwdrivers. It would have a kitchen with professional knives, a weight room with dumbbells, some light enough to throw and some heavy enough to use as war clubs. On the upper level, there would be extra housing, rooms with bedsheets that could be tied together to be used in an emergency exit, ripped to strips to act as choking devices. There would be first aid kits with medicines he could toss in an opponent's eyes, and there would be a pool with canisters of chlorine he could use for the same purpose as the medicines.

Time to set up camp.

Time to come up with some kind of plan.

Chapter 28

To anyone listening, please understand that you cannot trust anything narrated by the Professor from the time he and I met outside of the condemned building that used to be a YMCA. Whatever you have been told has actually not come from the Professor. He is using the characters most like himself, the Red Headmaster and the Dark Doppelgänger, as impersonators, so he can mislead you and tangle my plans with misdirection.

This is Cody Kennedy. I will communicate as long as I am able, but things don't look good. The Professor's gone rogue, and it didn't have to be this way. I have made a journal of this experience so that if I die, there will be an honest, official account of what really happened here in Murdertown.

Journal of Cody Kennedy

It started out well enough when he popped through from what was our normal existence, and I demonstrated how powerful his electric fence was with a glass soda bottle. Next, we tried to figure out what to do. Clearly, we needed to stick together, to write this together, and first on the agenda was deciding where to set up camp, you know, get off the street instead of sitting out in the great wide open like targets.

We decided to use the YMCA, of course, because there were a lot of defensive advantages. There would be bows and arrows to use as warnings, deterrents, and a tool shop where we could fix things. There was probably a kitchen, hopefully with some dried foods we could eat, and a weight room for personal conditioning in case this conflict was to go on and on. There were first aid kits we could use if we were hurt, and if there was upstairs housing, we would have a place to sleep better than a gymnasium floor or the pool deck.

We ventured in, but didn't get farther than the lobby. It was dark back in there, pitch black, and we couldn't find a lamp or light switch. There was a dull glow coming from the long rectangular transom window back above the entrance doors, and close by in the foyer area, we found a pair of modular cushioned seat benches like you'd find in a dentist's waiting room. In the gloom, they looked like toadstools belonging in Alice's Wonderland. We sat and talked about options.

"So," the Professor said, "who do we try to kill first?"

"That's a bit gung-ho, isn't it?"

"Just playing the hand we've been dealt."

"I think it would be better to figure out which characters are going to rise as the leaders before we do the bloodlust thing, looking for scalps."

"When you say 'us,' you mean me and you, teaming up … "

"Yes."

"Do you think we can die here, Cody, like really die?"

I took in a big sniff for emphasis.

"I can smell the mold in the walls, and I can feel the dampness like an old dungeon, or more for real, there was probably a leak and there's a pool of old standing water somewhere close by."

I clapped my hands and felt the Professor jerk in place.

"Sorry," I said. "I felt that, however, and it made my palms sting. I can smell and feel and see and most probably die, and I don't want to be proven right by a bullet to the heart, getting my blood sucked out, or walking into a booby-trap worse than bamboo spears slathered in shit in a pit like the fucking Vietnam jungle wars."

"Interesting."

"What?"

The Professor crossed his legs.

"Interesting," he said, "that you mention actions that would be taken by my characters alone, the Red Headmaster shooting you in the heart, Lucifer's Gal sucking your blood, and the Dark Doppelgänger setting a booby-trap."

"Yeah," I admitted, "you're right."

"My guys and gals against yours."

"At first, yes," I said. "Makes sense, don't you think?"

"What makes sense to me," said the Professor, "is that you wound up stacking this deck by killing off my Beekeeper, making it so we start this game with your four to my three."

There was a silence, his words hanging dead on the air, and he added, "All of it an unintentional by-product of your situation, I am sure."

"I don't want to discuss it," I said darkly.

"Sorry," said the Professor. "You miss her, don't you?"

"Yes."

"All things being equal, Cody, you created a fabulous character, living and breathing and beautiful. Cassidy Claybourne was a triumph regardless of her fate in this drama."

"I shouldn't have gotten high on my own supply," I muttered.

"Yeah," said the Professor with a shrug and a sigh. "Yeah." After a moment, he sat straighter and folded his arms. "So," he said, "do you think there's a day and night here?"

I laughed hollowly. "Yeah, it would be nice to be able to see what we're doing, right?"

"Yes." There was a pause. "How wide is the road outside, do you think?"

I closed my eyes. "I'm not good with this kind of math," I said. "Kind of like guessing how many jellybeans are in a jar, but I would say it's something like twenty-five, thirty feet from the buildings to the invisible fencing."

"You think it goes all the way around the block, like a high school track?"

"Yes, I get that feeling. Why?"

"Don't know. Seems it could come in handy somehow, but I don't have a context yet." He leaned back, crossed his feet at the ankles, and webbed his hands behind his head. "So let's circle back," he said. "Who do you think are the leaders of the two gangs?"

I didn't hesitate. "My group is led by Tito, the Rock Reaper. Yours by the Red Headmaster."

"Why not the Dark Doppelgänger?"

"Too evil. Even amongst tough guys, you gotta have some kind of charm."

"Hmm. Tell the truth, Cody, I don't think we go after any of those characters."

"What? Why not?"

He stood up and put his palms to the hips, stretching his back.

"Three reasons," he said. "First, in a perfect world, the one to kill off right away would be the Mod Goddess. You take her down, you might, keyword *might,* inherit the control of Savage Alice, and then no one could come near you, supernatural powers or not. That said, forgive the contradiction, but my second point is that turning up every loose piece of plywood looking for a snake isn't the best way to spend such precious time, especially considering that the Savage Alice thing is such a big maybe. The more rational strategy would be to find the world-famous drum kit somewhere in this block of buildings, because we know for a fact it flicks Wolf Shadow on and off like a light. And third—"

That's four, I thought, and I stood up as well; didn't feel right having the Professor looming over me here in the shadows, and when I did, he darted away toward the entrance doors, his hand on the crash bar.

"Lastly," he said, "I'm not the Professor, and I'm not just good at setting booby-traps. I'm also quite skilled at getting information, so thanks."

He pushed the door open and made his way off into the night, and before it quite closed behind him there was a sharp percussive *bang!* from where I had just been sitting, not like dynamite, but more powerful than an M80, bursting up flaming flecks of pleather and burning specs of cushion filler spattering the side of my face and my neck.

I rubbed at all of it hard, knowing it was going to leave a mark, a few actually.

And I was lucky.

The Dark Doppelgänger could have killed me. I had laid myself open to him like a lamb on an altar, and I wondered if it would have killed me had I stayed sitting. Maybe, maybe not. But I would have been wounded, balls torched, ass blasted, looking like a lame duck waddling all around Murdertown.

Either way, this was sport to him, as if he were the master of foxhounds on a royal hunting expedition, riding a great black steed, grinning like the devil, and holding out some poor soul's flaming head like a lantern.

Chapter 29

The Professor found Cody's journal. He started reading the entry and sat down slowly. This wasn't the Professor's characters versus those of Cody's invention. This was the Professor against Cody mano a mano, and the kid was smarter … no, not "smarter," but *way* smarter than the Professor had given him credit for. This was a war of disinformation, a salute to the new American way, and Cody was winning this race by leaps and bounds.

Anything the Professor did would either be omitted, misrepresented, or even passed off as the work of the Dark Doppelgänger, including the entry the Professor was writing at this very moment. Of course, the fact that the Professor was advancing his *own* journal in third-person limited should have made it clear that Cody's recollection of events was suspect. Common sense, the whole project had been penned in third person, so Cody's first-person entry wasn't consistent with the greater whole on a structural level; plus, in terms of semantics, it just sounded shoddy and rough, a bit of a chore sticking with the "I" character as Cody, as there were moments that the Professor couldn't picture who was talking. But all that didn't matter. This was Cody's attempt at his own sort of controlled chaos, imperfect, deeply flawed, stylistically hideous, yet effective in mixing the cards, so to speak.

And more, this was worrisome on another metatextual plane, because Cody had predicted that the Professor would enter the YMCA, feel around under the front counter in the darkness, find the flashlight, and then discover the aforementioned journal entry, written in sloppy cursive in a pocket notebook that had been sitting on the keyboard of the PC next to the defunct ID scanner. Moreover, the interpretation of what was real and what was being manufactured went another level deep, because there was no clear way to disprove that the Professor might very well be impersonating Cody writing a journal entry and the other way around, turning everything backward like a funhouse mirror in a hall of more mirrors.

The lights blared on both inside and out; in fact, the glare through the glass above the entrance made the Professor wince, rub his eyes. Then from outside came the music, a cheap shrilling organ and a snare drum sounding like a toy bat hitting a popcorn tin, and it was that circus song everyone knew but couldn't name, and it was getting louder, evidently coming down the street and in the Professor's mind drawing up bizarre images of freaks and geeks and blood-spattered mimes, headless magicians, deformed fetuses fed to pigs and wild dogs, a tightrope walker slipping, a fire breather burning and some lady in a leotard getting a knife in the neck spinning on the wheel of death to the sound of raucous cheers and the clatter of coins being dropped in the tip-bucket.

The Professor had to see this; face your fear, no hiding in Murdertown. All around him, the lobby looked collectively as he had pictured it: walls of dull polished block and water stains on the ceiling in the far corners, a pamphlet carousel with flyers and brochures, some of them curled down at the edges, and a pile of dust-covered folding chairs stacked on a truck dolly against the wall with the corkboard. He went to the door, pushed it open a bit more than a crack, and carefully wedged himself half in and half out.

Coming up the road was Cody the Clown, and the idea that the real Cody could impersonate this character and the other way around was something to check off the list as a no-go. This circus creature was huge, like a helium parade balloon at least thirty feet high. It was Cody's likeness wearing forest-green joker tassels with the jingle bells, his fat face slathered with white greasepaint as a base with blue diamond shapes around the eyes and a red laughing mouth with black border trim going all the way up the cheeks to the blush-dots. The straw-colored ruff collar looked like that of a scarecrow, and the jumpsuit was a vagabond's smorgasbord of red stripes, yellow polka dots, purple stars, and neon pink checkerboard. The humongous black clown shoes had bayonet blades sticking out of the toes; his eyes were just whites like the *Evil Dead* fiends, and he was laughing, teeth pointed as if he'd taken a file to the tips. His black oversized tongue was out like that of a slobbering dog.

He had a street organ strapped on and was turning the crank with one hand while the other was thrust into a man-sized puppet that evidently took the place of a monkey, sitting atop the musical contraption as if driving a horse and buggy through rough terrain, smiling idiotically and clapping together a pair of cymbals.

It looked like a thinned-down, skeletal version of the Professor himself, wearing a white collared shirt, a blue tie with a gentle floral pattern, a brown vest, and a tweed jacket with patches on the elbows. There were no pants, and the penis and scrotum bumped along the top edge of the street organ like a curious aardvark sniffing at an anthill, the spindly legs jerking and jangling as if pulled on strings.

It was the Red Headmaster, dead as a doornail with his insides scooped out, his legacy for creating mind-blowing tableaux made into a grand mockery as he played out the heinous vision of a twenty-seven-year-old guitar player who never went to college, never published anything, and wrote with holes in the logic so huge you could drive trucks through them.

The giant looked over, and though the dead-white eyes were impossible to read, it was obvious that the Professor had been spotted, the clown's mouth in a huge oval like a child surprised with cotton candy, ice cream, and Christmas gifts. He stopped cranking, but slowly for effect, the music winding down like air from a balloon, and he took his other hand out of the Red Headmaster puppet, letting it sag to its side in a rumple of bones. He started unstrapping, again like molasses, and he set the instrument down on the street.

He stood up tall and smiled—all teeth, brow high, shoulders scrunched up toward his ears as if to say, *Quietly, quietly, or I'll get in trouble,* and he took a long, sneaky tiptoe toward the YMCA building and in one step crossed an area of at least twenty-five feet. The Professor, as if woken from a mesmerizing nightmare, backed in and pulled shut the door. Luckily, it had pull tab locks top and bottom, and he shoved all four of them home.

He backed off a few steps. Nothing.

The silence was killing him.

There was movement above him, and shadows colored the lobby. It was the clown blocking out the sun, looking through the transom windows, his eyes big as monster truck tires with tiny black pinpoints for pupils you couldn't see from a distance. The Professor stared back, so weirded out that his mind went to odd logic, a writer's sort that measured whether this could actually work "on paper." Well, there was no way that thing could contort itself to bend down like this. Christ, he was so big out there, he must have been down on his knees like a kid looking under his bed for a frisbee.

The shadows around the Professor moved again, this time receding like the foam slipping back toward the ocean once the wave hit the shore, and suddenly there was a *ka-pow!* like a sledge hitting an anvil, and it was one of those oversized bayonet-blades the clown had sticking out of his shoes, punched hard through the door as if he was punting a football. The blade was as long as a canoe, at least a yard wide, and the tip of it was an inch from the Professor's crotch. Before he had trained with Eliza, he would have stood here in dumb awe, thankful it came up short, but he crouched and sprang to the side, landing on his hands, tucking in chin to chest and somersaulting away.

It was instinct, muscle memory, but it was also motivated by textual backstory. Cody had written in the original version of Cody the Clown that he thought it would be peachy-keen to squirt acid out of a flower instead of water, and back where the Professor had been standing, the tip of the blade sprayed a clear liquid that fanned out a spatter that turned to smoking holes in the vinyl floor tiles like Swiss cheese.

The Professor turned and ran for the back. The hall was darker, but not dark, and straight ahead, there was a door with a nameplate that said "MEN'S LOCKER ROOM AND SHOWERS," and next to it was the ladies' version, and the Professor took the dogleg left, passing the gymnasium with its doors open, revealing the basketball courts. There was a stairwell up to the right, and the Professor ran for it and pushed through, his footsteps clapping echoes back at him. He wanted to go as high as the steps could take him. It seemed logical that floor two would have aerobics rooms and weight-lifting, and if there were living quarters, they'd be above all that in order to give the most effective illusion of privacy.

And maybe some of the tenants left stuff behind, like a gun or two.

He burst through the third-floor entrance and exit door, since the half-turn staircase above him stopped at the halfway point, leading to a steel ceiling hatch door that was padlocked. He slowed; it was a hallway that looked like that of a cheap hotel with worn and thin green carpeting and shabby lighting that tried to look Victorian and fancy. The Professor tried a door or two, was not surprised that they were locked, and jogged the rest of the way toward the chamber that had "Public Space" tagged over the archway. Yeah. The cheap seats.

Inside, it looked like an infirmary, smelling vaguely of old sweat and Pine Sol, yet the latter was faint, like a hint of heartburn. There were around thirty cots, and the fourth bed in the row to the right had something sitting on the pillow.

A pocket notebook.

Closer up, the Professor could see writing, cursive writing, Cody's writing. He picked it up for a looksee.

"All right, you waste-case," it said, "enough is enough. I realize that you have been bitching and moaning, feeling cheated because I knocked off your precious Beekeeper before jumping into Murdertown, but I want to call things the way I see them for once. First off, the changes you imposed on Cody the Clown make him entertaining but almost useless. He can't fit inside buildings and is not nearly strong enough to bust through any of the steel roofs here, all multiple slopes with right angles, you know, hip style as opposed to gable, and meant to withstand cat five hurricanes and fucking tsunamis. You have made him a sort of sentinel that walks his beat along the oval street surrounding Murdertown, and while it does make for an interesting limitation, he is like the 1970s 'Pong' game compared to a current Grand Theft Auto game or Call of Duty-Modern Warfare 3.

"Do you see what I'm saying, Professor? You eliminated the possibility that Cody the Clown and I could impersonate each other, while inheriting a bowl of Lucky Charms, since the Red Headmaster, the Dark Doppelgänger, and you—the Professor—have all had the opportunity to twin yourselves all over the place with a shit-ton of mathematical possibilities. Lucky for me, the three of you are a triple-shot of 'Village Idiot,' and the Red Headmaster was dumb enough to trust the Dark Doppelgänger, thinking they could find Wolf Shadow and put her on a leash."

There was a space in the writing for emphasis, and then Cody wrote:

"Wanna see? How 'bout some charming backstory? Look behind you."

The Professor turned. On the fifth bed to his left, there was now a camcorder on the pillow, same as the one he had at home, a Samsung vlog type with night vision. He stepped closer and paused. It *was* his camcorder; it had the small chip in the lens hood from the time he dropped it, taking it down from a high shelf in the downstairs coat closet.

He edged in and stared at it as if he was a cautious lab chemist. True, he was a horror writer, but he was privately bothered by found-footage stuff. He had felt that the Blair Witch movie was slightly unnerving, and he had actually turned off *Megan Is Missing* when they found the picture of one of the girls with the steel brackets embedded in her terrified face, keeping wide open every orifice.

He had to know. He was falling for every trick, going exactly where Cody had predicted he would, but he had to know.

He picked it up and hit Play.

It was dark and grainy, then movement, but nothing discernible except some faint streaks like dim falling stars. The light came up, and for a moment it was all over-bright and piercing, settling abruptly into a viewable focus: a small room with lockers, a central round table, and a number of desk-chair combos, a small kitchen area, and on the floor a big American flag that apparently was being used as a blanket. All in all, it could have been a break-room in any number of businesses, but the Professor knew that it wasn't. It was a break-room turned into a classroom, with hall lockers, those teardrop-shaped desks, and a flag to pledge to. It was the hideout of the Red Headmaster.

"Looky, looky here," a voice said, moist and revolting, like the odor of an outhouse that hadn't had its tanks emptied for four or five months. It was the Professor's voice, sleazed into this grotesque imitation, and it seemed clear that it was the Dark Doppelgänger filming this invasion. There was the sound of a door opening, and the camera tilted and jerked to the side. There was an odd slanted angle of a corkboard with notices and essays pinned to it, and the Professor could only assume that the Dark Doppelgänger had slipped behind the far corner of the lockers.

"Knock, knock, who's there?" another voice said, clearly farther from the camera than its operator, and this version of the Professor's intonations felt just as bad as the former, though it was more the color of a slick-talking liar than the sickening malice of a devil.

"I know it's you, Doppelgänger," the voice continued. "Do you know how I know? I am not yet dead. It means you are open to working together, if only for a while, and I say let's unleash a storm, strike first, lead the charge."

The camera angle flipped downward, and there was a view of the floor, moving now as the Dark Doppelgänger stepped out of the shadows. Watching all this intently, the Professor smiled wryly. Of course, the camera was still facing down, because you had to hide the monster, or in this case, the both of them.

"How about this?" said the Red Headmaster. "We will document our rise to glory, you filming me, and later editing in voice-over to narrate the journey. And please, I know what you're thinking. Why would I be the lead character instead of you? Answer: yesterday, I discovered Wolf

Shadow's lair. It is in a tunnel, part of a network of them running under these buildings, and I'll give it to you, share her with you, maybe have you join in a threesome when we transform her, the two of us controlling her as her masters, and of course, I would next shoot her in the brain. Then, as the Mod Goddess painted out sarcastically to the Professor in her criticism of these supernatural characters, we'd hack her to bits with these battle axes that I found in the half-emptied war museum half a block down next to the tire farm. Here, no, grab it under the head, there you go."

"Thanks."

"No worries."

"I just don't know."

"What's not to know, Doppelgänger?"

"Seems a waste, killing the beast who could win it for us."

The Red Headmaster chuckled.

"You know, I might just shoot you in the heart after all. Pay attention. Wolf Shadow can't be killed, she's supernatural. And again, conflate that with the accidental prophecy the Mod G gave us, with the bits and pieces of the beast turning to wolf rats and multiplying, the tunnels perfect for the breeding, and when we unleash them on all the others through the secret opening I found in the building that I am going to adorn with public school signage, it will put us on the level of the Beekeeper, who was so unfairly taken too soon, and in an emblematic way it will make us like gods."

The Dark Doppelgänger laughed this time.

"I get it," he said. "The school markings make this one of your famous tableaux."

"Damned straight," the ex-teacher said. "Every rat represents a fallacy and failure of public schools, vomiting out of the pedagogical façade I will have erected, spreading and over flowing into the streets with rot and disease: biased tests, school shootings, power-hungry board members, racial unrest, ageism, unequal real estate taxes keeping the rich-rich and the poor in the gutter, suspensions, class cutting, expulsions, school fights, bullying, drugs and alcohol, parents banning books with no real knowledge of literature, abusive teachers, unqualified aids, bells and classrooms like buzzers and prison blocks, human factories made to produce nothing more than more of the same, as we whitewash history, all of it finally consuming all of us, damaged mortals, the products of this environment we created come back to haunt us, swarm us, devour us, and everyone's last thought will be that we have been consumed by our own waste, and the devastation will be as complete as it is dark and glorious!"

"You really are the sage on the stage, aren't you?"

"Well, you have to admit, it's engaging, no?"

After a long, pregnant pause, the Doppelgänger said,

"What if I were to simply overpower you, torture you, force you to give me the location of the tunnel entrance and a map to Wolf Shadow's lair? We don't possess the hand-to-hand ability the Professor himself learned from Liza Nicolescu, but darkness like mine trumps ego like yours all day, every day, though I do admit you are enormously dislikable."

"Thank you."

"Don't mention it."

"I have a gun," the Red Headmaster said. "Don't you remember? I shoot people in the heart and then put them on display. You should be on your knees thanking me."

"Well, cunt, as you guessed about me, I can safely say that if you wanted me dead, you would have done it by now, so no kneeling, no bluffing, and no more metaphorical cocksucking. Bring me to the wolf-bitch before I find your gun and shove it so far up your ass it makes your nose bleed."

The picture went dead, but jumped back into focus to reveal what looked like dark catacombs with spreads of black moss and algae dully glistening along the walls with stalactites dripping down from the curved ceiling like wax.

"Yes," the Dark Doppelgänger said, the figure of the Red Headmaster about fifteen feet in front of him, battle axe on his shoulder like a foot soldier's rifle. "We are presently in the network of tunnels under the abandoned businesses and tenements, and as promised, we creep along to the lair of the wolf."

The Professor felt the blood rush to his face. Shit, shit, and more shit, they sure hadn't filmed what building led to the tunnels, now had they? He felt the muzzle of a gun pressed against the back of his head, and he took his fingers away from the keys of his laptop, slowly putting his hands up like goalposts.

"No, motherfucker," a voice said. "Lower your hands and keep typing in your journal. I want you to go back four paragraphs and have the Dark Doppelgänger and the currently starved and dead-as-a-doornail Red Headmaster film the entrance to the tunnels."

"And why would I do that?"

"Because I'll kill you if you don't."

The Professor grinned like a kid.

"No, you won't, Mr. 'Rock Reaper.' To paraphrase the Red Headmaster, who, as you indicated, is currently deceased and being made to clap together cymbals as a hollowed-out circus monkey … if you wanted me dead, you would have done it already. So let's cut the hyperbole and the melodramatic threats. You need me, as you have also indicated, to invent the location of the tunnel entrance."

"Yeah, Professor, so spill. I might not kill you just yet, but I also have no problem torturing you. This place has to have a maintenance shop and a chest crammed full of hand tools made for grabbing and ripping. You don't need a tongue to type."

"Let's not get ahead of ourselves," said the Professor. "To be honest, I don't know where the tunnel entrance is located. I don't outline. I discovery write, and I literally made the Red Headmaster and Dark Doppelgänger jump past it in the video because I hadn't figured it out yet."

Tito moved the muzzle from the base of the Professor's skull and came around to the side. Now the gun was pressed to our grand narrator's right knee, and he didn't lower his hands, didn't dare look, and the light was shining off of Tito's bare head, reflecting brazenly in the corner of the Professor's eye, and hot dang, the dude wasn't even wearing the reaper's hood! Then again, why would he? Cody had used his own real name from the start, and the true identity of "The Professor" wouldn't be difficult to unearth, especially since he'd already been out in the open, on the steps of the YMCA, and inside it where there could have been cameras. He tried to think back and determine whether or not he and Cody had discussed camera placement, and it was tough to nail it down, tough to concentrate when the Rock Reaper, real as day, was about to root around downstairs looking for a pair of locking pliers.

Then …

"Hey," said the Professor, "I've got it. The answer is in the foreshadowing that I didn't even realize I'd planted. I've always been lucky that way, sort of inventing—"

"Shut the fuck up," said the Rock Reaper. "I don't want to lick your ass, hearing about your process. Tell me where the entrance is, or I'll take out your knee just for the fun of it."

"But it's not a location, per se," the Professor said. "It's more like a riddle relating to you, Tito Quinones, the Rock Reaper, the answer buried within something the Red Headmaster and Dark Doppelgänger were discussing that directly and indirectly involved you, lighting the fuse so to speak to propel you headfirst into this part of the story!"

The Rock Reaper pulled back the hammer of his pistol.

"It's the Dark Doppelgänger!" the Professor said, talking fast now. "It's what he said when he described the Red Headmaster as 'a sage on a stage.' That's actually you! No one here knows how to work a stage better than Tito Quinones, lead singer of Saint Diablo, and we're talking proscenium arch, three-quarter thrust, and black box … bar-room staging, grandstands, festivals, and arenas. The secret is there, somehow, some way. It's a code meant for you all along, sitting in the great wide open for you to crack!"

There was a sudden sound that was haunting and hollow as loud music always sounded from another room, and it was farther than that, coming from outside the building, a guitar, an amazing riff, and there was some kind of sustain on it that made it luscious and deliciously evil, and it was a violin-guitar combo, a "guit-fiddle," and Tito pulled away the gun from the Professor's right knee.

"That's my song," he said. The Professor turned to look up at him, and Tito Quinones was a shirtless sculpted god, his arms and abs shredded like some sort of Olympian. Otherwise, he was clad in ripped jeans with a rope belt, and his eyes were black as night, similar to the ones he had in for the video for the song "Voice on the Phone."

From outside, the vocal came in, strong but feminine, growling the first verse in a solid imitation of Tito's original, but delivered with a girly flair that made it more hypnotic than aggressive. Tito bared his teeth, jerked his glance down, and pointed the pistol at the Professor's forehead.

"I've got to fly," he said. "This is business. No one steals my song and lives. You, on the other hand, will stay here. If you tail me and wander outside, I will kill you, no lie. I don't really need you, because you aren't the only creator. Speaking of which …"

He reached behind for the back of his waistband, from which he drew a pocket notebook.

"Here," he said, tossing it to the Professor. "Some reading for you. Think of it like homework, time to get started."

The Rock Reaper sprang off and burst from the room. The Professor was about to follow despite the warning, but having Cody's notebook delivered so smoothly was impressive; in fact, it was irresistible, calling him like crack to an addict. He opened the notebook.

"Hi, asshole," Cody began. "Time to catch up and also look back. See, me and Tito came into the YMCA building together, but not just three minutes ago. We had been expecting you, waiting on you, hiding out in the hall while you watched your found-footage home movie camera with your Red Headmaster and Dark Doppelgänger walking through the tunnels. Did you realize you make little moaning noises when you watch video, as if you're a kid having a bad dream? Anyhoo, I have a slightly different problem than does Tito. Of course, I was disappointed that you skipped over the part that would have revealed to us the tunnel entrance, but you also neglected to give us the way the Red Headmaster died, like visually, the capture, you know, the whole ball of yarn. And since you don't presently know for yourself, perhaps I can be of assistance, because when you put the camera down a few minutes ago to go take a piss in the bathroom at the far end of the public space, then more recently decided to document your moves so far in your laptop, you never checked back under bed number five where you 'hid' the camcorder. See, I've got it now, and I've watched the whole thing. It's four weeks yesterday-past that the Dark Doppelgänger filmed your Red Headmaster creeping into Wolf Shadow's lair.

"And, Professor, I can tell what you're thinking. You want to see Tito and what's going on with the music playing outside. Well, consider this a warm-up act. A show-opener. Shit, man, I never believed that a flashback was a bad thing, and instead of lecturing me about interrupting your precious present action, I remind you that fucking with the timeline is chic, sick, super-cool and you really should know a bit of the background info before you go putting up your hand horns and rocking to the live theft of a Saint Diablo hit single.

"And so, it was dark, and the two wannabe rapists-to-be had their battle axes, and they came upon an abandoned bar, a pub built into the wall of the tunnel. Below the burned-out neon light tubing that said 'The Red Eye Saloon,' the entrance was covered with a black cloth that the Red Headmaster tore down dramatically. I mean, it made perfect sense, no? In the Cody the Clown story, Candi was some sort of medical assistant, but in the Wolf Shadow bit, she was studying to be a bartender!

"Tables to floor, the seating area was draped over with cobwebs like the masts of ghost ships, and the bar, the stools, and the mirror glass behind the mantels lined with bottles all looked frozen, calcified, as if years of lime deposits had preserved it all like a skeleton in a tomb.

"What are you doing?" said the camera operator.

"Getting a drink."

"Have you lost your mind?"

The Red Headmaster turned, face pale in the vlog light.

"I'm about to have rough sex with a lovely young woman in order to turn her into a killing machine. I need a fucking drink."

There was a pause.

"'The Jameson," the Doppelgänger suggested. "Over there, middle shelf. And pass it along when you're done."

They had taken two sips each when they heard it. A drumbeat, slow and rhythmic in a tribal jungle vibe, coming from downstairs. Scrambling, they found a door behind the bar, and the camera jumped and tilted as the Dark Doppelgänger followed his eager 'teammate' down the narrow staircase.

At the bottom, it opened up to a lighted room, the drum set nestled to the front wall, covered in sheets and blankets, including that all-important kick drum with the canvas draped over it. The Red Headmaster had his hand pressed to his breast like a damsel being proposed to, and he bent down to look under the canvas.

He gasped.

The drum had no front resonant head, no Wolf Shadow logo; it was Cajon style, an empty shell all the way to the back, where there was the primary batter head for the kick-peddle.

"Fuck," the Red Headmaster said.

There was a primal screech, female, and a tall figure flew into the shot, all knees, nails, and elbows, and she crashed into the Red Headmaster so hard they both bashed into the drums up across the tom-toms, collapsing the snare stand, skidding the floor toms, and pulling the crash cymbals inward under the blankets as if they were polite opponents bowing to each other.

The woman was on top in a wifebeater and jeans, long straw-blonde hair loose and hanging over her face, and she reared way back and brought her fist down, hard like a hammer again and again, and it sounded like a baseball bat hitting a side of beef, and though the rims of the drums hid the Red Headmaster from view, after the fifth blow spots of dark red spattered upward.

She reached in and pulled him up by the necktie, yanking him back over the drums, his face a red smear, and she jerked him to the floor to pull him along as if she was an eager child with her little red wagon.

Against the far wall was the prison-cage, bare floor, door open, all the cushy pillows and silks in a pile out here over by the heater and water boiler.

She tossed him into the crate, a rumple of bones crash-landing in a heap in the back left corner. She clanked shut the door like a judgment and turned toward the camera as she flipped the long hair back off her face to flow down her back.

"And, Professor, no lie, Candi Kennedy was spellbinding, hot as fuck, I shit you not. There she was, filling the camera screen, a woman so … visual, so stunning that I pictured her image on fancy porcelain like artwork or on the ceiling of a church or something. And LORD, she was pissed, face flushed, cheekbones high, eyes sharp like knives, the cat's-eye makeup, long, slick and daring like wingtips."

"Doppelgänger," she said, "you get to live another day for the 'Red' piece of shit I've got in that cage."

"I told you that you could trust me."

"Fuck off, I don't. I still think you're like every other pervert coming to fuck me and make me transform. No one even considered the possibility that I could win this thing myself, no one."

"Including Cody Kennedy?"

The screen became huge with her face, and the angle jerked to the right. Clearly, she had grabbed the camera operator's shirt.

"Don't you ever," she said, "*ever* mention the Creator's name in vain again."

"He's not a deity," said the Doppelgänger softly.

"I don't know what he is," she returned, letting go of him. "He's a myth to me, a superhero, a legend, a god. And one thing I do know is that we will be together someday, like the stories he told of our marriage. But it won't be in a dream state. It will be in the real and the now."

"I fucking love you."

"Now, that I do believe, dark one," she said. "Even the purest of evil feels lust, feeling like love, but always with a flavor profile of tragedy."

She let him go.

"Same orders as before," she said. "You steer clear of Cody the Clown. He is a simple soul made in the image of the Creator. He is my pet, and I am now in the process of making him a new toy."

The camera shot moved to the right over her shoulder, and the auto-focus took a second to read the background. The Red Headmaster back there was starting to stir and moan.

"That's right," she continued, "and I want you to come back once a week for a month."

"So long between visits?"

"Yes, but for good reason. I want you to take pictures of him with your phone and record each pic on your camcorder. To remind you, and anyone else who sees the footage, of the consequences if you betray me."

"Why not just film him?"

"Still shots are more potent."

"So long between visits?"

"You're a broken record."

"If the shoe fits … "

She brought up her right hand like Rocky showing his gory paw in the meat house. Her knuckles were smeared with the Red Headmaster's blood, and she raised fist to face to rub high on each cheek like eye black, like war paint.

"You want to see me more often than just once a week?" she said. "Okay. Then get the fuck out of here, start getting busy, make yourself useful, and bring me the Soldier."

"Yeah, Professor, so then the camera went dark. And … nothing. And more nada, and dude, I was about to give up on it, but a still-shot flashed up, titled at the top of the frame: 'Week 1.' It was your spitting image, Professor, a close-up of the Red Headmaster behind bars, gripping them, face between them, his bruises in the purple and yellowing phase, one eye still mostly closed with a film of pus gleaming in the slit. He was shouting, evidently at the top of his lungs, mouth open wide, neck taut and strained.

"The camera darkened again, Professor, and this time it took longer, almost as if the Doppelgänger and Candi had planned it that way, making me wait on the jump scare.

"The screen brightened suddenly with 'Week 2,' and the difference from the last week was wicked. He was naked, sitting in the back left corner of the cage, knees up so his heels were against his butt, arms hugging those spindly legs together like kindling. He was grinning at the camera like a mental patient, no bruises or cuts on his face anymore, but dang, man, he had lost so much weight that his neck looked longer, his head sitting on top like the knob at the end of a branch. His cheeks were sucked in like a kid imitating a fish, and his wide eyes were marbles in craters.

"The screen darkened. Suspense. My dear God, Professor, I didn't think I could take it! Sudden brightness! Still shot! I almost screamed like a final girl; I swear it, I swear!

"It was a close-up, and he was on the floor of his jail cell, head turned to the side, and he was biting the bar on the cell door as if trying to eat it. His lips were threads peeled back from his rack of buck teeth, his face sunken in like bad fruit. He was hairless now, dirt clotted on top of his skull, or it could have been age spots, tough to tell the difference, but his eyes, Professor, his eyes were the worst of it, glazed sightless blue, protruding rude and crude like Mr. Potato Head accessories bugged out and staring.

"And finally, my good Professor ... after long last, it's high time to give you what you've been waiting for. The present tense! A promise is a promise, and so off you go!"

The Professor was so absorbed in the writing in the notebook that it took him a second to adjust to the fact that he was outside in the brightness now, disoriented, lying down on his side in a rough patch of grass, face to face with a mask from hell, his own image twisted through a nightmare that had deteriorated the skin to patchwork on bone, the wide curve of teeth clenched in a brazen grin, the nose nonexistent for all but the dark cavities on either side of the paper-thin nasal spine. And those eyes, my fucking God, the glazed and lifeless blue eyes were hardened and preserved somehow, dangling in their sockets by the optic nerves like gum balls on strings.

The Professor screamed, but it was drowned out by the music, the guitar solo going on, heavy squeal, endless sustain, mountainous bends, and poetic vibrato, the action so sensitive you could hear Lucifer's Gal moving her fingers along the strings between frets like feathers from heaven, and you could feel down to your backbone the satisfying percussive click of her pick before each pass of multi-note sweeps and exotic scales that were boisterous, haunting, and achingly sexual.

The Professor screamed again as a humongous gloved hand came in close and wrapped its fingers around the dead Red Headmaster's waist, lifting him, making the eyes go "googly" on their threads, and the Professor got to his feet to scramble away before Cody the Clown realized that his creator's chief rival had been lying right next to him.

Of course, the circus giant had not been looking down; he had simply reached for his lap puppet where he had left him, and the Professor moved off, crawling at first, getting to his feet, half running and half looking back to see the clown with both hands in the air, the left holding his toy, the right doing the Ronnie James Dio devil-horns, bopping his enormous head, the joker tassels jangling.

And heat, massive heat, and the Professor had started running away at full speed, but he stopped; he just had to have a look-see, and he turned back toward the music, and they were in a vacant lot, probably a few properties down from the YMCA building. In front of them in the street was a long outdoor theater stage at least twenty feet high with a wall of Marshall amplifiers along the back edge behind the blonde metal guitar queen, playing that guit-fiddle as if she was teaching it a lesson, long-ass honey-colored hair flowing far past her shoulders, sleeveless red sequin vest, a short leather skirt, and studded black boots running high on the thigh.

Heat again, Christ almighty, she had a shitload of pyro going on, and the only things the Professor could compare it to were Kiss on the Destroyer tour in 1978 or, more currently, the fiery circus Rammstein unveiled. There were salamander flame columns blasting up intermittently at the front of the stage, far left and right, flame jets behind those in fan shapes, and center-stage backdrop fire-pillars crisscrossing each other from a pair of swiveling heads mounted into the staging.

Lucifer's Gal never even saw the Rock Reaper coming.

Tito Quinones had scrambled up on the stage, and he was an inch or two shorter than Lucifer's Gal, but that didn't stop him from approaching fast, gripping her by the throat, lifting her off her feet and holding her there. The musical instrument came unstrapped and clanked to the stage with an amplified pop and dissonant echo, and Lucifer's Gal reached for the chokehold, clawing at it, feet kicking.

The Professor had a moment where he froze, thinking that this was his creation being brutalized by Cody's invention, and maybe there was a duty here to intervene, or was this only hubris, and wait a sec, why did the Professor want to protect her when he wouldn't mind seeing the Dark Doppelgänger bite the dust, and maybe this was a gender thing, or maybe the Professor thought he could use his knowledge of hand-to-hand to take on the Rock Reaper and maybe more, he wasn't so sure he could take him.

Run away, now. A no-brainer. In all, the Professor needed to be the last contestant standing, and one of the combatants taking out the other was a freebie regardless of who thought up the character portrait. That said, he didn't run after all, but rather, he began backing up, glancing back over his shoulder at his escape route every five steps or so, heading for the far side of this lot, hoping some other monster wasn't waiting for him around the far corner.

In front of him while he peddled back, the Rock Reaper was holding Lucifer's Gal off her feet with two hands now, clearly squeezing with everything he had, and she had transformed into more of her vampire self, a long face of smooth bone and fang shaped like a crescent moon, eyes dark scarlet and slanted, honey-blonde hair giving her a witch vibe, and she was thrashing like a wildcat, biting at the air, and scratching at the Rock Reaper's face giving him red tiger stripes, making him madder and then he was doing the shake-the-baby thing, her head bucking like whiplash and hey, wasn't she the supernatural one? How was this even a fight, and also, where was Tito's gun? Was it less effective on her than brute strength? The Professor laughed to himself as it was becoming more and more clear that Cody's creations had major issues of warped logic, generalization, and inconsistency, and that is when he fell backward into the void.

The Professor plummeted six feet into the chasm that smelled like a strange mix of earth and Italian food, and his crash landing was cushioned by what must have been a hundred pounds of garlic cloves, making a "bed" of death for one particular bloodsucker. The Professor marveled at Cody Kennedy's surprising cleverness and his own foolhardy unpreparedness.

They had discussed the supernatural characters as if they were untouchable and immortal, but garlic was never mentioned when it came to defenses against vampires. Did the fact that the Professor hadn't brought it up make it fair game?

He pushed to his feet and jumped to get his fingers over the edge of the freshly dug grave. Cody had planned all this, having his Rock Reaper act that he was surprised to hear Lucifer's Gal steal his music, and banking on the idea that the Professor would follow, would have to look while making his escape and literally "fall for it," tumbling backward into a booby-trap, the type that Cody had been prepared to recognize and therefore set for unsuspecting others.

Gosh darn son-of-a-biscuit, the Professor's greatest creation was to be buried alive with him on a bed of "kryptonite," possibly rendering her helpless but to gnaw on the closest potential victim like an infant sucking on a baby bottle. Their new shared eternity under six feet of backfill.

The Professor pulled himself up high enough to see over the edge, and it might have been too late at this point, as the Rock Reaper was maybe thirty yards away, coming toward him with Lucifer's Gal slung over his shoulder, her body limp as a corpse and son-of-a-bitch, he was doing a slow-walk like a bad horror movie trying to add drama to a paper-thin bad guy, and suddenly the concert stage in the background exploded.

The percussive *BOOM* was followed close by a massive burst of sheer white and vermillion orange that mushroomed up, sending an undertow of billowing smoke to both sides, the overall sight of it speckled with chunks of splintered timber and shards of hard plastic and steel flying through the air on all sides like shrapnel.

This was "slow-walked" as well, and it gave the Professor an extra second to keep watching before ducking for cover, and from the smoke and rubble of the decimated grandstand came a figure, a horse and its rider both made of flame, galloping hard, kicking up sparks, and of course, that was where the pyro was coming from … Savage Alice hiding under the stage, and suddenly everything ramped up to live speed, and the Professor let go and fell back to the bed of bittersweet garlic.

Scraps flew overhead like missiles, and the Professor waited only a second more before he jumped again for a grip on the edge of the grave, and as he pulled himself up, there was the distinct high whine of a chainsaw cutting through the numbness the explosion had put on his ears.

He got his sightline over the lip. The Rock Reaper had dropped his victim to the earth face down; she was stirring; he had turned to face his aggressor, stage-scrap stippled all over his back like buckshot, and Savage Alice was almost upon him, flaming chainsaw held high like a war-flag, her long thin face flowing into itself like hot steel in a forge.

She only needed one pass, flying by, stroking across the chainsaw like a tennis pro executing a hard forehand blast.

She got the Rock Reaper straight through the neck, his head flipping up into the air, and while the Professor expected blood to pinwheel off like a carnival ride with an oil leak, there was no spillage; the heat of the flaming saw had cauterized the wound, and the head landed next to its headless body that had curled to the ground.

On her approach toward the grave now, Savage Alice slowed to canter, then a trot, and she came up close, looming over the Professor, who had just let go of the edge and was looking up at her from the void. She yanked the reins, drawing the horse up on his hind legs, and raised high the chainsaw, not revving, just flaming.

"Men should beware, Mister," she said.

"Right," he said. "You're here to protect women from being manhandled, no exceptions, got it."

She brought the horse down to four legs to stamp gently in place.

"Lucifer's Gal is—"

"Fine," said the Professor. "Of course. Tito dropped her the second there was an explosion behind him. She landed face down, and it was as good as 'hitting the dirt,' as they say."

"Yes, but there's a problem now. There was friendly fire."

"Is that a joke, like a pun?"

"Collateral damage. Go check out Cody the Clown."

Her horse started to transform beneath her, the long flowing mane becoming ape hanger handlebars on a chopper, the fore and hind limbs spinning into the circular shapes of dual compound motorcycle tires, the dock and skirt of the beast's bushy tail hardening to the configuration of the muffler, the pipes, and the headers.

He pulled himself up to watch this grand exit, and she gunned it, kicking up dirt and grass behind in a spray peppered with streaks of wildfire, skidding around the grave and peeling out to the far side of Murdertown.

The Professor looked across the lot space on a diagonal. Like a small mountain range, Cody the Clown lay dead on his back about ten feet from the stage area, his fat middle peppered with debris from the explosion, the guit-fiddle buried in the center of his chest, with the guitar neck clearly having punched through his breastplate like a javelin hurled by a giant.

Lucifer's Gal got up slowly, rubbing her neck, hair in her face, stumbling along like a drunk at first, and the Rock Reaper's head was conveniently in her path, and she kicked it away with a short scream, and now she started walking with purpose, striding over to the corpse of the clown. She started at the arm splayed out to the near side and climbed him like a kid at a party on a bouncy castle, half crawling, half shimmying all the way up to his big, bloated middle. She gained her feet. Stood tall for a moment. Bent to get back her property and grabbed the base of the strange musical instrument with both hands and pulled upward with a vengeance.

There was a sickening, moist sound like the heel of a boot squelching up out of wet, muddy ground, and when the guit-fiddle came free, she almost fell back, just managing to keep her balance. From the Professor's vantage point, the instrument seemed to have escaped real damage, though the neck was streaked with bodily fluids and the headstock was covered with thick, beefy gore that was dripping.

She positioned the instrument for walking, holding it in the center bout groove with the guitar neck slanted down as if she was a gunslinger using the belly carry technique with her rifle. Hopping down, she disappeared on the far side of the circus giant, heading off to wherever there was a shadow to hide in, a bed to sleep on, and a door with a good lock on it.

The Professor hauled himself out of the grave, thankful that Eliza had made him bulk up. As his "old self," he would have been foiled at the "breaking point," where you'd have to struggle a knee or an ankle up over the lip, but now he stood out on firm ground.

In a sort of sick fascination, he wanted to look closer at the Rock Reaper's remains. Same with Cody the Clown; in fact, he wanted to climb on, maybe jump up and down like a kid on a trampoline to see how much blood he could make shoot up from the wound like a geyser. He wondered why he had such a thought, and wondered further why it seemed more morbid than all the rest of this happy splatter-crap he and Cody had created.

There was a scream, hollow and muffled, wretched and rageful. From below. From the tunnels.

Candi Kennedy must have found out that her favorite pet was put down.

News traveled fast through the bowels of Murdertown.

Chapter 30

Everything I say is a lie. That was a lie. Did I just lie?

Yeah, kid-stuff, right? But figuring out that childish, annoying riddle is way easier than having you (the audience) trust the fact that I have the laptop now, and I have taken over this narrative. Well, believe it and believe less all you have been told up until now. Everything I have done has been interpreted through what the Professor claimed to read out of my pocket notebooks, so you have never heard my real writing voice. Instead, you have gotten the Professor's interpretation of events through his paraphrase of my writing (often actually) and direct quotes (less regularly).

And he's gotten a good number of things wrong or warped or slanted so his Red Headmaster would seem smarter than he actually was and especially his Dark fucking Doppelgänger coming off far too "nice" for being pure evil. In fact, it was difficult for me to see any difference between the two, so killing off the Red Headmaster was actually the Professor's cheap cop-out so he wouldn't have to work too hard continuing to build this cheap cardboard character.

But let's go back and chart some "facts" he gave you that are simply not true. First, we have to discuss the entrance to the tunnels. The Professor wanted to keep it secret to build suspense or some such horseshit, but having his "Professor character" simply say to the Rock Reaper that he hadn't thought it up yet was cheesy, cheap, shifty, and stupid. I mean, c'mon, readers of a possible book and viewers of a potential future podcast would never believe it. As usual, the Professor has been all talk and no substance, so let me man up and tell you a few things.

I do honestly believe there are many entrances to the network of tunnels, but the one the Dark Doppelgänger found was right there in the YMCA. Remember the uncomfortable scene where I was talking to the Dark Doppelgänger who was masquerading as the Professor in the darkened lobby of the Y? I am making the claim that your discomfort didn't come from a horror reader's fear and apprehension, but more a result of bad writing. The Dark Doppelgänger claimed that he wanted "information," and was actually given nothing more than projections of who might lead each group of characters, which didn't really give insight to the grand scheme here. Then, to make matters worse, there was the wimpiest, lamest booby-trap ever concocted, with the exploding chair cushion sending up flaming bits of foam core. Really?

It was actually a much more serious assassination attempt that I barely escaped.

When The Dark One revealed his identity and hit the crash bar on the front entrance door to escape, I ran the other way in the dark toward the hall behind the counter. I just made it. See, under the pamphlet carousel in the lobby, there was a trap door leading to a basement area. The Doppelgänger had found that trap door, pulled it open, and duct taped a stick of dynamite underneath with a detonator he had in his palm like a clown's joy buzzer. But don't get me going about the Professor's gross inability to properly depict the big fella, Cody the Clown, hey, I'll get to it, trust me.

So the explosive blew a smoking hole in the floor about twenty feet across, and it was a gamble and serious miscalculation on the Doppelgänger's part. If he killed me, yes, the game would have been over, giving the Professor carte blanche to win this whole thing himself, but if he missed ... well, sir, here I am, telling you that when the smoke cleared and I dropped down into the basement, where they had stored a shit-ton of old file cabinets, boxes of moldy invoices, and broken-down exercise equipment, I found the tunnel entrance farther in, under the basketball courts. It was a dark, open hole about as big as the one up in the lobby, a dark hole with a steel stepladder leading down into the blackness of the tunnels.

So there. Secret revealed.

And yeah, there are more issues with the Professor's writing, oh fuck-yeah, there's more. Cody the Clown was not just some mindless idiot. He was a savant of sorts and a good speaker; he told stories, mostly weird stuff no one would ever bother knowing about the circus. Example: he loved the idea that "circus" was another name for "circle," or an arena ring, where Romans actually filled the coliseum stage space with water to do naval scenes. He loved knowing that acrobats and jugglers were like halftime acts for men who rode horses in circles as the headliners, and before the Civil War, a famous clown, Dan Rice, endorsed political candidate Zachary Taylor by saying, "Get on the bandwagon." Plus, the circus was always a traveling show and started using tents to be "under the big top" in 1825, and ...

Yes. Wait. I get it. Now the Professor is trying to tell you (or at least he will wish he could have told you after first reading this) that I am a "poor writer," because I "impose on the reader lists of expository text," and he'll say that "Cody tells instead of shows," and that Cody fucking Kennedy does his "research" by going on Wikipedia and copying shit word for word, but what he doesn't tell you is that a shitload of articles and books he uses in his own classes as examples of "good writing" list things frequently, like Sherman Alexi's "Superman and Me" and Mortimer J. Adler's "How to Mark a Book," which even uses bullet points. Hypocrite! Fucking liar! Fucking ... *teacher*, always twisting the game so students can never figure out the code, fighting dirty and shitting on what's really important, just like Mrs. Borowy did to me in third grade, when she caught me looking at my "Circus Journal," the one I created myself from newspaper and magazine clippings and pages from books. It was my go-to, my babydoll, the work of art that I had brought to school and hidden in my desk so I could have something to sneak quicky-looks at to keep me awake during her boring-assed science and civics lessons. Well, she caught me, of course, since teachers are always experts at "catching you," instead of "teaching you," and she stopped her lecture to scold me, and that afternoon I faked like I brought it home. I didn't, though. Instead,

I hid it in my cubby, which she rooted through after school in a totally illegal and immoral search, and the next morning I found it in my desk again, marked up all through it with red pen. With red pen. WITH RED FUCKING PEN!

That journal was my soul, man. It was a beautiful scrapbook with all the pics and quotes carefully cut out and carefully placed to make the ultimate circus joy-ride. I had a tent section and a ring section and one for acrobatics and tumblers, a prop section and a history section, a behind-the-scenes section and a makeup and face paint section, and then I cut and pasted special pages for animals and clowns.

And Mrs. Borowy hadn't only corrected the grammar in the parts I spent hours printing in perfect fancy penmanship with a Sharpie. She put red slashes across pictures she found "inappropriate," like the one I had of Grady Styles: The Lobster Boy, and General Tom Thumb, and the Four-Legged Lady, and the Human Unicorn.

She trashed my creation. For no fucking reason. So, Professor, it's time that I took my red pen to your raggedy, uneven, biased interpretation of the events here in Murdertown.

First, stop giving me these patronizing compliments about how my notebook entries are such works of "genius." It sounds like you're my "mommi", building my "self-esteem." And rolling it back, by the way, your repeated "use" of the transom windows above the YMCA's entrance doors is repetitive and amateur. The scene where the Dark Doppelgänger finds the Red Headmaster's hideout is confusing for all us regular folk, trying to figure out who is talking. The Red Headmaster's tableau with the rats coming out of the school building is rushed past too fast to "see," and in the tunnels, c'mon, stalagmites from the ceiling? So it's a cave?

And, Professor, "yo," as you would say with that irritating Philadelphia accent that sort of whines and yowls like a cat in heat, I mean, when you talk about Candi tackling the Red Headmaster into the drum set, you totally fucked up her hair, man. I'm just saying … I can tell what you were *trying* to do, like having her long straw-blonde mane hanging over her face, making the blood spatter up when she was pounding the dude in the face … like, maybe you wanted it to look like a scary veil or bloody burial shroud, but again, it's the cheap work of a proud idiot. See, it would never happen in the first place. Candi loves her braids, just like Cassidy Claybourne, and she would have had them tied back.

And there's more.

Yo.

What's up with this timetable, man? How long have some of these contestants been in Murdertown? It takes four weeks to starve the Red Headmaster, so you are expecting us all to believe that he, the Dark Doppelgänger, Cody the Clown, and Candi were all playing this game for a month just waiting for me and you to arrive? What about Lucifer's Gal and the Rock Reaper? They seemed pretty acclimated to the surroundings. Were they here for a month as well?

Fuck you.

We're going on a journey now.

Into the tunnels. Time for the Dark Doppelgänger to come into his own.

The Dark Doppelgänger dragged the body along the tunnel floor, which was damp and gritty, like cellar dirt. The body was in a burlap sack that the Dark One had snagged from the storage room of the paper mill on the far side of Murdertown, and this was a bitch of a chore, like rubbing sandpaper on sandpaper.

It was also dark, and even though the Red Eye Saloon was just twenty or thirty feet away at this point, the faint light drifting up from the basement left everything out here in a shadowy dreamscape, like outlines drawn on black paper with charcoal.

Candi had told the Dark Doppelgänger to bring her the Soldier.

She had never specified that the guy had to be living.

The Dark One adjusted his grip, switching hands so he was pulling the corpse along his left side, the non-dominant one. This slowed him down more, almost to a crawl, and he switched it up again, using both hands to grab the mouth of the burlap that was corkscrewed closed, and he tried walking in reverse, putting his back into it.

"Dark One … " a voice droned, Candi's voice, amplified but cheap, like a microphone made in the 1960s plugged through a boombox from the '80s, shaping her tone all wispy and breathy with the dead echo of the tunnel beneath it.

The Red Eye Saloon lit up like Times Square on New Year's, the neon light tubes flickering hot pink, the seating area wiped down and clean, the bar actually a long glass fish tank with exotic Veiltails and Flowerhorn Cichlids, Zebra Plecos and African Butterflies darting every which-ways, and while there was no evident underbar, the backbar was a wall of gleaming mirror-squares with three long shelves stocked with liquor, liquor, and more liquor.

Candi was standing at the back of the seating area now with the megaphone she'd been moaning into, and her hair was tied back in a big fishtail braid, and why the theme was nautical was a mystery, probably coincidence, and the willowy medical-assistant-become-bartender was wearing a tight black asymmetrical strap hollow top showing waist on one side and an undertow of sweet navel, and she had on tight black leggings and black stiletto heels she kicked off to go barefoot.

"You've brought him," she said.

The Dark One was still breathing heavily, and he let go of his grip on the twist of burlap, bending to put his hands on his knees.

"Yes," he said. "Clearly."

She walked between tables to the open entrance archway. "Is he dead?"

"Clearly."

"How?"

The Doppelganger paused. "Whatever do you mean?" He straightened. She was still a head and a half taller.

"I mean," she said, "how did you off him? This guy was supposed to be the ultimate warrior, and I am curious as to how you overcame him when you could barely manage to drag the body here."

He gave a short, hollow laugh.

"I didn't kill him. I cut him from his power source. He is AI-generated, a weird kind of humanoid bot, and he was charging up in the middle of the microgrid on the far side of the deserted multi-story car park. I got him at low energy—what we would consider sleeping. I unplugged him from the main system by removing the male jack from the female set in the back of his neck, opened him, and removed the equivalent of his heart, his CPU, and tossed it into the bottom of this body bag." He smiled, though it was with a curled lip. "And, darling, I was out of breath because the hardware is heavier than I had anticipated."

She stepped closer. "What's he look like?"

"Go ahead. Have a peekaboo, be my guest."

"Tell me first."

The Doppelgänger shrugged. "He's wearing army fatigues, you know, camouflage colors and high lace-up work boots. He's neither tall nor short, he's totally jacked, and he has no face."

She blinked at him. "What do you mean?"

"I mean, he has no face. There is an outline and a flat blank with code running through it top to bottom like a waterfall made of typed numbers and letters flowing so fast you can't read them."

She dropped to her knees at the mouth of the burlap sack that had started to yawn open.

"Hold on," said the Doppelgänger, moving into the bar space and over to the left by the vintage jukebox. "I don't trust that thing," he said. "I'm no techie, but what if it has some sort of emergency ignition system or something?" The Dark One grabbed the battle axe he had left leaning against the wall at the end of his last visit to the Red Eye, and he moved behind Candi in a ready position.

"Okay," he said. "Go ahead."

She giggled.

She tucked the lip of the sack under the head, and next she peeled it back from the face.

It wasn't a soldier-bot. It was the very human and very, very dead Red Headmaster, skinless now, crack down the middle of his forehead with one eye missing, the other dangling low on his cheekbone.

Candi made to push up quickly, but the Dark Doppelgänger was quicker, and he reared back and brought down the battle axe hard, sinking it into her back between the shoulders with a meaty *thwunk,* and she screamed and jumped up and hopped around, face warped and bloodless, and she was reaching back with her hands, straining to get hold of the axe handle, which was within reach, yes, but impossible to pull back and dislodge, there wasn't an angle that would allow it, and she was whimpering, choking out short screeches of pain and frustration.

The Doppelgänger kept his distance a few paces away, and he folded his hands behind his back patiently.

"Now, now," he said.

She screamed at him a long, sweet nothing of rage, and made to jump at him with her fingers curled like claws. The Dark One stepped out of the way, and she kept her balance, turned a 180, and burst past him, back toward the bar, and she rushed at it, through the checkerboard pattern of tables, trying to bash against the fishtank semi-sideways to make a glancing blow that might loosen the awful obstruction, but she more hit the surface dead-on, wedging it farther into her back.

That brought her to her knees, and the Doppelgänger padded over.

"Let's talk about your options," he said softly.

She screamed at him, face wretched; her voice had blood in it.

"The way I see it," the Doppelgänger continued, "you can die right here on the floor of the Red Eye or you can tell me where you hid the Wolf Shadow bass drumhead."

She tried to spit at him, but didn't go far enough.

He smiled.

"Darling, you are going to die in a minute, maybe seconds, and the only way you are going to beat this thing is to take your supernatural, immortal form. Since I am the one who will fuck you—and, my dear, I do intend to go hard and fast—I will become your loving chieftain, using your ferocious wolf side to win Murdertown, take over Philadelphia, and then capture the East Coast, the country, the world. We're going to be famous, you and I, so where is the fucking Wolf Shadow drumhead, please, pretty please …"

She looked up at him, eyes steely.

She took a deep, painful breath.

She lurched back to her back, popping both knees, landing hard. The sound was thick like a cleaver running through tough meat and gristle, the axe head surfacing out through the front of her chest, stretching the gauzy fabric of her blouse in the shape of a pup-tent. Blood poured down the sides of her ribcage, and her eyes fluttered shut.

"Option B," said the Dark Doppelgänger. "Fair enough."

"No, no, no, fucking no, Cody!" typed the Professor. "You take control of the laptop; you are required to finish the scene. That's the rule. It's what we discussed. I feel as if I am emailing a student to remind him of the course orientation on page three in the Canvas platform, where I have specifically decreed that one cannot 'make up' work in the last week of the semester just to get by. Time is money, and every day that goes by past the due date is like currency the given student is stealing from the other given students. Your work, Cody, is horribly incomplete, and you have failed, and you can fuck off.

"And what's more, you left the laptop out in the open here in the shelter space in the YMCA, on bed number five. You left it for me to finish the scene. So not only do you not do the work, but you imply that you want me to write your damned paper for you, as if you're entitled to sit back on your laurels because you were 'man enough' to kill off your own character.

"Well, two can play at that game. We are far enough into this where Murdertown is starting to write itself, and your lack of story-recognition is astounding to me. No one murders, much less manhandles a female character 'round these parts, without suffering existential consequences. C'mon, Cody, you know this!

"So come with me, Sir Cody Kennedy. Back down in the tunnels. Where the shit has only just begun to gum up the fan."

The Dark Doppelgänger was about to turn Candi over so he could plant a foot into her lower back and rip free his battle axe, when he heard it … that inhuman, insectile, high-flying whine, all gas-driven and pistons a-pumping … all cylinders, crankshaft, and knuckle gears gunning.

The tunnel flashed in shadows and waves, as if the ocean had become a stepsister to the light of the sun, and it was coming from deep inside the undertow beneath Murdertown, and it was advancing quickly up the tunnel, the revving of the chainsaw becoming the dissonant lead guitar to the rhythmic mechanized shriek of the motorcycle.

The Dark One didn't panic. On the other hand, he didn't reason to himself that a possible refuge might have been the basement of the Red Eye, since the flaming bitch might not have been able to work her chopper down a thin flight of stairs, and he started to run back toward the YMCA and the tunnel entrance going up through its basement.

The fire queen was closer. He could feel the heat of her now, and suddenly it seemed he was in a funhouse "Barrel of Love" where the room was spinning all around you like vertigo, and he lost his footing, pitching forward on his knees and his elbows, skinning both to the bone. Fuckin' A! She was riding up and down the concave cylindrical tunnel walls—or was that convex?—and why the fuck was the Doppelgänger playing word games with himself when he was about to be made into shish kebab?

She was almost on top of him, the tunnel walls bright with the reflective shapes of flames spatting and whipping in the hot breath of murder.

He turned to face her, to beg for his life, and she was already half past him, swinging the blade-bar of the saw down and back up like a child scooping sand on the beach with a pail, and like a flash of lightning it cut straight through his balls, up through his guts and between his eyes out through the scalp, a red-hot butcher knife splitting in two a sculpture made of butter, cauterized, French fried edges, no blood, just the twin halves leaning together for a moment at the forehead, then the left side dropping back, the right half falling forward, both simultaneously hitting the tunnel dirt with the receding reflections of Savage Alice licking back across them like a polite round of applause.

Oh, bravo, Mr. Professor-man! So you can kill off one of your characters, too! Yay, you're such a prize, such a talent! Well, guess what. I just found another laptop in the Museum of Artistic and Cultural Artifacts, three doors down in the antique weapons wing. If you are reading this, you have regained your position in the YMCA and are using the original laptop, of course, so instead of "telling" what the audience can already figure out, let me show you something. I have a surprise.

And not just for you.

(Exactly Eleven Minutes Before the Fiery Murder of the Dark Doppelgänger)

The Soldier hauled himself up into Engine 17, the Ladder Truck parked next to the Quint with its 300-plus-gallon water tank and the fire pump that could manage a thousand gallons per minute. Above the garage were the dormitories, and the adjoining building to the right housed the day room with its wall-mounted fire lockers, contractor's storage chests, office chairs, and card table with a training room in the back and a kitchen behind that.

The Soldier quickly and efficiently turned the battery dial, switched on the ignition, hit the two starter buttons, and pressed the starter motor to stereo. The engine rumbled to life, and the Soldier engaged the reverse control system to back up the rig so its rear was sticking twenty feet outside the garage.

He shoved open the driver's side door, hopped down to the garage floor, and walked past the front bumper to look down into the orifice he had uncovered by moving the truck. It was six feet in diameter, cut roughly through the cement with octagonal edge angles, indicating that someone had cut a rough diameter in multiple passes with a cut-off saw, probably minus the blade guard, so they could use an eighteen-incher.

It was black as midnight down there, and the Soldier turned to head over to the wall where he had leaning against a stepladder rack, a man-sized bracket hood that he had welded together in the shop. It looked like a huge waffle iron, and he bent, lifted with the legs, walked it across, and carefully set it down to cover the black hole. There were multiple openings in the bracket hood, each with a curved locking device made to hold in place one-, two- and three-inch hoses. On the metal shelving fastened to the wall, there was a Ramset stud gun, and the Soldier brought it to the edge of the bracket hood to fasten it down with two-and-a-half-inch pins on opposite sides; they banged through only half sunk to the heads. He should have used stronger loads, but it was good enough for him to continue to execute the mission. Time to move, let's move.

There was no way to properly angle the deck cannon on top of the rig, but the Soldier was going to use everything else that was available, and in the front bumper of the truck, there was a small hose, usually used for garbage and car fires. He took it out and walked it over to the orifice in the floor, setting it in the hood bracket, locking it in place.

He moved to the side of the truck, chop-chop, and he opened the storage compartment and hefted out the attack hose, unfolding it over to the bracket hood. The hose, of course, was connected to the cap water tank, and when engaged, it would pump out a thousand gallons per minute, check.

He moved to the back of the truck and yes sir, he got out the big boy, the heavy-duty three-inch supply line, and uncoiled it to the street to hook it up to the fire hydrant, which did admittedly have a couple of small leaks he'd scouted out before, needing the O-rings replaced in the bonnet and upper stem, but it was good enough; wouldn't affect the pressure in any measurable way. He walked the hose back to the garage and locked in the nozzle to the center of the steel grid.

There was a sudden and muffled sound of a high-pitched engine that vibrated the concrete beneath the Soldier's feet, and he checked his watch. He had wanted to utilize the smallest time window possible, exposing his location with the rig sticking out of the garage, but there had been a slight miscalculation on his part, leaving him a few seconds behind schedule. He dutifully sent record of this to the internal electro-magnetic correction system in his machine brain, and he backed off just in time to avoid the *whoosh* of flame that burst out of the tunnel opening as Savage Alice roared past underneath. If his reconnaissance operation had yielded accurate results, it would be over quickly down there, and he needed to carry this through before she turned back around after killing the Dark Doppelgänger, as he had figured she would.

He moved quickly to the truck and engaged the pumps, pinning the dials. Water bellied into the hoses, and he raced out to the hydrant. He took the wrench with his opposite hand on top of the operating nut and turned the valve counterclockwise. There was a *hiss,* and the hose bulged with water. He jogged back to the bracket hood to check on the massive deluge blasting down into the hole.

Mission accomplished.

He'd successfully started flooding the tunnels.

Okay, Cody. Dueling laptops it is. Let me take it from here. Maybe I have a surprise up my sleeve as well.

There was only one tunnel, though there was what could be considered a "network" of entrance/exit openings starting all the way back east in the basement of the YMCA. The second was four buildings west in a broom closet at the Suds n' Sparkle dry cleaners, and the third was two doors down from that in the employee bathroom in the Trading Post Pawn Shop through a trick wall that rotated like Batman scenery, leading to a short flight of stairs. Five buildings past the Red Eye Saloon was the fourth opening, cut into the floor of an empty warehousing unit the police precinct had used as a holding area for contraband attained during search and seizure operations. The fifth opening, as you pointed out so illustriously, Cody, my good friend, was in the firehouse in the garage under the ladder truck, and the sixth was in the last building on the west side, in the auto repair shop, behind the lift, in the form of a ramp. That was the exit Savage Alice needed to reach, but the cylindrical tunnel suddenly seemed smaller than it had initially looked, and water was gushing in at an alarming rate. She was at the wrong end of the tunnel for this, and at full speed, she turned the motorcycle around by pulling into a skid halfway up the curved wall underneath the tunnel entrance in the basement of the YMCA.

As an escape hatch, it wasn't an option. The drop from the edge of the opening up there to the tunnel floor was fifteen to twenty feet at least, and someone had taken the ladder.

The water was gushing in all around her, and by the time she had gotten the bike started back up the tunnel, her wheels were halfway submerged, the footpegs too, and she could feel a hollow, numbing cold that spread through her ankles and halfway up the shin. Her soul-fire, her lifeblood, was being drowned, flushed into frozen nothingness. In response, the parts of her that were yet unaffected burned hotter, and her flames were torching upward, scorching the ceiling black in the shapes of storm clouds. In front of her, the terrible deluge was coming so hard it was frothing at the top in whitecaps, churning and swirling like some massive beast, rabid and vengeful.

She passed the Red Eye Saloon, and it was partly buried, the tables in the seating area sticking up above the rising surface like islands.

Too quickly, then, Savage Alice was numb from the waist down, the bike totally engulfed and stalled, and she floated off of it, knowing that it had been a fool's game, thinking she could drive fast enough to make the auto repair shop and get to its ramp. If only she could last until passing beneath the police precinct's warehouse, maybe using the water to float up to the cutout in the floor! But the tunnel was filling just too goddamned fast, and she was engulfed all the way to the neck now, treading water with arms she couldn't feel, her head, her face, her eyes, and her scalp broiling in shooting flames so hot they were white, her expression black slashes of desperation and fury.

By the time she reached the opening, the water was an inch from the tunnel ceiling, and she had been submerged for more than a few precious seconds. She floated up through the cut-out and drifted a few feet in off the edge. Her body had utterly shed its fiery flesh and was now a shadowed sketch of a girl who had burned to death in an equipment barn, her features skeletal, her skin like black parchment with small specs of it floating around her on the pulse of the overspill coming up through the entrance hole.

Savage Alice had finally met her end.

In the damp.

In the dark.

On the concrete.

Oh, no, you don't, Professor. Savage Alice is both of ours. You don't get the grand death scene alone. So let's add to it, shall we? How about starting it with, *"But then …"* (heh heh)

But then …

The Soldier had turned off the hoses, mission accomplished, and in the police precinct's basement warehouse space the floor was covered with an inch or two of water, a couple of old evidence inventory sheets in triplicate floating and bobbing along with a clipboard, three pencils, a crushed Dunkin' Donuts cup, and a red rubber glove used for handling acids.

And of course, there was the corpse of Savage Alice lying a foot from the edge of the tunnel opening, knees bent and hands curled in like a fetus, charred skull-face half in and half out of the standing flood water.

Across the room on a diagonal, there was a stack of wooden pallets, and something was moving between the slats of the second skid from the bottom, just above the water line. It was a dark, slippery vertebrate sliding over the splintery wood and cutting along the water's surface, a long serpentine body moving in capital S-shapes feeding out from one another.

Altogether, the snake was fifteen feet long, a few inches in diameter, and it had the face of a saurian goddess, dull silver skin smooth and patterned with diamond shapes, cold and reptilian as it was human and female.

The Mod Goddess approached Savage Alice and entered her mouth, slithering far down her throat to the bottom of her stomach. Much like the Soldier's fire hoses, the snake's body suddenly swelled from the trachea down the gullet, past the heart, liver, and spleen. When filled to the anal plate and the undertail, she withdrew, coiled herself up like the pet of a snake charmer, and spat out the fetid water to the side in a long stream.

Savage Alice jerked, and there was a *pop!* and tendrils of smoke that came from her exposed ear-hole, nasal cavities, and optic voids. Again her body jolted, and she sat up with her head hanging to one side as if her neck was broken. Abruptly, she straightened it, and her frame went rigid as if shocked by a defibrillator on steroids, and her eye sockets burst with jets of blue flame. It spread through her face like orange molten steel in a forge, broiling and running into itself, blossoming out to roils and ruptures of billowing hair with the accompaniment of machine-gun bursts of sparks and hot static.

She stood, her body ablaze, all but her feet, submerged yes, but the watery disease did not metastasize to infect her shins and knees, and Savage Alice walked to the stairs, at first awkwardly, half limping, half dragging and sloshing along, but by the time she reached the foot of the flight she was walking tall, mounting the first step with purpose and verve, and halfway up the staircase fire shot out of her toes and behind her heels as if she had been baptized in the river Styx and come out on the other side with new moxie and strength where Achilles fell short.

She climbed the rest of the way to the first-floor level of the abandoned police station, crossed the space, leaving scorches on the smooth epoxy flooring, and Savage Alice, back to true form, pushed through the door to the mean streets of Murdertown.

Cody, man, that's not cool. I wrote the perfect death scene, and your "sequel" or "phoenix rising from the ashes" bit just … kind of sucks to be honest.

217

Hey, Prof., why the harshness, my bro?

We agreed from the beginning that honesty has to rule supreme, Cody. We both look at art the same way, that commercial art like rock or podcasts are part of a machine that feeds off money and views, likes, Facebook friends and X followers.

Then what exactly is the problem with my chapter segment, man? People love this kind of shit. That's why there are sequels.

As I said, Cody, her death scene was perfect. She's the best thing I ever wrote, and once something like that is dead, you just don't do a cartoon awakening. This might be hard for you to understand, but when you are part of the aforementioned "machine," you have to be a magician and make it look like you're not. Having this gross rebirth shows your scaffolding behind the illusion. It's like playing poker, cheating, and showing to the whole table the device up your sleeve that you used to palm the seven of diamonds.

Whoa Nelly, back it up, Professor. First off, why would you say it might be hard for me to understand? I'm twenty-seven years old, not five. Also, we had the "machine" discussion a year ago, and I am the one who coined it, referring to the music business and therefore the podcast business. Not that it is some "new expression," but you have this sort of sneaky skill at claiming ownership of one thing and assuming equal co-ownership of others that were created by me, as if time makes me forget.

Savage Alice is mine, Cody.

Fine. The Soldier, Cody the Clown, the Rock Reaper, and Wolf Shadow are mine, but so is the Dark Doppelgänger. That's something our audience would be surprised at: that I both wrote it in your voice and criticized it in mine. That's the best part of this thing, not your one-dimensional "win" with Savage Alice. And by the way, you did not in fact write her story all by your lonesome. I helped with it; at least acknowledge that much.

I'm not playing this game anymore, Cody. I can't feed your ego with your self-proclaimed embellishments just because you feel that if you "put it out there" I will just "agree" to avoid confrontation. Let's start keeping this real. If you divvied up who wrote what, at least in reference to the original story of Savage Alice, it was ninety-five percent me, a short five to you, if even that. What parts did you write again? Oh, right. You looked up the brands of the motorcycles the dad collected, you came up with the name of the town in Nebraska, and the idea that she plays "Candy Crush" on her phone in the principal's office. Big whoop. "The Legend of Savage Alice" is mine, and I am going to remove it from this mess we created and try to sell it as a short story to a small-press magazine or something. Yeah, maybe I'll get a penny a word, or a contributor's copy, or a fucking T-shirt. But wait, Cody. Where did you say you were again? Three doors down in the Museum of Artistic and Cultural Artifacts, the antique weapons wing? Well, wait there for me. We have some things to ... discuss face to face.

The Professor pushed up from his chair and closed the laptop. His heart was pounding. He had a slight headache. The museum was about a minute and thirty seconds from the YMCA, and it wouldn't be all that difficult to find the antique weapons wing. He was so furious he felt it up in his ears, the roots of his hair. He was almost shaking with the trepidation and thrill of real confrontation, and yes, this had to be done face to face. When you broke up with someone, you didn't call or send a fucking text.

He'd almost made it through the door when a voice made him pause.
"Professor ... Michael, please stop."
The Professor felt an icy thrill down his spine, yet also a warmth in

the pit of his gut. It was Ralph Romano, lead singer of Wolf Shadow, dead since January 1, 2023, of cirrhosis of the liver, and the character he and Cody had politely named "Ghost."

"I've missed you, man," said the Professor, hand still on the doorknob.

"Same, Michael. Look at me."

The Professor turned. Ralph was right here, in this room, in the flesh, or so it appeared. He was standing between the rows of cots in the middle of the YMCA's public shelter space, wearing his rock clothes: all black, sleeveless drawstring leather vest, silver-studded wristbands covering his forearms, baggy leather pants tucked into high lace-up motorcycle boots. His black hair was long and straight, coming down far past his shoulders, and he was wearing a super-large Christian cross with those German flairs at the edges. He put his arms out and angled his head like, *C'mon, man. Show me some love.* The Professor hesitated, like … the guy was dead, for Christ's sake … but he shook it off and walked over, hugged his friend. Ralph was strong, the embrace robust, and there was a faint aroma about him that was like the sweet musky oil colognes they sold in vape shops and street vendor booths, warm as day, cool as fuck.

The embrace was altogether too brief, but Ralph extended his arms and held the Professor by the shoulders an extra sec.

"It's nice to finally meet you in person," he said.

"Ditto," said the Professor. "You're shorter than I pictured from the Zoom meetings and podcasts."

"And you're taller than I had thought you'd be," Ralph said. "I pictured four foot nine at the most, and you're at least five foot three."

They both laughed heartily. Ralph went and sat on the nearest cot in the left row, and the Professor chose the one across from it on the right, both men with their legs and feet hanging over the given steel footrail.

"So," said the Professor, "what's it like, anyway?"

"What?" Silence, and Ralph smiled, looking up at the ceiling for a moment. "You mean out there? When I'm not here?"

"Why are you here, come to think of it … "

"You wrote me in."

"Never expected you to actually show. So, give it up, why? In the end, you're no murderer."

"Neither are you."

"Not the point."

"No," Ralph said. "Not even a little bit, you're right." He gently squeezed his nose between his thumb and the middle knuckle of his index finger. "Let's just say," he continued, "that I am the equalizer, the advisor, the friend. A therapist of sorts."

"You think I need counseling?"

"Have you read what you and Cody are writing?"

They both laughed, but it was short-lived.

"Michael," said Ralph. "Or rather, *Professor* … you are about to go have words with Cody, face to face in the museum in the exotic weapons wing."

The Professor smiled at no one.

"You're a good reader and listener," he said. "You must have paid attention in school."

"Right," said Ralph. "Maybe so, maybe not, but I've been around long enough to know when I'm being baited. You should have seen this coming."

"What are you saying?"

Ralph looked at the back of his hand and flexed his fingers.

"He's playing you," he said. "Remember, you are the writer, but he's more of the gamer, different generation, different skill set. It's not Cody waiting for you at the museum. It's the Soldier. And the idea that it's in the exotic weapons wing is no accident."

The Professor stood. "Bring it on."

"I wouldn't," Ralph said. "Please, Professor, relax. Have a seat, and talk a few minutes more."

The Professor sat. Ralph tucked the long locks of hair behind both ears, making him look boyish and, at the same time, ancient and wise.

"If you go," he continued, "you will fight bravely, skillfully, even heroically, and you will also lose your life violently."

"That's from a movie."

"Yes," Ralph said, "not a quote, but it's close. It's from *Zorro.*"

"Right! With Antonio Benderas and Anthony Hopkins."

Ralph made the six-gun shape with his hand and pointed. "You got it," he said.

"But wait," said the Professor. "This is all fake, right? Cody invented you to tell me this right here and right now in order to change the trajectory. Maybe it's Cody waiting there after all, and he just wants to avoid an argument live and in-person, you know, as if he painted himself into a corner, and now you're his escape hatch. Maybe I do go to face him, and this is where he starts losing and I start really winning this thing."

"See, that's what I mean," said Ralph. "The thing I would love for you to understand is that this isn't about winning. Whether it's the Soldier or Cody Kennedy waiting there for you by the medieval crusader swords and French naval cutlasses, this is all about blood running hot in all the wrong ways ... anger and hubris and ego and loss."

"But wait," the Professor said. "Just say it is the Soldier after all. Don't I deserve the chance to beat him? At least give me that. I'm a good author in my own oddball style, and I can write my way out of any angle he tries."

Ralph gave a slight smile and closed his eyes for a second.

"This isn't just a piece of writing anymore, Professor. Some of it has bled into the real. The Soldier is a machine, and he can hurt you. It will also be dark with the overheads shut down and the after-hours accent lighting coming up from the floor, illuminating the weapons and leaving the fighting space in shadows as if you're underwater. The Soldier can see in the dark. He doesn't tire, and he can execute his techniques with mechanical precision. He will record every move you make and note the probabilities for the success of his future attacks and counter-moves according to your every weakness."

"So I don't have a chance? Not even one potential scenario?"

Ralph looked off to the side and for a moment juked his head ever so slightly as if there was a tune in his head playing at low volume like some precious whisper.

"There are instances," he said, "where you might last longer than round one. I see that you could survive the medieval needle swords and a round with the Scottish claymores, but only because you miss with an overly exuberant fendente, shattering the glass case with the museum's fire axe. This distracts him. Amazingly, then, I can see you pulling a quick mirror-strike on the other side of his neck, partly decapitating him. Still, every round past that goes to the Soldier, even with his head lolling up and down toward his shoulder like a zoo balloon on a stick. When you wield the chiseled European rapiers, he will inevitably carry off an empty fade and run his blade straight through your stomach. Or there are the US Civil War swords, and the way he pulls a Hamlet and gets you with a poisoned edge scratched on your arm, or at the end of your duel with the Kyu Gunto army swords, when he fakes a lunge and pulls off a backhanded slash across the meat of your throat, making you gush blood like a Hawaiian volcano."

"Oh."

"And it's the same thing if it's Cody waiting there in the exotic weapons wing, don't you see?"

"How?"

Ralph put his palms on his knees as if about to stand up, but it was just to take a deep breath.

"It's an analogy," he said finally, "or maybe it's a parallel or a shitty metaphor or a rock singer's poor attempt at aligning the stars to make a point. And so, here goes. You confront Cody face to face, and you start off as if you're joking, needling like the needle swords in the Soldier's scenario, and with an angry smile he rolls his eyes and asks if you're serious, do you really think your characters are as good as his, and you say sarcastically, 'Oh, yeah, Candi is such a fucking gem,' and he laughs too loud and says that the Red Headmaster is a pompous, condescending blowhard like you, and then Cody grins showing all his teeth and slaps you on the back a bit too hard, and the fake smiles vanish from both of your faces."

Ralph paused a moment to clear his throat, and the Professor rubbed the back of his neck.

"And you move on to the next phase," Ralph continued, "the display with the Scottish claymores, yeah, the big 'n' heavy two-handed numbers, the big guns, each of you accusing the other of creating the weaker exchanges and dooming this project from the get-go, and taking this further, you move on to the chiseled European rapiers, except instead of stabbing each other through the stomach, it would be straight through the heart, you attacking his guitar playing, with the reminder that he never quite got out of playing the club circuit just as he would bash your work in the small horror book market with your overwriting and limited commercial success."

The Professor's head was hanging between his shoulders at this point.

"I see what you mean," he murmured.

"Not finished," said Ralph. "Not quite yet. When you move on to the Civil War swords with poisoned edges, you both start to play exceptionally dirty, hurling insults that will stick with the other forever just like, of course … poison … a sickening disease festering, infecting you both down to the soul, with your comments on Cody's weight and how that is what really kept him from ever being signed to a big record label all these years, and from Cody's worst instincts, he talks about your height, your bald head, your goofy glasses and big ears, and you call him 'obese' and he calls you 'troll,' and finally the two of you brandish your Kyu Gunto swords, slashing each other's throats and ending this thing forever."

The Professor glanced up, and Ralph was looking back, clear-eyed and sober.

"Professor," he said, "we are artists, the loneliest people on earth. We have a creative vision and few friends for all but those we do projects with. And even those so rarely last. Don't make the mistakes I did: so many bands with so much potential, always crashing and burning because we'd argue over writing credits and royalties, expenses and practice times, hotels and whether or not relatives could be roadies or interim management or financial advisors, and most of all we bitched and moaned about whether the bridge was better in G minor or E diminished, or whether the guitar solo was too long and cocky, or whether the drummer's fancy fills in the verses were overkill, trashing the vocal track."

He paused, he smiled, he shrugged.

"It always came down to those damaging words, having words, everyone pushing out their chests and insisting that they knew better, that they had been in this business for longer, that they had dealt with people like you and learned the fucking hard way."

He studied the Professor's face. "One more thing," he said.

"Like I don't feel bad enough already?"

"Not important; content is crucial. Professor, do you want to know why Cody could so easily kill the Candi character through the Dark Doppelgänger? Do you want to know why he acted as if he didn't want someone in the house to know Cassidy Claybourne was waiting for him out on the stoop?"

"Yeah, sure. Yes, of course. You're going to tell me he isn't married?"

"That's right."

"Then who—"

"His dad. He doesn't make enough at the music shop to support himself, so he still lives with his father. He's twenty-seven; he's still a kid."

"A baby ... "

"Now don't be ashamed, Professor, at least not too much."

The Professor gave a brief chuckle. "I'm more envious than ashamed."

"Of Cody?"

"Of youth in general."

Ralph nodded. "Yeah, man, mid- to late twenties," he said. "Wild times."

"No, my friend," the Professor said. "I'm talking younger. I'm thinking seventeen maybe."

"Why seventeen?"

"Because when I was seventeen it was it was great to be alive, man. 1978: think about it. I was a junior, and my high school experience from the start, from tenth grade on, was a rock and roll fantasy. We didn't have cable television back then or bank cards, computers, or cell phones, but we did have the greatest album-oriented rock in history, brand spanking new, all ours, the world in the palms of our hands. First, we were blown away by Boston's self-titled debut in August 1976, then Kansas *Leftoverture,* that October, followed by the Eagles with *Hotel California,* in December. That next March it was Foreigner's self-titled debut, followed by Styx's *Grand Illusion* in July and Queen's *News of the World* the next October. We didn't think it could get any better, and lo and behold, we were soon given Van Halen's self-titled debut in February 1978. And that was also the year I joined the band Man of War, not to be confused with Man O War, the metal band who in 1984 made the *Guinness Book of World Records* for the loudest show. No, Man of War was my cover band and a good one, playing keg parties, two a week in my senior year, as well as Battle of the Bands competitions, dance halls, back patios, parking lots, and old movie theaters, anywhere we could plug in and turn up the amps."

Ralph nodded and absently fingered the German cross around his neck.

"That's the project that turned into the '80s club band that did all originals, yeah?"

"That's right," said the Professor, knowing he'd told Ralph this part of the story a hundred times, but unable to help himself. "Our biggest gig was playing the Empire Rock Room on a Saturday night in 1987. We opened for a band called Metal Wolf. They had an album out through MCA Records, and Lynn Kratz, a DJ from the biggest Philly rock station, WMMR, introduced us. It was sold out. We rocked the living shit out of that joint." He smiled reflectively. "The night before we played, Cinderella had performed there at the Empire. The night after us, it was Skid Row. I sang out of the same house microphone as those dudes, and I'll always be proud of it."

"That's awesome, Michael."

"But Ralph, it's not Man of War that I'm talking about, though if I could go back and relive every practice and performance, I would."

"What then?"

The Professor looked at the floor, shrugged like a kid.

"I'm talking," he said, "about the part of being seventeen for me that always gets overshadowed by Man of War, because that was the superior project. I'm talking about Hughie McGillicutty, my very best friend since seventh grade all the way through high school graduation, tall Irish kid, so we looked funny hanging out, but good funny, you know, the Catholic skyscraper and the pesky little Jewish guy, friends for life and all that. See, Hughie played guitar, he loved the guitar, he lived the guitar, and I'm saying that music was so central to everyone's lives back then that it wasn't just the 'superior products' that mattered."

"So he wasn't ever in Man of War … "

The Professor laughed heartily.

"Naw, he wasn't good enough for Man of War. The guitar player for that project was this guy Lou Pastalone, and he was the best axe grinder any of us had ever seen, at least from around our hometown. He had a Stratocaster and a Les Paul, the latter of which I preferred, but he loved playing that 'scratchy-Strat' like Eddie Van Halen. Lou was the first to figure out that two-handed maneuver where you hammer on with both index fingers simultaneously, you know, tapping. He could play the Freebird solo note for note, and he could shred Ritchie Blackmore's entire catalog. But my lifelong pal Hughie? Hey, man, while he had heart and verve, he had only a smidge of real talent, sort of run-of-the-mill and mediocre. I was the vocalist for Man of War, but I didn't sing with Hughie. That's where I got to play drums."

"You're a drummer?"

"Aw, hell no. That's the point. It wasn't about being 'good,' but it was all about having fun. Any night I wasn't practicing with Man of War, I was at Hughie's house, jamming. He lived in one of those little saltbox brick houses that didn't have a driveway. His mother was a nurse and worked nights, and Christmas 1977, Hughie's younger brother Jimmy got a drum set he never bothered learning to use, so it wasn't long before we hooked it and set it up in Hughie's room. The set was totally rinky-dink ... a tiny Ludwig with that woodgrain finish that looked like basement paneling you would see with a singing fish on the wall. It didn't even have a floor tom, just the kick drum, the hats, the snare, one tom-tom, the ride cymbal, and a crash. I was excited, because this was a chance for me to rock out on an instrument instead of doing the more 'formal' Man of War vocals, so I figured out a simplistic 4/4 beat, consistent on the high hats, which I always kept closed, and then bass on one, snare on three."

He sighed.

"And that was pretty much the sum total of what I could do," he continued. "Though I did learn to move the bass kicks in other patterns around that consistent snare, it never got more complicated than most of the AC/DC drumbeats or the one from 'Just What I Needed' by *The Cars*. And so we 'juice-jammed' mostly with beers, usually Michelobs that Hughie took out of his mom's stash she kept in the laundry room."

The Professor looked at Ralph as if startled with himself.

"Hey, sorry, man. I shouldn't have mentioned alcohol."

"No worries," said Ralph. "There's no liquor where I'm hanging out now, so therefore no addiction anymore. Did you smoke too?"

"Damned tooting we did. Parliaments and sometimes weed. Hughie had a Gibson SG. He didn't have a Marshall amp, I forget the brand, but he had an effect box that made it sound pretty grand when he cranked it."

Ralph was smiling like a kid hearing his favorite fairy tale.

"You two played well together," he said like a statement. The Professor grinned.

"Well, yes and no. Hughie was a better guitar player than I was a drummer, but that doesn't say much. It was all relative. Hughie was no more than a beginner's beginner, playing bar chords well enough, but his scales were basic as fuck. He was always hopeful, though, and once in a while he'd put together a pattern that shined. That's why 'good' had nothing to do with it. I could play a solid backbeat, and it sent Hughie flying, trying new things, falling on his face, and then saving it with his go-to runs. For me, as said, I knew one or two beats I did really well, and as for fills, I only had two drums to work with anyway, so I had about three … no, *exactly* three rat-a-tat-thump-a-thumps that I could use as transitions if I wanted to get fancy."

The Professor's voice lowered, almost as if he was trying not to choke up.

"Hughie liked my playing," he continued. "That's what was important. I remember during the typical smoke-break or time-out we took to chug a beer or three, I'd sardonically mention that I sucked, and Hughie would always say the same thing, sincere and serious. 'I think you're pretty good,' he'd say. 'I always know where you're going, so we always get there.' And so I rocked the fuck out of those one or two beats, jamming with my best friend all day, every day, sound-pounding the house and shaking the foundations just for the fucking fun of it."

He looked at the floor.

"It was an absolute blast," he said. "No judgments, no competition, just playing our hearts out together, and it was the happiest I'd ever been in my life. Still is, by far."

Silence.

The Professor raised his glance. Ralph was gone. Dang, what a disappointing "outro." No fadeout, no goodbyes, but one thing was for sure.

It was not the time to go see Cody Kennedy.

Chapter 31

The Soldier was actually policing the firehouse, and he had backed out the #47 pumper engine, the #4 aerial ladder truck, and the quint. The rest of the apparatus bay was in a bit of disorder, only because he had done a lot of prep and pre-testing of the hoses before flooding the tunnels, and he had to reorganize the gear lockers and mobile work stations, as well as replenishing the cylinder storage caddies that had been only partly stocked when he'd first gotten here.

In the garage, in front of the open door to the old watch tower, was a coil of three-inch hose that he had knotted with a length of two-inch blue PVC. Next to that, on an angle, was a loaded mobile hose dryer rack that needed to be moved flush to the wall, five feet over to the right.

Something moved. The Soldier saw it, recorded it, and replayed it through his retina webcam, and there was definite movement down in the twists of canvas and PVC hose piled on the floor. The Soldier took a step closer. A huge silver snake popped its head out of the bottom of the hose-mound left center and, flicking out its black forked tongue with a distinct hateful *hiss,* it withdrew back into the honeycomb as if its own private nest.

The Soldier was about to spring right for the flathead axe in the first workstation, but the Mod Goddess seemed to have different plans, slithering out the back side and sliding through the doorway into the old watch tower that years ago had become a bell tower, and a few years after that, a defunct cylindrical space sixty feet high and eighteen feet in diameter. It was made of firebrick and, unfortunately, OSHA had used the EPA's "Good Neighbor Rule" to force the township to cement in the dome at the top, because it looked so much like a smokestack that could burden downwind areas with emissions. Originally, there had been a wide spiral staircase in there and a decorative fireman's pole going down-center, but those had been removed, leaving nothing but the fixed ladder on the wall with the see-through safety cage leading all the way up to the concrete underside of the dome.

The Mod Goddess was corkscrewing her way up the ladder, and the Soldier almost burst off to the maintenance closet where he had stashed his wide-jaw snake tongs with the extension pole and the heavy-duty reptile bag. Still, climbing the ladder wouldn't be practical; doing it one-handed while toting up the snake-catching equipment was like managing a shopping bag and a broomstick in the crook of your arm, left-handed and trying to play hopscotch uphill. Plus, with Savage Alice drowned and neutralized, there was no reason to capture the snake alive to hold it hostage.

Option number two: the Soldier's computer-brain worked the calculations and time-probabilities of starving the Mod Goddess to death, shutting the door down here, and turning home the captain's wheel lock.

Negative. Too long a process.

He would do it by hand, rip her in two. He had her dead to rights; there was no other point of entry or exit in the tower.

With his foot, the Soldier nudged and slid along the hose pile to the side, and he grabbed the heavy door with one hand (powered by his hydraulic tendons) and swung it with him into the base of the tower, pulling it home with the bracket-shaped pull-handle on the inner side. And though he couldn't turn the big captain's locking wheel from in here, his calculations indicated that even if she managed to get past him on the ladder, the Mod Goddess, at approximately fifteen feet in length and eighty-eight pounds, would not be able to budge the door even a millimeter, considering that it weighed just over one thousand pounds.

Oh, he had her.

Dead to rights.

*

The moment the Soldier shut himself inside the tower, there was movement amongst the hoses hanging on the mobile dryer rack back in the garage. It was subtle at first, only a quiver, but then there was something black and gray pushing out from between the heavy lengths of canvas.

It had a head like an oversized rat, face pruned and exaggerated like a bitter child, and it had worked its way to the outside now, clinging to one of the hoses. It spread its wings like skeletal fingers slowly unfolding, webbed together by sensitive membrane and colored like the devil's underbelly.

She released, flapping her Halloween, circus-tent wings like a pterodactyl beating upon the air, bobbing, hovering.

Suddenly the black bat burst into a gray puff of smoke, then a mist swirling and dancing around the tall figure now standing there as if she owned her own private breeze; and when the wisps disappeared, Lucifer's Gal took a brief look around, long blonde hair flowing in her face, tiger skin spandex, pleated black mini, and thigh-high studded black boots.

There was something coming from outside the station, and Lucifer's Gal shielded her eyes. The garage heated up, and the air tasted like fire.

"We ready?" the voice said, dry as the desert.

"Yes," said Lucifer's Gal. "It's time. But … are you sure he won't hear us?"

"Don't worry," the voice said. "The Mod Goddess has a rattle that will pin all his meters and dials straight to the red zone."

"Let's go then," said the blond metal freak.

Savage Alice readied herself to cross the threshold into the base of the tower.

The snake was a fast climber.

After four rungs, however, the Soldier's machine-learning algorithms had processed the data and better timed the step, release, and grab of the next crosspiece, and he was moving in a rhythm now that tripled his original speed. Approximately twenty feet above him, the Mod Goddess was twisting up the siderail. She suddenly rattled her tail, the hollow air-filled scales shaking, the sound violent and sheer, and the Soldier measured it with the monitor in his left eardrum and flashed it up on his retinal graph. The volume indicator lines were up as high as they could go in the red, and while yhe Soldier didn't pause his advance, he brought up the digital audio interpreter, and across his right optic screen he read that the nearest equivalent to the rattle amplified in this enclosed space was sitting on one of the engines of a Thunderscreech Bomber during takeoff.

Once Savage Alice had gained entry, Lucifer's Gal made to re-shut the door. This was more difficult than the opening had been, since in order to accomplish the initial task, she merely had to hold the wheel lock and lean back to pull using her weight. Here, the best she could do was give it a shoulder, pushing forward, the soles of her boots slipping on the cement. Christ, it was heavy, like a bank safe made of lead in a spy movie.

She finally got it closed.

She turned the wheel three full revolutions to lock it and felt it click into place once the bolt was shoved home.

The distance between the Mod Goddess and the human battle machine had shrunk to ten feet, and he had turned off his audio intake to silence the massive rattle that sent vibrations through the steel ladder like electrical current. The snake was presently wrapping her lower half horizontally around a rung like the spiral pattern on an old-fashioned barber's pole, and once she secured herself there, the top third of her body rose, her head and neck erect like a cobra facing the inner wall of the tower. She seemed for a brief moment to study the surface, then honed in on one particular firebrick, pushing forward the top of her head.

The loose brick slid into the wall; it fell off somewhere outside, and she followed it through the small opening.

The Soldier's heat indicator was flashing code red, and the tower was filled with shadows that flickered and danced.

He looked downward.

*

He immediately engaged the machine gun in his heel, pounding the low floor of the brick silo with shot, all passing harmlessly through the fiery apparition down there, the figure of a girl in a portrait of flame, and she was atop a motorcycle chassis that was ever-growing beneath her, with its engine and tank aflame, rear suspension and then the front forks, blue fire shooting out of the tailpipe, and she looked up at him, face roiled with rage, her long black mouth stretched open in a scream with her flaming hair snapping at the air like serpents from hell.

The Soldier made calculations of possibilities versus probabilities, and the water cannon in his other heel was an option, though he knew it wouldn't have a positive measurable effect, like bringing a water pistol to a gunfight. Jumping down and making for the door was the only choice.

But below him, Savage Alice had already transferred her weight to the front of the motorcycle, switching to first gear, light on the throttle, holding down the front brake. The back tire screamed as she held the bike in place, and she worked it up to full throttle in a magnificent static burnout that would have left scorches of tread-patterns blackened on the asphalt, and the bike was screeching, and flames torched upward engulfing the tower from the bottom to the peak in a violent golden pillar of combustion within what now resembled a blast furnace: hearth to bosh to barrel to stack at 2300 degrees Fahrenheit, and though the Soldier had leapt off the ladder, mid-flight he became stock for the forge, a "billet" whose ABS, polycarbonate, and polyurethane parts and accessories turned to gummy toxic waste and all his steel became molten metal and slag, bitter bedfellows with the steel of the stepladder, all falling down like rain through the fiery ghost of a girl like baptism as she hit the gas one last ceremonial time like a coda defined by the liquid steel finally gathered in the crucible beneath her in grand unholy cremation.

Chapter 32

Cody was about to risk everything, walking out to the great wide open while there were still killers within the perimeter. But he had to get out of here. Now. Yesterday. There had to be an exit.

The problem was that neither he nor the Professor had written in an escape hatch, and making one up at this late stage of the game would be sloppy and forced like cheating, and there was a name for pulling a fast one like this, some froo-froo French word Cody couldn't quite bring to mind … something like "douchebag-sex-machine" or whatever.

Fuck it, he had to try to get out of here. This was an emergency; no more fun and games, real life had to prevail. There had to be an exit somewhere, in one of these buildings, and he was going to have to comb through every single one of them or die trying.

He pushed out through the doors of the museum into the brightness and heard it, immediately recognizing Wolf Shadow's best song by far, the one the Professor wrote a review on in 2015, the essay the band loved, the work that brought the Prof into the fold as he became what would become lifelong friends with Ralph and Cody too, for that matter. It was "Cauldron of Deceit," one of those tracks featuring Ralph's traditional vocal just bursting with passion and power, more "pop"-oriented than their later stuff, but too heavy to be called anything but good old-fashioned ass-kicking rock.

Still, the original version of "Cauldron" was all guitar, fingerpicking to power chords on the build in the chorus, but this adaptation was being played on a church organ, old school yet distorted with incredible broadband and crunch, as if the player was pulling a Jon Lord of Deep

Purple and running a Leslie-Hammond through a Marshall stack. It sounded like the beginning to a horror movie, one with Frankenstein monsters, opera phantoms, and Claymation beasts.

It was coming from the building to Cody's left, no storefront signage, no display window, no banners or awnings, just chipped concrete block and dead center, a red steel door with diamond-patterned wire in the peep window. The idea that the door looked more like an internal one than the type used for the exterior was odd, but Cody was in a pinch, no time to figure out the trivial details anymore, as if he was kicking back, writing a novel. Cody pulled open the door.

It was a warehouse, empty of any shelves or racking, with a portable metal rolling staircase in the back left corner leading to a catwalk with a safety rail running up along the high perimeter. Here on the floor, there were a couple of heavy plastic tilt carts, a forklift, and a hand truck dolly lying on its side.

At the far corner to the right there was a massive pipe organ, and sitting on the piano bench facing away was Ralph Romano, hitting the keys dramatically, bunching up his shoulders on the high screechy notes and swaying to and fro on the lows as if mirroring a crowd of twenty thousand fans holding up their lighters and waving back at him in slow motion.

Cody took a step forward, and the music abruptly stopped, which was somehow louder as a silence than the music it had followed, and that was just weird enough to write lyrics about, but Ralph had already moved on to more pressing matters.

"You're leaving," he said, still facing away. It had an echo to it, making him godlike. Cody continued to cross the space, and Ralph put up his hand like making a pledge.

"No," he said. "There's no time for hugs and hellos. Your father is in a bad way."

"Yes."

"He needs you."

"Yes."

"Do you know the ailment?"

"No, but it isn't hard to guess," Cody said. "He's going to take out the recycling and trip over the curb, or the infection in his lower back flared up and he's lying in the bed unable to move, or he has hesitant bowel syndrome again, or he's going to try to cook pancakes and slip and fall face first into the stove, then hard to the floor, breaking a hip and an elbow."

Ralph stood. Turned. He was wearing the leather vest, baggy leather pants, and motorcycle boots, but he also had on a black tuxedo top, of which he'd cut off the sleeves. He walked forward in careful, measured steps.

"Cody, my good friend and musical brother, you can go, but I have to tell you that there will be a cost."

"There always is."

"Yes, but this has two consequences, one for you and one for another."

"For why?"

Ralph spread his arms wide.

"Just because," he said. "There's a rip in the seam, right here in this room, but before you go, you have to be made aware that when you make your exit, the Professor might not ever be able leave as a result. He might, keyword *might,* be stranded."

"Might? What's that mean, *'might'?"*

"What's anything mean?"

Neither smiled, yet neither frowned.

"What's the other consequence?" Cody said.

Ralph looked at his feet for a moment.

"It's good to see you, man."

"Same."

Ralph looked up, his expression blank and unreadable.

"The other condition is that you have to give me one of your memories, Cody. One you have of the two of us, the very best recollection you've kept with you."

"I don't understand."

"Sure you do. You just don't believe it. Trust, however, that I collect memories now, memories I take with me back to heaven to cherish."

"What's the catch?"

"No catch really," Ralph said. "But you can't have it back. It will leave a void you will never be able to fill, even if someone were to tell you the story of that memory line for line, move for move. So what's it going to be? What will you bestow unto me that will show me your perspective of a special shared experience of ours? Will it be one of our songwriting sessions? One of our late nights mixing and setting levels at the soundboard in the studio? Maybe one of our gigs, like your first with us when we opened for Faster Pussycat at the Troubadour, and there was no room for all our gear because their set-up took up most of the stage space, so you put your amp and effect pedals on the floor in the mosh pit and said,

"'It's ok. I like being right in here with the people anyway.'"

Both had said that part together, Ralph with fondness, Cody in a murmur.

"No, man," Cody said after a reflective pause. "The memory I'm going to surrender to you is the road trip to Oakland, when we remixed the first version of the 'Meat Tree' demo on Ronnie's eight-track."

Ralph nodded. "That's a good one."

Cody gave a bit of a laugh. "His wife was a trip."

"Right?"

"Yeah. Rules for every room are on a list on the fridge."

"The checklist in the bathroom, with the pencil on a string."

"Where you could have your sneaks on, and where only socks were allowed."

"How to straighten up your room and the complicated way you had to make the bed, folding the sheet and blankets like they were precious origami." Ralph paused. "She was nice, though."

"The best," said Cody. "Total peace, love, and kumbaya, just a bit uptight about cleanliness and hygiene. And hey, she loved our music." He closed his eyes briefly and shook his head. "I loved our music, man. We had it. We nailed it that weekend. We were a hundred and ten percent solid on the vision for the first time, talking until the sun came up the next morning about makeup and costumes, and how we were going to incorporate big-venue magic and illusions into our live shows, opening with a vampire-lift out of the fog like rising out of our coffins, and how we were going to figure out how to fly on cables the way Pink does it at her shows, and flaming Bibles, a model wishing well with beasts creeping out of it, and contacts that made our eyes glow, the works."

"We were together on it. That's for sure."

"We had plans," Cody said. Then he said it again, this time heavy with feeling.

"Yes," Ralph answered. "We had plans."

Cody smiled crookedly. "Hey, you know what they say. You know that you're serious … "

" … if you pull an all-nighter," Ralph finished. It was a treasured phrase between them from the night they cut that demo right up until the moment Ralph had been on his deathbed.

"So go for it," Cody said. "Take the memory."

Ralph studied him for a moment, almost as if he was determining whether Cody was gifting this as a precious token of their friendship or rather, that he was self-medicating … setting himself free in a way.

"I'll take it," Ralph said finally. "Here goes." He closed his eyes, and Cody immediately felt a "pull," from behind his skull and his spine and the backs of his legs, not painful but more like centrifugal force, almost as if he was being held to the inner shell of a Tilt-a-Whirl ride during a hard spin, and there was a relief as something in his head released itself, pulling the other way like a splinter coming out, and then the force was gone, and Cody felt sad, missing the memory that he could no longer quite place.

Ralph opened his eyes, and it was done. His face was filled with emotion, and Cody was spent, as if he had just wept himself dry. Ralph smiled sadly.

"I wish you could remember this with me," he said, "but everything has its price."

"Yeah," Cody said dully. "I feel like I've lost a piece of my spirit."

"Understood," said Ralph, "but I hope you can believe that I don't under-appreciate this gem. I didn't remember our brainstorming session the way you saw it, with such vivid colors and friendship and faith. It was a blur before now, you know, because the alcohol always robbed me blind."

Cody looked off, shrugged.

"When I said I felt like I lost a piece of my spirit, I wasn't talking about the memory."

Ralph looked downward, nodded.

"Yeah," he said. "I let everyone down."

"No, man," Cody said. "You built us up, always taking us where we never thought we could go." He shook his hair out of his face and followed it up by palming it back off his forehead. "So, hey," he continued, "Ralph, please. Where's the rip in the seam? My dad, I mean, don't ask me how I know, but I do. He needs me."

"Right," said Ralph. "The stairway on wheels over there. Take it up to the catwalk. In the shadows back there is an opening for a vent, a big one—you know, industrial ductwork. Go through it."

"Check," Cody said, turning to go, stopping. "Hey, wait," he said, half looking back. "The Professor, I mean, I can't leave him stranded here, I just can't."

Ralph smiled a little, mostly with his eyes.

"You leave the Professor to me," he said.

"You'll intervene?"

"Don't know that I'll have to, but I'll do what I do. Now get going, take care of your pop. Oh, but wait." He reached under his lapel and pulled out a screwdriver. "For the grate up there. It has four set screws."

Cody took the small hand tool. Gave a farewell salute and turned on his heel.

He strode across the warehouse floor. He climbed the mobile staircase. He took off the grate, pushed in headfirst, and went and got the fuck out of Murdertown.

Chapter 33

Ralph was in the woodshop, a few doors east of the warehouse where he'd just guided Cody to the rip in the seam up on the catwalk. He was sitting at the bench, working on a Porter Cable plate joiner, the armature more specifically. Suddenly, the walls were filled with dancing shadows, and the temperature rose almost hot enough to burn.

"What are you working on?" said the voice from the doorway. There was heat in her tone, old rage, older tarnished innocence, but also a longing. Ralph spoke to the wall-shadows.

"Repairs," he said.

"I used to fix things," said Savage Alice.

Ralph turned. He had a shop rag and he was wiping off his fingers.

"I could use a hand," he said. Alice was still mostly aflame, but there was an outline in the head now, the shape of a face, the face of a girl.

"You backed up in the weeds?" she said.

"Yeah."

"How many?"

Ralph pushed up and moved left to the steel rack with the red plastic repair bins.

"Looks like maybe twenty," he said. "This Makita drill needs brushes, the Milwaukee Sawzall needs a new cord, the Dewalt cordless needs a C-clip and a new shift collar, and this Skil circular saw needs a clean and lube."

"I want to help."

Ralph came over. "There is a cost."

"I'll pay it."

"No," Ralph said. "This is one that I have to pay. An exchange. I will give you my greatest, fondest memory in exchange for your worst. I am willing, but you have to be as well. You are going to have to let it go."

Her face burst hard to flame. "They hurt me!" she said.

"Yes."

"They deserve to pay! Everyone does!"

"Yet," said Ralph, "at this point, I am the only one who is making an offer. And those two boys are dead."

"As am I."

"As am I as well," said Ralph. "All I have are my memories, and I will give you the one dearest to me."

"What is it?"

He smiled, but his eyes filled.

"My wedding," he said. "When I married my soulmate, Lisa."

"You'd give that to me? What's the catch?"

"No catch," he said. "Just maybe a bit of simplicity."

"What's that mean?"

"What's anything mean? Except that maybe it's the simple things in life that are truly the best things to cherish, to think about. Not the big stage appearances or albums or royalties, but more the people-to-people stuff. The experiences that count. So, please, do the exchange with me, Alice. Let me bear the pain of what happened in the red equipment barn. Set yourself free of it. Let's keep it simple."

The fire around her face ebbed off to flickers, and she seemed almost human again, as if the fire was just an accent for the outline.

"I feel," she said, "that I'm not allowed to forget what they did to me. That I owe it to myself to relive it over and over, like for some reason it's my duty."

Ralph nodded affirmation.

"That somehow it's your fault," he said, "even though you know it isn't. I get it. But I have a duty as well, and I have my own demons to fight here in the afterlife. Let me take on this horror you keep stabbing back into yourself, Alice. Let me do this."

Her shoulders drooped, and she looked at the floor.

"What was she like? You know … Lisa."

That rocked him for some reason, like a punch in the gut, and he brought his right knuckles up to wipe under his eye.

"She was my everything," he said, "my sweet and beautiful angel. She was all that was good in life, almost as if she had magic invisible fairy dust that she swirled in the air wherever she went. And we knew we wanted to marry only a few months after we met each other, we just knew. We wanted to tie the knot on Halloween, actually, but one night, I said, 'Let's just do this!' Still, Lisa knew her son would want to be there, so we decided to wait until the next week and do it at the Hall of Records with only a few friends and fam." He smiled. "Lisa was practicing signing her new name all week, and she borrowed a black dress from her friend, you know, totally metal to the hilt, and I wasn't working at the time, so I borrowed a jacket from one of my bandmates along with a shirt and tie. Lisa ordered the silver wedding bands online, and the day of the wedding when they came in from FedEx, she tried hers on, and it was too small. She freaked and went to the mall, begging them to stretch it, crying, the whole deal, and so when we met at the place, she hadn't had the chance to do her hair or her makeup, and it didn't matter, because no one was ever so beautiful to me, like a sunrise on the ocean, ducks on the pond, mist on the meadow and all." He stopped, closed his eyes, picturing everything. "We picked up the cake and went to the Olive Garden for dinner, then El Torito for drinks. And we were married." He took a deep breath. "Trust me," he said. "My re-tell here doesn't do it justice. You have to live it. You have to …"

"I'm in, I'll do it," said Alice. "Give me the wedding memory and take these rat-bastards out of my head."

The exchange took but a moment, but the effect was violent. Ralph was thrown back into the racks with the repair bins, #43 tumbling down and striking him on the forehead, corner-first. Down on the floor, he wiped at it and smeared blood across his brow. He still had the shop rag in his other hand, and he patted his forehead dry. Ten feet from him was

Alice, human now, no flame about her, overalls and hair pulled back in a ponytail, and she was wrapped in a ball on the floor, shaking with tears.

"So beautiful," she was saying, muffled but pure. "So warm and cozy and human and good."

Ralph shook his head to clear it, but this wasn't going to clear easily. The flashes of Alice's experience in the red barn were savage and horrific: the violation, the roughness, the hideous laughter.

He stood.

She pushed up, came over to him, put her head to his chest, and let him embrace her, his chin resting on the top of her head.

"I'm so sorry," he said.

"I'm grateful," she said. "But I miss my pop."

"I never had a daughter," said Ralph.

"So maybe it's a rebalance, a new start, you know, heaven."

"Yeah, so, let's get there."

They started walking toward the door, and Ralph was talking about the rip in the seam, saying that there were machine repair shops in heaven filled with tools that needed fixing … and that he would check in on her every day … and that the memory of hers that he'd eaten was going to stay right where it was for eternity … and that his memory of Lisa was one of many and that it was but a loan … and heaven was the place where he could be with all his memories, wrapped in them warm and cozy and human and good forever and ever and ever …

Chapter 34

The Professor had gotten the note from Ralph about the rip in the seam a few minutes ago, and he made his way out of the YMCA and over to the empty warehouse with the red steel door and the peep-window that made it seem like an internal door instead of some more fitting design meant for exteriors.

Inside, it smelled like WD-40 and hand nails, and he walked across the floor to the rolling staircase.

He'd had enough; he was out of here. The place had no allure anymore, not without Cody. Real life had gotten in the way, the same as all the other projects that always got sidetracked so we could pay the bills, do the chores, work late, live life as if on this endless treadmill, wearing blindfolds, lost in the depths of the salt mines. Damn it. He had enjoyed this, and now, who did he have to go home to? *What* did he have to go home to? The teaching? Sure. He had to admit that he liked it, admired himself for it, but the whole thing was no more than "the good fight" in the end. It was work. Good work, but work just the same. Where was the passion? Where was that feeling you got as a kid when you burst into a run for no reason or climbed a tree for no reason, or joined a theater group or youth baseball team or an ass-kicking rock band for all the right reasons?

He climbed the mobile staircase.

So, what in the end had **The Kill or Be Killed** project given him? Memories? Hey, that was good for Ralph—no, cancel that thought, it was *great* for Ralph—but the Professor wasn't dead.

No, not at all. But all he had waiting for him back in his small office at home was a security training he had to do for Delaware County Community College so he would better recognize malware, a set of analysis papers for UDEL, and at least sixty multi-modal projects from Immaculata. He had two recommendations to write for students he barely remembered, and there were his ten hours of Friday Zoom tutoring. He had to buy more Post-It notes, another roll book, and his leather bag was looking raggedy. He had to clean the bathroom. He had to go to the store and buy half-and-half and American cheese.

Atop the catwalk, he could see the void of the duct he was going to crawl into, the grate over to the side leaning against the wall. He crawled into the duct.

When he crawled out, he wasn't at home in his office, sitting in front of his personal computer. He was in a store, darkened, after hours, with a display window filled with guitars, a book carousel shaped like a Christmas tree, and the far wall busy, occupied first by a pegboard filled with cords and packages of strings and then wind instruments: saxophones, trumpets, oboes, and clarinets, even a tuba on a stand as you'd see in a museum, and more toward the rear, there were the stringed instruments including banjos, guitars, fiddles, bass guitars, and cellos, all leading way back to where there was the shadow of an open door leading to the bathrooms, the practice studios for lessons, or both.

The Professor walked farther into the store, moving left so he could run his fingers over the glass of the long display counter filled with collections of stomp boxes, microphones, drumsticks, guitar picks in glass jars, electric keyboards, small amplifiers, and vocal effects processors. He heard movement in the back, far left, where a light suddenly poured through the door of what was most probably the manager's office or the small repair shop.

The store smelled like cobwebs and books.

The Professor went past the counter and walked into the back repair room.

It was a ragtag sort of happy mess, with an Explorer guitar on the bench with the humbuckers taken out to be replaced next to an array of lube sprays, solder coils, glue guns, and snipping tools, and on the shelving against the wall there was a trombone in three pieces, a flute with a rusted dent in the fluttering hole, a number of guitars, some of them neckless, three piccolos, five snare drums without the heads, and parts that looked as if they belonged to a harp.

Over by the rinse basin was a woman, long blonde hair, black sleeveless Burning Witches tee, and tight jeans ripped at the knees. She had her guit-fiddle strapped on, and it was plugged into a Marshall. She had her fingers over the strings so she wouldn't get feedback.

"Where are we?" said the Professor.

"New Jersey."

"You going to hang me upside down on that hook behind you?"

"Thinking about it."

There was a flicker of a smile on her face, just not with her lips.

"Wanna jam?" she said. "We got all night, you and me. I don't open the store until nine A.M."

"I'm not worthy," the Professor muttered.

She was chewing gum, looking him over.

"I hear you're pretty good," she said. "Plain and simple backbeat I can use to go flying. Sort of like I'll know where you're going, so we'll always get there together."

She walked over to the corner by the racking with the parts of the harp, and there on the floor was something covered with a length of blue plastic tarp. She leaned over and slid it off.

It was a rinky-dink drum kit, a Ludwig missing the floor tom, woodgrain finish, like paneling you'd see on a wall that had a singing fish on it.

The Professor was almost at a loss for words. Almost …

"How long can I stay?" he said softly.

She smiled. "As long as you want. Time is funny around here."

"Hmm."

She raised her chin.

"Hey, man," she said. "I gave up on considering myself 'worthy' or not, and you know what? I've never felt so free. I threw away the New Jersey Devils drinking cups with the famous guitarists named on the place cards in front of them, because I realized I didn't need 'em. Maybe I'm not the fastest shred-wizard in the grand wide scheme of things, but I've got soul, a love for the sound, for the groove, for the way bending a note and turning that harmonic feedback into a squeal makes me feel like a superhero. Professor, I might be kind of plain, but I have nice hair, I got good legs. There's Michelobs in the mini-fridge over there and an opened pack of Parliaments on the bench by the coffee can with the wood chisels. Take a seat on the throne there and start rocking those drums, dude. Hit 'em good and hit 'em hard, I'll adjust to you, I'm a quick learner."

He went and sat on the stool. There were drumsticks resting on the snare drum, big ones like the "telephone poles" used by the guy in Pink Floyd back in the day. Across from him, Lucy Phirsgail took a stance, spread her feet, and the Professor picked up the sticks, held them up, and started to click them together, giving the universal war call that made every kid in a band or just playing air guitar get a chill down the spine … balanced on the razor's edge of a rock and roll power chord.

One, two, three, FOUR!

Chapter 35

The Mod Goddess slithered along, checking for survivors. She made her way through the YMCA, the break room of the ACME, where the Red Headmaster had set up shop, and the Town Hall auditorium, where he had planned to put up exterior signage like that of a school so he could release symbolic rats out through the entrance doors. Outside, she double-checked the tire farm and the vacant lot with the pulverized concert stage and the grave seasoned with multiple cloves of garlic. She wormed her way to Ralph's carpenter shop and all through the museum, then through the firehouse. She checked the Suds and Sparkle Dry Cleaners and the Trading Post Pawn Shop. She wriggled down the stairs into the police precinct's basement storage room and checked all the offices and garage space of the auto repair shop.

Finally, she slid across the threshold of the near-empty warehouse. The interior red steel door with the peep-window had been left open, almost like an invitation, and she made S-shapes along the gritty concrete floor all the way to the mobile stepladder.

She snaked up to the catwalk and passed the immense industrial draft hood that belonged in a junkyard. The grating for the vent was leaning against the railing, but the vent itself was no longer a void. It had been sealed with a thick metal plate fastened with heavy-duty self-drilling tek screws. The Mod Goddess figured it was Ralph Romano who managed to do this somehow, but to this very day, it remains the greatest mystery of Murdertown.

Regardless ...

There was no one else in this block of abandoned buildings besides

Blood Red Meta

the Mod Goddess.

She had won the *Kill or Be Killed* competition.

And she was alone.

Chapter 36

The Professor grinned ear to ear, and he adjusted the mouthpiece of his headset.

"Hey, Candace," he said to the screen. "How have you been?"

Fine," she said, leaning down, coming full into the shot of the Zoom call, putting her arms around Cody's neck. He was smiling like a damned fool himself. He turned, kissed her cheek, and she backed off playfully.

"Do you two have any idea what time it is?"

"Not a clue," said the Professor.

She rolled her eyes. "7:15. In the morning!"

Cody looked as if he'd just unearthed buried treasure. He peeled off the Post-It note he had covering the time at the bottom right corner of the computer screen, and he put both fists up in the air.

"Another all-nighter!" he cried. The Professor peeled back his mini-Post-It note and raised his fists as well. *God,* when they really got going, they lost track of time! Candace backed off enough to rest her arm across Cody's shoulder.

"So, hon," she said, "was I 'Candi' this time, or did you use my middle name?"

"Both," the Professor said for him. "He split you in two, using 'Candi' as the wife and 'Cassidy' as the girlfriend."

She pursed her lips, mock annoyance. She looked at her husband.

"Did I die this time?"

Cody answered this one.

"Yes, darling, but Cassidy died a heroine, overcoming her biggest fear to save my life, and Candi decided to leave her supernatural powers unused, making her death three times as triumphant and sad."

"How nice." She looked right into the camera.

"So was this a go?" she said. "Do you have yourselves a podcast yet?"

Cody and the Professor looked at each other for a long moment. Then they literally said at the same time,

"Naw … "

They both started laughing. Harder; they couldn't seem to stop. Candace smiled at them up the side of her face, shook her head, and had long left the room by the time they finally got themselves together.

"What time is it again?" Cody said, using the bottom of his shirt to wipe his eyes.

"7:15, now 7:17."

"You're keeping your clock hidden on the screen there, right?"

"Of course."

"Always better not to know," Cody agreed. "No bonds, no restrictions, because … you know that you're serious …"

" … if you pull an all-nighter," finished the Professor. He looked suddenly pensive, introverted, and saddened.

"I miss Ralph," he said.

Cody's face went blank, his eyes lowered.

"Me too," he said quietly. "We had plans." He shook his head as if to clear it. "Hey, man, don't you have to get ready for work?"

"I gave them all off, especially being this close to Thanksgiving," said the Professor, "but I promised Eliza that I would wake her up and drive her to her—thing, her dance lesson."

Cody laughed with his hand over his mouth for a moment.

"Wake her up?" he said. "You mean she's back?"

The Professor smiled and shrugged.

"We're better together. We're getting on better than ever."

"Even with your horror stories and would-be podcasts?"

"Yes."

"Even with your weird fantasies of being a rock star, a master swordsman, a famous rock columnist, and a best-selling author?"

"Absolutely."

There was silence for a moment.

"So," Cody said.

"Yeah. So … "

Cody leaned back in his chair and webbed his fingers, resting on his stomach.

"Maybe," he said, "maybe we could break down the musical equipment, you know, describe it, like the stuff Wolf Shadow was going to take on the road for their first national tour before the pandemic came in to steal everybody's dreams."

"Yes!" said the Professor. "Real nerdy, totally narrating the behind-the-scenes geeky technical gear."

"Yeah, man!" Cody pulled forward, his hands in eager fists on the desk in front of him. "We could start with my 2005 Schecter C1 Exotic quilted maple red, and the way I plug into a Boss GT 1000 effects board with a drop pedal attached that runs into a Mesa dual rectifier to four by twelve Celestion speakers."

"Right!" the Professor said. "And maybe I could talk about books and scripts and movie soundtracks, and the effect metal music has on creating suspense and jump scares …"

"Right times fucking two!" Cody exclaimed. "Then I could take it to the next level by showing actual live gigging with the remaining members of Wolf Shadow!"

"Yes! A live blog! I think they call it a 'vlog.'"

"Dammed right they do."

"And," the Professor continued, "you could do the narrating as you go, you know, maybe opening for one of these old '80s hair metal bands still touring or maybe doing a residency in Vegas."

"Yeah, man! And then you could take over the narrator's role when I am on stage playing, sort of talking about the crowd and how rock and roll is the root of the theming in all these great films."

"And," said the Professor, "why couldn't we have the equipment be haunted?"

Cody's eyes widened.

"Fuckin' A, yes!" he cried. "The audience would be lulled into thinking it's just a regular old live band vlog, and then we switch it up with our own soundtrack haunting us."

"Yes, yes, Cody, my man," cried the Professor, "and not only do we bring the soundtrack out of the background and into the forefront, but it becomes a lead character!"

"Damn straight," Cody added. "In the end, we'll have a studio album, a live album, a book, and a movie all at once!"

"Damn straight," said the Professor.

They both were silent, almost "stunned," as if they'd just eaten a big meal.

"I miss Ralph," said Cody.

"Me too."

"He would have known how to put this together."

"Damn right he would."

Cody brightened.

"Don't worry, Professor. Someday we'll come up with an idea that will put us right into the big time."

"Sure, we will. The world is our oyster."

"We're on the brink of it for sure."

"Absolutely."

They both thought about it for a minute.

"What if ... " Cody said slyly. "What if we vlogged for someone already famous?"

"Okay, sure," said the Professor. "Let their notoriety, already established, do the heavy lifting!"

"Then," Cody added, "when the equipment gets haunted, the audience won't know whether it's real or if we're the ones staging it, acting all sweet and innocent!"

"Then," said the Professor ...

"Then," said Cody at the same time...

(Outro—Fadeout)

Short Epilogue

The Professor padded downstairs to eat the other half of the Wawa hoagie he'd bought earlier that day, and in sunny California, Cody was headed toward the basement where he thought he'd left the box of guitar picks he had bought at the store with his employee's discount, half price. Back up in their dens, the chairs in front of both PCs seemed to fill with floods of darkness, shadows taking human form like silhouettes.

Shadows of Ralph.

He became all the shadows.

He wasn't going anywhere, anytime soon.

This novel is dedicated to Ralph Buso
1968–2023

About the Author

MICHAEL ARONOVITZ is a horror writer, college professor, and rock critic. His published novels include *Alice Walks*, *The Witch of the Wood*, *Phantom Effect*, *The Sculptor*, and *The Winslow Sisters*, and his published collections are *Seven Deadly Pleasures* and *Dancing With Tombstones*.

Aronovitz has published more than fifty short stories and has appeared in magazines and anthologies such as *Weird Tales*, *Searchers After Horror*, *The Castle of Horror*, *Penumbra*, *Shunned Houses*, and *Apostles of the Weird*. His short story titled "How Bria Died" was featured in *The Year's Best Dark Fantasy and Horror*, 2011, Prime Books.

Aronovitz writes the site copy and press releases for new signings at Eclipse Records, a rock and metal label out of Pompton Plains, New Jersey..

About the Artist

Born in Pennsylvania, MICHAEL SQUID is a horror author and filmmaker. His unique and chilling stories have appeared in several books, anthologies, podcasts, and comic adaptations. A film lover and horror devourer, he began bringing his dark concepts to film with his debut short, *The Chrysalis*.

GALLOWS WHISPER